THE GOD OF IMPERTINENCE

ALSO BY STEN NADOLNY

THE DISCOVERY OF SLOWNESS

THE GOD OF

IMPERTINENCE

STEN NADOLNY

TRANSLATED FROM THE GERMAN BY

BREON MITCHELL

VIKING

VIKING
Published by the Penguin Group
Penguin Books USA Inc., 375 Hudson Street,
New York, New York 10014, U.S.A.
Penguin Books Ltd, 27 Wrights Lane,
London W8 5TZ, England
Penguin Books Australia Ltd, Ringwood,
Victoria, Australia
Penguin Books Canada Ltd, 10 Alcorn Avenue,
Toronto, Ontario, Canada M4V 3B2
Penguin Books (N.Z.) Ltd, 182–190 Wairau Road,
Auckland 10, New Zealand

Penguin Books Ltd, Registered Offices:
Harmondsworth, Middlesex, England

First published in 1997 by Viking Penguin,
a division of Penguin Books USA Inc.

1   3   5   7   9   10   8   6   4   2

Originally published in Germany under the title
Ein Gott der Frechheit by R. Piper GmbH & Co. KG.
© 1994 R. Piper GmbH & Co. KG, Munchen.

LIBRARY OF CONGRESS CATALOGING IN PUBLICATION DATA
Nadolny, Sten.
[Gott der Frechheit. English]
The god of impertinence: a novel /
by Sten Nadolny ; translated from the German by Breon Mitchell.
p.   cm.
ISBN 0–670–87301–2 (alk. paper)
I. Mitchell, Breon.   II. Title.
PT2674.A313G6813   1997
833'.914—dc21   96–52431

This book is printed on acid-free paper.
⊗

Printed in the United States of America
Set in Minion
Designed by Sabrina Bowers

THE GOD OF IMPERTINENCE

A QUASI RESURRECTION

The ship cut through quietly lurking waters. Something bad had happened here, and it might happen again. It was cold. Two days till Greek Easter.

The young woman was the only person on deck.

The cruise ship approached the narrow passage between two islands of melancholy aspect. On one side, at the point of greatest proximity, a steep cliff of black stone thrust upward like a mighty fortress. Not even the tiniest plant had found a foothold. From a distance the wall resembled a scar, healed and hardened. As they drew closer, the bare rock took on a metallic sheen. Power radiated from the spot, menacing, stretching from water to sky, vibrant and invisible. A force gathered to leap, a lightning bolt still dark, poised to strike.

The woman pulled her scarf closer around her neck, hunching her shoulders against the cold. She tried to read the black wall as she might a book. It was covered with ledges, cracks and hollows, bumps and grooves, discolorations fading toward pink or pale. As the ship drew nearer, the stone appeared even more complex and fissured. But it remained illegible.

Then, in the center of the basalt labyrinth, the woman spied a human figure. Startled, she cried, "Dear God!" and stiffened, her eyes wide, watching for a movement. No, he must be dead. The man was as black as the background, but she could still make out his head, shoulders, arms, and legs clearly. He was naked. A cultic figure, carved in stone? If so, it was a strange cult, for the figure was in chains. The man had heavy iron manacles about his hands, ankles, and neck. Someone sentenced to death? Then he must have died recently; all those hungry birds would quickly turn a corpse into a skeleton.

She heard a sound, a low, rumbling reverberation, which seemed to come from the cliff or, rather, from everywhere at once, growing in intensity. It swelled to a booming roar. The woman tore her gaze from the stone figure and looked anxiously toward the other island, the site of an active volcano—was it choosing to erupt now, a picture-postcard volcano doing its part to liven up the season? More likely a fresh mass would shove itself above the surface of the waters, a third island, brand stinking new and wreathed in sulfurous fumes. Nothing of the kind occurred. There was only a loud splash. A stone must have fallen into the sea. She looked down in time to see the water close upon itself and shoot upward.

She turned back to the rocky cliff, the ship having now drawn closer. A crackling sound reached her, and an insistent buzz like hornets. She watched as the cliff split open. A crack raced along the black surface, widening to a gap at its starting point. A pen line, she thought. This was really something, as if someone were drawing a line down the wall. In spite of the uneven surface, the line was as straight as a string. It ran directly toward the human figure and seemed about to split it in two—but passed instead behind, reversed, zigzagged, and then continued as before. Now a rattle as the manacles and chains fell away. Fragments of iron bounced off the wall and splashed into the sea. The lifeless body slid partway down and remained sitting slumped on a ledge.

The roaring and groaning lessened. No tidal wave yet. But now what? The arms of the figure were moving. The man was attempting to rise; he was flexing his wrists, testing their mobility.

Was she the only witness? Was it all happening just for her, the rumble, the release, the figure rising? The other passengers must be deaf, the Greek skipper on the bridge blind. She stumbled toward him and tapped on the windowpane, but the man only smiled, eyebrows raised, staring straight ahead. They were past the straits now; the cliff appeared narrower. But the figure was still clearly visible. He had stepped to the outer edge of the ledge and spread his arms, head raised, looking out to sea. From the east, low on the horizon, something was flying toward him, a small, compact cloud, like an attacking swarm of bees. It enveloped him. Now he appeared covered with fur. At that same moment his feet left the ground and he lay horizontally in the air. He floated for an instant near the face of the cliff, then drifted away and was borne off at increasing speed, disappearing at last behind the volcanic island to the east.

All was quiet once again, empty and dead, but the sense of menace had passed, the vibrant power was gone. The passengers were only now ascending from the cabin area, grumbling because they'd missed Schmidt Cliff, a famous sight. They listened, smiling indulgently, as the young woman gave a breathless description of the figure in the rock. All the skipper could say was that a stone had fallen. There was a brief discussion between those who wanted to go on to the volcano on Nea Kaimeni, as planned, and be at Thira in time for lunch, and others, who wanted to go back to the spot where the rock had fallen. "The chains are still dangling from the cliff. You'll see," said the young woman. They wanted to see them. The skipper restrained his impatience and reversed direction.

No one believed the story. The young woman came from East

Germany and was taking her first trip in the West. She spoke far too rapidly, and she obviously read too much. The only other German on board was her exact opposite, a heavy man whose supply of beer seemed as infinite as his imagination was limited. He had a telescope and was now examining the black cliff face. He finally lowered the telescope and passed it on to a Dutch schoolteacher.

"No chains in sight," he said. The skipper nodded solemnly a few times, as if they had finally admitted his authority. He turned back to the helm.

"But there were some not long ago," the German continued. "There were five hand-forged iron rings for chains; three of them are still partially attached. We had ones like that in the stalls back home to chain the cattle—simple eyelets, pounded in for heavy duty. These haven't been sawed off; they've broken from metal fatigue, or they've been bent back and forth until they were worn out. At any rate, it was hand-forged iron. Cast iron breaks differently." The fat man had never spoken at such length before.

"Someone was set free," said the young woman, "and he'd been chained there a long time."

"What makes you think that?"

"Because he could hardly move."

They all peered closely at the face of the cliff, to no avail. The teacher with the telescope frowned. "Well, I can't see anything. How can you possibly tell what sort of metal it was?"

The fat man measured her with a melancholy gaze. "I'm a professional blacksmith. I know everything there is to know about the trade. I even shoed horses in my early days, with old man Münch in Freystadt."

"Oh?"

"When I see a piece of forged iron, my dear lady, I can describe the man who made it."

• • •

Over three thousand years ago, a large, circular island lay in the present-day caldera that forms the Bay of Santorin. It was thickly settled and known as Strongyli, and was even mentioned by Plato. Whether it might have been Atlantis itself is a matter of debate. Its center collapsed during a volcanic eruption or earthquake around 1500 B.C., and the sea rushed into the gigantic crater, leaving only small portions of the island's shores exposed. It's said that the tidal wave produced by this catastrophe was the Old Testament Flood.

The portions of the island's coast that remained were quickly settled, and the main city was given the name Thera, or modern-day Thira. The inhabitants harvested excellent wine from the volcanic soil. They were skilled sailors and traders as well, and for a long time they were the wealthiest island people far and wide.

In 197 B.C., a glowing mass arose from the steaming waters of the caldera, which cooled and formed a small, barren central island the Greeks called Hiera, or "The Holy One." They built a temple on it for Hephaistos, or Hephaestus, the god of fire and the forge. Decades passed before the first plants took root in the crevices of the black rock.

Over fifteen hundred years later, a second island was formed, by a volcanic mass that rose to the east of Hiera from the bottom of the sea, splitting the island in two. The new island, to the east, is known today as Nea Kaimeni, or "Volcano" (because it's still active), and the remains of the former Hiera are called Palea Kaimeni— "Ancient Charred One."

Schmidt Cliff, or Cape Schmidt, is the name of the almost vertical, forty-meter-high rock cliff that marks the point where the island Palea Kaimeni broke away on the east. A German geologist and explorer by the name of Schmidt surveyed it in the nineteenth century, and a German artist, also named Schmidt, spent a day sketching it in 1850, later painting it for the Greek Hall of the Neues Museum in Berlin. The painting was presumably destroyed by fire in 1945, although it may have disappeared during the evacuation. The artist is forgotten, the geologist still mentioned, no doubt because the cliff was named after him.

• • •

The old gods still exist, because they are immortal. Athena, Zeus, Apollo, Hephaestus—as long as mortals live, the gods cannot die, even if they wish. Unless, of course, they decide to self-destruct by destroying mankind. But then they would die even more thoroughly than humans. Some form of memory of men and women might yet persist in rats or bees, but the gods would be extinguished, they would have disappeared without a trace, as if they had never existed.

Eternal life has its drawbacks. Erotic pleasure diminishes over the centuries. And those aching joints require a daily diet of brawn or jelly to keep them flexible. Every ten or twenty years you have to change your shape to hide the fact that you aren't aging. The well-planned "sudden accidents" that end the lives of most gods enable them to go on existing in another form. If the gods still lived on Olympus, these problems would not plague them. But in modern times they need a good disguise to walk among mortals. And human interaction is important for them, for after all, they must maintain their cults. Being a god these days is a miserable affair. Temples are seldom built, let alone adequately maintained, and cattle no longer sacrificed. At the very least, the gods need to keep their names current and see that new stories are told about them. That's why archaeologists are important and, above all, people who dream, and more than just vaguely, about the gods and goddesses. Gods become listless without them and waste away in spite of their nectar and their athleticism. Then all the gods add to life is eternal crabbiness.

The fates of the various gods over the past few millennia vary greatly. In some cases, no one knows what has become of them, but hope remains that they might return. In others, mankind still recognizes the names but believes, mistakenly, that they have died. And a few gods are totally forgotten—Anteros, for example, the god of requited love. Only Eros remains active, he whose parents were Aphrodite and Ares, the god of war. He kindles love whenever he wishes, without worrying whether it awakens a response. In fact, this naughty child enjoys inciting jealousy and the thirst for revenge.

The gods cannot die unless mankind ceases to exist. But they can quietly vegetate, degenerating inwardly and outwardly, until they have decayed into debased forms. And some have departed into the dark depths of Tartarus, awaiting better times. All this has consequences.

• • •

Mankind was unaware of the role the gods played in their pessimism, which seemed sufficiently justified by current events and the general human condition. "The world has come to such a pass," said a guest in Bebra after breakfast, while paying his hotel bill, "that only a scoundrel can save it," implying that whoever wanted to do so had better be a fast talker.

Europe was more turbulent than ever, politically and otherwise, everything in flux, momentous possibilities envisioned, including decline and fall, and the future was by no means certain. The first to fall into confusion were those who, in quieter times, had been accustomed to telling others what was right and wrong. Disoriented and irritable, they blindly kindled both hopes and fears, trying to impress themselves and others. Such was their method of avoiding despair. Worst of all were writers' conferences, as the gods were well aware: "We shouldn't have given them language in the first place."

Only a scoundrel can save it, a man complained under his breath one spring morning in Bebra, without the slightest notion that this sentence, chiseled in stone, could serve as a momentous and infallible truth. But they sensed something, these mortals. In the Europe of spring 1990, a semblance of the twilight of the gods was in the air, indeed a morning twilight, an awakening. There was more talk of myths than in the entire two thousand years before, talk of reenchantment, of metamorphoses, sublimity and ultimate worlds, above all of gods and goddesses. And a few people began to recall Hermes, although he was doing nothing in particular to reinvigorate his cult.

But even those who placed vague hopes in Hermes had no idea who he actually was: a mischief-maker from the very start, a universal scoundrel and yet the son of Zeus. No sooner had the nymph Maia given birth to him in a grotto on Mount Cyllene than he peeled off his swaddling clothes, began roaming about, and stole a herd of cattle from Apollo, craftily leading them away and hiding them. Not long afterward he induced a tortoise, by means of coolly calculated compliments, to stick its neck out far enough that he could grab it. He used its shell and a cow's intestine to make the musical instrument later known as a lyre. But by the time Apollo caught on to his cattle-rustling tricks and consulted Maia, Hermes was lying again in his swaddling clothes, innocent as a babe, looking as if butter wouldn't melt in his mouth. Apollo grabbed him anyway, planning to drag him before Zeus, the highest judge, but Hermes, still prone to his lies, released such a powerful fart that the oh-so-proper Apollo was startled and dropped him, almost failing to get him to Zeus. There, too, the rascal so cleverly and impertinently denied everything that his father, Zeus, laughed with pride. Hermes was henceforth the god of those who steal their happiness rather than wait for it to be handed to them.

The world in 1990 had reached a point where, with divine aid, it might have been possible to reclaim the happiness that had been lost. But the ancient gods were not respected, and so desire for the divine remained vague. People knew the name Hermes, but in a form that hindered rather than helped to develop a serious cult. The Roman form, Mercury, was used for newspapers, ships, travel bureaus, messenger services, and businessmen's glee clubs. The more sophisticated Greek name designated entities such as space flights, credit insurance companies, mail order businesses, vitamin tablets, and silk scarves. There had also been a paddle steamer in Magdeburg by that name, which people still remembered.

Other recent indicators carried a bit more weight. Hermes figured in the title of philosophical works in France and Germany and as a character in plays and novels. A two-man band (harp and guitar) called itself Hermes; their album *Wild Sow with a Special Touch* led the charts. And in Paris surgeons recommended operations "à l'Hermès." At first people thought they were being flippant, but it was in fact a variation of a new figure of speech current in both East and West: "Hit the road with Hermes!" More and more people used the phrase, but no one knew what it was supposed to mean. It ranged in tone from ironic pessimism to hearty confidence.

Suddenly mortals all over Europe were referring to Hermes— on a British golf course, at a Frankfurt business seminar, in a psychiatric institute in Madrid, in the Lithuanian parliament, even during the emergency session of a secret service agency that had misplaced its government. Was he perhaps resurfacing, the god of merchants, thieves, orators, and wrestlers, Hermes, conductor of dead souls to Hades and messenger of the gods, with wings on his hat and sandals? This god of sudden change, clever tricks, windfalls, and impertinence—was he about to appear? The other gods, themselves neglected, were eager to find out, for they knew where he had been for the past two thousand years. Something new seemed to be asserting itself among the hypersensitive, the lunatics, and the notorious self-promoters of old Europe. Impertinence was a form of love for truth. It cleared away the lies of consolation; it was cold and distant. Hermes was the god of communication, renouncing the fog of mysticism.

A few authors had either written about him or were doing so. Kerenyi, Thomas Mann, Ranke-Graves, and Walter F. Otto focused on Hermes. Rombach launched an attack, which went largely unnoticed. Serres made observations with crystal clarity, but so brilliantly that the issue was clouded. Nadolny hadn't quite made up his mind, needing a little more time. Pictor composed a circumspect hymn, which could also be taken ironically (it was in classical Greek, which ruled out a broader audience). Freya Zangemeister wrote an essay for a professional journal of archaeology, offering the opinion that Hermes would never reappear, since his presence consisted solely in the fact that his absence was noted. "Time and again over the past two thousand years," said Zangemeister, "pleas have arisen to Hermes; at times entire societies have been gripped by the same desire. But he never arrives." Indeed his principal characteristic was to be a god always on his way, who never arrives.

A few female pen pals wanted to "live with Hermes." What that meant remained to be seen.

The young woman in the Bay of Santorin, who was the only witness to his release, had suspected he was Hermes. She had watched him, black and ungainly, as he stood testing his limbs, only to be borne across the sea to the main island by a swarm of bees. She would have been glad to prove it, but no one supported her. The fat blacksmith had sunk into lethargy. By the time they were peering into the sulfurous stench of the volcano on Nea Kaimeni, he'd lost all interest in the story. Why remained a mystery, in spite of all those cans of beer.

• • •

The island had an expert on the gods, and the innkeeper's wife at the Selini knew where he lived. Henry Pictor was an alcoholic Englishman who'd arrived and never made it away again. He had a house high on the mountain in Pirgos, where there was no water, which made no great difference to him. When she arrived, he confirmed her suspicions at once. "Oh, of course, that was Hermes. So he's finally free? Jolly good! That means he was held captive for— just a moment—exactly two thousand one hundred and eighty- seven years, with the first three hundred at the exact center of the cone. Yes, that blackens you, all right!" He told her about Hermes and his own attempt at a hymn in his honor. "Don't fall in love with him," he said. "The gods maintain an ironical distance from humans."

He was either too drunk or too lazy to accompany the young woman to Schmidt Cliff. "I know it well enough. I've sketched it hundreds of times and painted it often, even did a mural of it for the Greek Hall. . . ." He emptied his glass, then lost his train of thought and focused on her earrings. She wore clips, half-moon disks that almost covered her ears. He said: "You have pretty ears—why the armor?" Since she barely spoke English, all she gathered was that he didn't want to come along.

Knidlberger, a Bavarian who had discovered Santorin and knew it well, had lived on the island forever. He received the young woman but gave no sign he knew anything about her story. Instead he offered compliments. "What wonderful Dutch-blue eyes you have. You should stay," he said. "I'm from Rott am Inn, and I'm not going back. This is the home of the gods. Where are you headed next? Have you been to Athens?"

She waved her hand. "I wanted to. But my travel agent . . . It's a long story; let's drop it. First I go to Venice, then back to Stendal."

He smiled and refilled her wineglass. "Then there's nothing to say but 'Hit the road with Hermes!' By the way, how can you hear anything with those half-moons blocking your ears?"

Her itinerary left time for nothing more. The ship was scheduled to depart the day after Easter. This Hermes business, was it some crazy notion, some dream? Why had the blacksmith suddenly lost interest? The sulfur fumes had either cleared his mind or clouded it. The result was equally strange.

• • •

Black and crusted, Hermes crouched between two small bushes of thorny spurge, his back resting against a rock, slowly flexing his hands and feet to limber the joints. They popped and crackled like fire. At any rate, he could still hear. The cries of seagulls came to him, and he saw swallows. It must be a cold spring; they hadn't flown north yet. They were keeping their distance, so he couldn't ask them what it was like up north.

Memories returned. How as a child he had loved to sit in forests and fens, by springs and in splendid meadows, but above all at the crossroads of human commerce, motionless and lonely as a stone marker, imagining he was invisible. Later he received the staff that made this possible, and he enjoyed invisibility. Lying there lazily, unseen by all, feeling the salty wind and watching with cool amusement the life of beetles and dragonflies, of men and gods, he longed to have all that again.

Unfortunately it was precisely his sight that bothered him, for his eyes were as dehydrated as dried fruit. He squinted out across the caldera, trying to see the volcanic island in the middle, which had served so long as his glowing, stone-throwing, sulfur-stinking prison. All he could make out was a gigantic black tortoise that lay in the middle of the bay, a desolate, lurking dunghill. Close by he could make out fennel, rosemary, red and pink herb blossoms, thistles, cacti, all of which required little moisture. It was arid and dusty here. A few steps away, steps he was as yet unable to take, stones were piled on top of one another, clearly by design. Were there still humans who worshiped him, then? But perhaps such pyramids had acquired another meaning over time.

The bees, following unknown instructions, did not carry him to the home of a mortal or the temple of a god. Their buzzing conveyed no information, nor did they realize that he was once their lord. Now they had another. Demeter perhaps? Strange, too, that none of the gods were there to greet or help him. Iris must have taken over as messenger of the gods in his absence, as she did in the Trojan War, when he hadn't wanted the job. Or was it dreamy-headed Pan? But he was too easily frightened, even by himself. Perhaps Athena, but that seemed unlikely too. She stuck her nose into too many affairs, nor was she diplomatic enough. The message she was supposed to deliver would invariably turn into her own. As in my case, thought Hermes, but with me no one ever noticed.

Acrid smoke assailed his nostrils. It was certainly not a burnt offering, but neither was it the stink of a volcano. Perhaps it was the fire the seagulls had mentioned. These seagulls! Instead of bringing him up-to-date about men and gods, they extolled the virtues of the warm updraft from a perpetual fire on a hillside near the city, and how they were borne upward upon it. Or they complained about the cats of Thera, who clawed the bits of fish away from them. What did birds know about anything? No one else had appeared, not even an Athenian; perhaps they, too, were afraid of Zeus and his judgment. For the first few centuries, he'd been imprisoned deep inside the volcanic island, with at most a brief message from Poseidon flashed now and then by a gleaming fish through a watery crack in the cliff. "You'll soon be breathing fresh air again." A bad joke, really. The island did in fact split in two, but his chains remained. From his spot on the newly created cliff wall he could see, at least for a time, the brightly whitewashed houses of Thera, until Hephaestus, with the usual display of smoke and fire, caused a new island to rise between Hermes and the mortals. His eyes dimmed from lack of moisture. The last movements he had been able to make out in the distance had been those of sailing ships. They were supplying a garrison on the mountain.

At least he could now move his ankles without the help of his hands. Immortality was but a burden. He recalled poor Tithonus. Zeus had granted him immortality at the request of the goddess Eos, who hadn't stopped to think that her lover would need eternal health, beauty, and youth as well if he was to retain the form she cherished. Tithonus had grown grayer and more wrinkled as he aged, shriveling up, his voice turning falsetto. In the end she carried him around in her jewelry box. He was probably crawling about somewhere even today, still immortal, the weariest cricket in the world.

He took a few steps. What he had previously thought was a pile of stones turned out to be a small mountain of tin containers, still stinking with decaying food. Scattered among them were half-rotten fish heads, partial skeletons, tail fins, a bleached cat's skull. Rusty, six-sided pieces of metal with an interesting threaded hole in their center. No life except for bluebottles and lizards. He recalled sadly how he could once glance at a lizard and, in the blink of an eye, count the number of spots on its body. His pulse was gradually increasing, and with it his mental acuity and memory. On the volcanic cliff, his heartbeat had been slower than a hibernating hamster's. He spied a clump of thyme. Breathing heavily, he bent over, pulled it up, and took a bite. Yes, he needed courage now, and thyme, mixed with Hyperion's flower if possible, would provide it.

His situation? He was at the beginning of something that was probably the end of everything.

After another twenty wobbling steps he came to a rusty metal frame, twisted and half overgrown. An animal trap? Wheels large and small lay scattered about. Humans had invented all sorts of things since his time, and Hephaestus, who was so undivinely in love with mankind, had obviously instructed them in his art. If Hephaestus loved you, it was best to flee. If he hated you, the same was true. The gods all knew how little difference there was between love and hate in Hephaestus' case. Both led to inordinate demands.

The idea that a wheel was more than a symbol or an instrument of torture came from Hephaestus. A new man could be created in this form. He built a manlike body, but with eight legs instead of two legs and arms. The oversized feet, stretched in all directions, formed a wheel. Instead of walking or running by placing one foot in front of the other, this artificial man tumbled along like a ball of dry seaweed before a storm. Zeus, shaking his head, refused to breathe life into this wheel man, which, with its eight legs, struck him as unerotic. Hephaestus apparently didn't realize that the gods were more interested in a pleasing sway of the hips than in speed. He grumpily withdrew, growling and muttering, and made more wheels. What were no longer to be "legs" he called "spokes." He then

invented the carriage, beloved of Helios and many others who had to carry heavy loads. It was a mistake to underestimate Hephaestus, even if he was a born loser. Immediately after his birth his mother, Hera, threw him out of Olympus because he was so ugly—he hadn't got along with her since—and he fell into the sea. Later, when he became a blacksmith, his father, Zeus, grew angry with him and threw him out again. This time he landed on the isle of Lemnos and was permanently crippled. But there he learned the ultimate refinements of his craft before returning to Olympus. He was a master artisan, but he viewed the serenity of Olympic life with hate, envy, and contempt. He preferred to be with humans. He knew he could count on them to be orderly, faithful, and respectful of art— everything the gods were not.

His most obvious shortcoming was tenderness in the throes of desire, and so he inevitably attracted little tenderness in others. Eros made a wide detour around him, as did Anteros, the god of requited love. Although Zeus forced Aphrodite to marry the sweaty hammer man, she soon tired of him. "Beauty and labor, symbolically united"—what a formula for boredom! She preferred the joys of Ares' lance, by far the most pleasant around. No one but Hephaestus was particularly upset or even surprised. Not even Zeus took Hephaestus' side. He reacted quite normally, roaring with laughter and slapping his thighs. That was the good old Zeus, before his irascibility stretched from eternity to eternity. Bad temper alone led to Hermes' harsh sentence. Aphrodite's seduction, which was only to be expected, was still acceptable, even in an increasingly torpid and gloomy Olympian world. But not Hermes himself, the god of mercurial agility and practical jokes.

The metal frame was not a trap but a former bed. The cow skin stretched over it had disintegrated. Were humans sleeping on metal spirals now? It was a bitter fate to be an ignorant, laggard god. But the thyme was having its intended effect. What was a god without courage?

The gulls' cries had changed now; they were baying. No, wait—

dogs were approaching, spotted dogs with lolling tongues. Hundreds of dogs—horrible. And in their midst who else but Hecate, the goddess of dogs, with her bandy-legs and lady's beard. She was wearing Hermes' flying sandals and his winged hat, even his butterfly staff, the Phalaion. Was *she* now the messenger for the gods? What had happened to Iris?

Hecate, with her bowlegs, tried to mimic the traditional floating gait of the messenger approaching the recipient. Good: she'd probably come to report that Zeus had commuted his sentence and to hand over his attributes, including the magic staff. He nodded to her amiably. After all, she must be excited to be delivering a message to Hermes from Zeus, which, god (and goddess) knows, is a somewhat daunting task.

Hecate took the most dignified stance she could in all the dust and began to speak. The dogs sat down in obedient boredom. Hecate's language was simple and direct. Hermes barely understood it. Did she spend all her time talking to her dogs?

"Good afternoon, Hermes. The Lord of the Universe sent me. You're free to go on your way. But stay away from mainland Hellas and above all from Athens! If you disobey this order you'll be thrown back into the volcano. Follow the first woman you meet to the midpoint of the world. There you will discover what The Lord has decreed for you. You won't receive your hat, staff, and sandals yet. You'll find out when it's time for that. Here are some provisions to start you on your way. After this you're on your own."

She placed a basket on the ground. It contained lamentably small portions of wobbly jelly, nectar, and ambrosia. The dogs snuffled around and went for the basket. Hecate had to shout to hold them back.

"Is that all?" asked Hermes.

"Yes."

"You mean I can't fly, turn invisible, or put people to sleep with my staff? What, pray tell, *can* I do?"

"Whatever you could do before without your sandals, hat, and

staff. I admit that's not much, but it won't last forever. And don't forget, you're not allowed to go to Athens: that would mean a quick end to your outing."

With their mistress setting out, the dogs began to snarl again, jostling, nipping, and harrying each other. They made such a racket Hermes couldn't have asked a single question, although he had plenty. Where was the midpoint of the world? He had never bothered with such nonsense; questions dealing with midpoints were Apollo's affair. But she was already on her way, an old, overtaxed dame, the goddess of the dog, holding down the wrong job. How could Zeus have dragged her of all people from the Underworld to serve as divine messenger?

And why did she refer to Zeus as "The Lord"?

Hermes could see he was going to need a whole armful of thyme to counteract the melancholy effects of these miserable circumstances. Only one hope remained: the human race. After all, they were created by the Titans, and his own mother had been mortal. On the other hand, he was too much of an Olympian to view them as anything but playthings. Some had nice thighs; and it was fun to seduce them. As playthings they were constantly evolving, which made for a surprise now and then, even for bored immortals.

In the meantime it was equally clear to the Olympians that they couldn't exist without the minds of men. But there were enough of those.

Hermes set out on his way north, placing one foot laboriously in front of the other. He hoped the midpoint of the world wasn't too many steps away.

• • •

The bright-eyed young woman who claimed to have seen Hermes liberated came from Stendal in Altmark and was named Helga Herdhitze. She hated her surname. It stood for everything she wanted to leave behind. She was bound to her father in a love-hate relationship. She hated him because he fell far short of what she loved about him. He could, in his laconic way, measure and manufacture almost any useful object, but he didn't know how to love or live.

Her family name was the major reason Helga wanted to marry young. But she hadn't found the right man. Her most persistent suitors, declared and undeclared, were out of the question, since none of them bore the least resemblance to the small statue she had discovered in the Winckelmann Museum at the age of ten. It was a bronze of Hermes, and even aside from its cheerful and clever countenance, she couldn't imagine touching any man who, when naked, failed to match up to it.

She had turned nineteen on the ninth of December. A dangerous inner desire made her feel as if she might lose control, but it was perhaps a hidden strength as well. She meant to learn more about it.

She loved nothing static or predictable. Anything surprising, even sudden death, enchanted her. Boredom caused her physical pain. She held her ears in class to avoid boring lectures. She tossed to and fro constantly in her sleep, and by morning her bed looked like a battlefield. Her interest in geology had been kindled by volcanism and was limited to possible earthquakes or eruptions. These weren't that frequent, of course, so she was in for a long wait. Stendal was situated on a "lower terrace of the final ice age," a "dead ice depression with compressed moraines," so nothing was stirring there.

Johann Joachim Winckelmann, the "eloquent herald of classical art," was born in Stendal on the ninth of December, 1717, as stated on the bronze monument erected in his honor near the Magnet department store. Helga, who had been asking since she was in the crib whether the world was taking any notice of her, had often visited the statue of Winckelmann to see her birth date in bronze, even if the year was wrong. Sometimes she imagined having been around since 1717 and knowing a corresponding amount, her childlike body and speech masking a vast superiority.

LAUCHHAMMER and FUDIT were engraved in small letters on the back of the monument. Lauchhammer referred to either a city or a foundry, so someone named Fudit must have cast the statue. Her father could have done it; he knew everything there was to know about metalwork. It was a pity he rarely got to use the anvil and forge in his workshop near Tangermünder Gate. He was the company locksmith for an agricultural collective and spent most of his time there. When he was at the forge, he was making new axles for old cars, not noble bodies and clever countenances. Ever since her mother's death, eleven years before, her father had drifted deeper and deeper into despondency, and now he talked openly of "putting an end to everything."

In the meantime she'd learned that *fudit* was the perfect tense of a Latin verb: Lauchhammer, the foundry, "fudit"—had cast it. And she was no longer taken with Winckelmann. She distrusted his concept of universal eternal beauty, as she did all sweeping generalities. She connected Winckelmann's "noble simplicity" with the lies of a falsely posited social unity surrounding her. And "quiet grandeur" was always a code word for sacrifice! She would rather die than be sacrificed.

She was always the "skinny one," almost anorexic, pale, freckled, and so spider quick that her face never made much of an impression. As a schoolgirl she was an outstanding table-tennis player. Then she dreamed of powerful motorcycles and got her license, yet she spent all her time studying or reading, often on a bench beside the statue of Winckelmann or Lenin. When people talked to her, she spoke so quickly she had to repeat herself. At night she was often alone in her father's deserted smithy, sitting in a circle of light cast by a strong work lamp.

After completing school she worked for a time as a librarian at the German Railway Maintenance Facility. She liked being around books and thought of studying geology or archaeology. The only interesting things in this country were underground. She longed to travel too, to see if the world beyond the border might be more interested in her than the one she came from. She learned the languages of countries she might one day visit: Polish, Hungarian, even Serbo-Croatian, although she had little hope of ever making it to Yugoslavia, which was already practically the West. Languages were easy for her, and when she got hold of a foreigner, she was soon repeating his words flawlessly.

She spent time in the workshop because she saw it as the beginning and center of all misfortunes, including her own. The tools, whose names she'd known since childhood, rusty or gleaming with oil, the floor covered with soot, dust, and metal shavings, the anvil deformed by the blows of the hammer, with its massive beak and the square hole for the hardy, the setts and sledgehammers, the swages, the long-handled tongs, were all memorials of a former diligence, now blunt and blind, dead iron like Lenin by Tangermünder Gate.

If the smell of a place could drive a person to suicide, it would be this scent of cold grease and ashes. But here was where she was to begin life. Every object in the room seemed to be urging her to "hit the road." Half-finished repairs, broken chains, busted carts, mounds of iron shoes from long-dead horses, rigid piles of worn-out shock absorbers, all constituted the once honorable past, which, at some indefinable point, had taken a turn toward loneliness, boredom, and corrosion. At some point the blacksmiths had carried out their great betrayal of the forge and anvil. As a child she had watched her father forging garden gates, and even a few inventions—a bicycle for the armless that could be steered with the feet, a new type of fox trap. He made everything from scrap, quickly sensing possibilities, improvising. He could do anything, but he no longer saw any sense in it and so betrayed his abilities from lack of courage.

Here she sat and read about Greeks, volcanoes, romance, ships on the high seas, golden jewelry. Here was the iron prison from which she longed to escape, the ashes from which she would rise to head West, where ideas could be developed, where life consisted of more than dos and don'ts, where everything was alluring and well crafted, awakening pleasure, not fear and melancholy. And she would never, never return. She loved the West, the inaccessible, as a concept, a place where mistakes and misadventures were recognized as opportunities to be incorporated and exploited, reformulated as new sources of inspiration and profit. In the East, mistakes led only to greater inefficiency, larger deficiencies, additional proscriptions. In the East, mistakes were simply mistakes.

Father had no one else. In the spring of 1990, when he hadn't been home for days, she heard that a man had been found at the garbage dump, bound with a clothesline in a plastic tablecloth. She rushed in alarm to the police, but it wasn't her father, and in fact he wasn't even from the area. It turned out that the man had tied himself up and got into the dumpster, hoping to be transported to the landfill. He survived and, when questioned, replied: "My name is legion, for we are many." He left and was never seen again.

This event took place shortly before Helga's departure. She was determined to see Athens and had borrowed money from a table-tennis friend who was now living in Munich. She went to a newly opened travel bureau and bought a ticket on a cruise called "Eternal Greece," run by Bob Cazzola's Mythic Tours. She was assured that Athens was always included on the itinerary. Boarding the ship in Venice shortly before Easter, she learned to her dismay that they wouldn't land at Athens after all. She would see Ithaca, Delphi, Olympia, Corinth, Mycene, and Naxos.

Santorin was the last stop on the way back.

CRUISE WITH MUSIC

Evening was drawing nigh on the second day of his deliverance, or at least his release. Before the night was over, Hermes intended to take his place among men and gods.

Now he could account for the smoldering fire on the hill: it was burning garbage, including a great heap of a papyrus-like material that seemed to be everywhere recently. The odor recalled Hephaestus' smelly forge—something he'd known from the first day the blacksmith god placed him in chains. He was familiar with that stench, both above and below the earth. That was how Hephaestus controlled men, by smell, bending them to his will with thick smoke when he needed their services. Was nothing else available—the fruity fragrance of the Muses, Aphrodite's perfume?

Pain in the left ankle. The shackles had dug in deeply. Hephaestus had probably wanted to make sure that Hermes would have a limp like his if he ever got free. Miserable weather. Wind, rain, and cold were hardly what he needed to make his limbs flexible.

Two days and a night crawling about like a toad in the garbage. But he was getting faster. He'd soon be finding gods or humans to recruit as allies in the search for his sandals, his hat, and his staff, so that he could finally fly—and make love. Two thousand years without a soft, pliable breast beneath his hand, no locks of hair, no thighs suddenly bare and waiting. He might be headed for a downfall, but he needed to seduce a few women first—human or divine, it didn't matter: they all encircled the slippery thrusts the same way. Hermes noted approvingly that, as in times of old, his most devoted friend had perked up at the thought and was already pointing the way.

All about lay a landscape of hard-baked black and yellow lava, formed into terraces like stone vineyards, but larger and uglier, with no vines growing on them. Just a broad depression, a stadium like a wound in the earth. Stones from the legacy of Hephaestus had been quarried here: tuff or pumice, hardened silver nitrate with variegated bubbles and pores, easily read by those adept at prophecy.

Hermes read that he would lie with a woman that night.

There were bees everywhere—had they built nests in the air bubbles of the rock? That seemed unlikely, for even wild bees were too respectable to turn to the arid waste of volcanic tuff. Now he saw an unadorned, four-story building staring wretchedly out across the broad caldera from the farther edge of the scooped-out ghost arena. That's where the bees were coming from, and buzzing off to.

In the center of the depression was a giant puddle left by the rain. He didn't care for his reflection: his hair had been baked into a black, crinkled carpet by the heat and smoke of the volcano. He washed his hair and body thoroughly with sand and water. He couldn't get rid of the blackness on his skin, nor would his hair straighten.

He found the building empty, half in ruins. Large sections of the walls, built with slabs of rock instead of stones, had collapsed. Probably an earthquake. The bees' nests were inside, high in the corner, between wall and ceiling. In the large, bare, empty room, their hum echoed like the nervous music that announced the arrival of the Furies. Hephaestus had been the guardian here: iron wheels everywhere, some with gear teeth, others wide and smooth for long leather belts, which stretched in turn to other wheels. Next to those, wheels with handles, wheels on rusted carts, innumerable tiny gear wheels in a broken box on the floor.

From a second-story window Hermes could see the houses of Thera. On a high wall he could read TAVERNA MYTHOS, in Roman letters, of course, which were far less familiar to him. Could the Greeks have all died out? Wine still seemed available anyway; that was important for dealing with humans. He longed to be traveling through cities again, gazing through brightly lit windows at men and women making love, drinking, fighting, or reading. Even as a child god he'd spent many a night that way, curious to see how much of the divine these humans retained when they felt themselves unobserved.

He'd wait till sunset, then be on his way. He wondered what the women were wearing these days. But the main question was whether he could regain control of his renowned leap through the right ear of a living being. Could he carefully wind his way once more past the eardrum, climb the hammer, anvil, and stirrup, avoiding any noisy slips or falls, and then begin his controlling whispers? No one had ever done it better, and some gods had never dared to try.

One thing was certain: he was not about to bore himself roaming about among men and women whose heads he couldn't enter. If he couldn't penetrate mortals, absorb strange worlds, leave his trace upon them, he preferred to return to his chains, doze off, and dry up in the smoke for a few more thousand years. Anything but a clearheaded boredom.

• • •

The climb was easier than he'd thought. He'd left the basket in the bees' bare palace. He headed straight toward the inviting sign of the tavern. The holes in the hardened lava offered a solid grip. A startled scorpion stung him on the thumb. Fortunately he could shake off pain the way a dog shakes off water. Then came a high, smooth wall, probably the battlements of Thera, the final barrier. But when he looked over the top, no tavern was in sight.

• • •

It must have been an outdoor shrine, with cypresses, stone benches, and an obelisk in the center. He could make out bas-reliefs with an inscription in memory of Greek soldiers killed in battle with the "Turkoi." Some new race, presumably, from the edge of the world. No mention of who won.

No one here either. Nothing but a dog that trotted up, sniffed him, and decided to adopt him temporarily as a master. Hermes wondered if he should risk slipping into the dog's head to make his own naked, black form disappear. But dog ears required additional practice and dexterity. They were protected by a shock of hair and had a tendency to flicker at the crucial moment. A further disadvantage was that animals showed almost no reaction to whispered guidance; you had to bypass the auditory nerve and make your way to the cerebellum. It was nothing more than a sport. They could serve as a hiding place or a disguise in emergencies; he'd fathered Pan while in a goat, which was no simple matter—in that case one had to penetrate a lot further than the brain. And it was important to avoid the butcher's knife and the hunter's arrow if you were hiding in an animal. It could be a real pain.

Now he needed something to cover his nakedness. He saw a tall pole at the top of which a rectangular blue cloth with white stripes fluttered in the wind. He mounted in a flash, loosening the cloth from the eyelets, noticing as he did so that it could easily have been lowered with the attached cord. He slid down, tied it around his waist, and walked on. A man with an amazing hanging belly was standing in front of one of the houses. He'd observed him stealing the cloth and was busily scolding him. His Greek was worse than Hecate's; he used words Hermes had never heard before. "Speak like a man, so I can understand you!" Hermes said. He thought of adding, "I'm Hermes and would appreciate your hospitality." Or should he enter his mind? The man had the standard lettuce-leaf ear of the informer, probably poorly washed. It certainly wasn't attractive, but he needed to begin his studies as soon as possible.

The fat one went back inside, and Hermes followed, in spite of his protests, waiting for the best chance at his right ear. But the man lifted a white bone to his head, put one end to his mouth, and covered his ear with the other, as if he were onto the god's trick and wanted to protect himself, while talking excitedly all the time. It was actually more like a small sculpture than a bone, polished smooth, with a slender cord dangling from it. At any rate, Hermes couldn't get into his ear. He didn't like the man anyway, and the interior of the house repelled him—gleams and reflections everywhere, sharp edges on everything. He went back out to look for the tavern. The dog was still there, lifting a leg against one of the cypresses.

A slim, pretty woman passed by and glanced at Hermes, her eyes straying for a moment to the cloth wrapped about him. She was alone, apparently on her way to the shrine to converse with the gods. She must be the one he was supposed to follow to the midpoint of the world! Her eyes were blue, her hair blond and surprisingly short. Her garment was totally unfeminine: a huge jacket with padded shoulders, her legs stuck in long blue tubes made of a hard, thick material. But the way she moved in this fortress was promising: graceful and supple, with a hint of special agility. He followed her and said with a smile: "You're in luck. I am Hermes. You will bring forth demigods and have a long life."

She laughed, shrugged, and said something in an awkward, sibilant barbarian tongue that couldn't possibly be based on Greek. She gazed long and hard at his body, with a curiosity that seemed a challenge but was surely surprise. He intended to help this wonderful young rogue of a woman out of that man's jacket and leggings just as rapidly as possible. She didn't seem afraid, which was good. Of course, one of the simplest tricks of all was to turn fear into joy, but he needed his winged staff for that, and for the moment Hecate had it. Before long, certainly, he would be in this woman's head, learning what she knew and where she was going in the world. He wanted to absorb her language, so he could whisper sweet nothings in the days ahead. She'd have to remove her metal earrings, which were so big they blocked his way.

A shrine was just the place for intimate relationships between gods and mortals. Hermes placed his hand gently on the woman's padded shoulder and turned her toward him. Her face was intelligent, pleasant, and lively, displaying an incipient devotion for which he had been waiting thousands of years. This woman knew instinctively to submit quietly at the approach of a god. I'll have her ride me, thought Hermes; she's not used to a shrine's stone benches. His heart beat rapidly, no longer in hibernation mode.

Suddenly men's voices. It was the fat guy again, accompanied by two tall men in stiff caps, with black sticks in their hands. Rough voices—they seemed to be barking orders. These men obviously didn't know a god when they saw one. Where to—into the woman's head? Her earrings blocked the way, and the magic leap didn't work if he had to clear the way himself. No, there was no way out; he had to forfeit her and run. He hadn't regained top speed yet, but the men in caps had difficulty keeping up with him. Of course, they knew the place better. Women screamed as he raced down a crowded street, narrowly avoiding a large glassy tortoise on wheels. People sitting inside recoiled at the sight of him. It was a dead-end street, so he slipped into one of the houses through an open door. People were sitting in front of a boxlike window that emitted a bluish, shimmering light. He dashed up the stairs and through a room, then pulled himself onto the roof and hid behind a chimney flue. One of the capped men tried to follow him, while the other shouted up directions from the street. The man who was chasing him stepped onto the roof, but he was too heavy. He broke through the tiles with a clatter, falling to the floor beneath. Hermes heard his groans and curses. On the roof stood a long pole with a comblike metal frame, a bird perch. So there was an avian cult now.

He heard the voices of men beneath the roof. A few long leaps across the houses back to the shrine seemed in order—after all, the young woman was waiting for him on the stone bench. He loped along without breaking through the tiles. Even portly gods don't weigh much more than a well-nourished cat, unless they intentionally increase their weight. A few people noticed him, but his strength and agility had returned—no one could follow.

The young woman had disappeared. Had the fat man seized her? Hermes went to his house and asked, and again the man picked up the sculpture with the cord. Hermes grabbed it, banged him on the fingers, and repeated his question. But the fat man no longer understood classical Greek. Hermes returned to where the woman had been last standing, near the obelisk, and inhaled deeply. She smelled like flowers. Where was the dog? He came trotting toward him. Hermes crouched to play with him, murmuring so that he cocked his ears and stood still. Then Hermes loosened his blue-and-white waistcloth; he had to be naked to enter a head. Just like that, he was in, no problem with the hair after all. He slipped cautiously past the eardrum into the middle ear—dogs were touchier than humans—and glided across the bridge into a world of scents and memories of untold canine generations. Among the freshest Hermes discovered the flowery fragrance of the woman. Even a beginner couldn't lose his way in the cerebellum. He quickly reacquainted himself with the layout of the nerve centers, stimulating and tickling the right spots. Stirring the hunting instinct was easy. He put the dog on the scent, and he was off, sniffing his way through town. Hermes inched forward to the optic nerve, which was easy to walk along, and looked out through the dog's eyes. He was startled to see another giant tortoise heading for him. He'd be in for a long, miserable time if he got trapped in a dead dog's head: he could leave only a live host or one totally decomposed.

But the dog knew what he was doing. He slipped along calmly with no problem, doggedly following the scent of the woman to her room. The dog glided through the hotel entrance as a porter tried to stop him. But an animal carrying Hermes wasn't about to be slowed by a few yells and projectiles. Then came a staircase, a long, dark hall, and the dog paused before a door, whining. Hermes sprang from his ear. Seeing him suddenly full size again, the dog took off in fright.

How did doors open these days? Good thing the dog had whined: the woman opened it from the inside. She wasn't even surprised, just laughed and let him in. A large vial stood on the table, with two narrow glass reeds standing in it, so that you couldn't take a drink without hitting your nose.

There was glass everywhere! One piece, the size of your forearm, was a treasure kings could once have sent a special ship for. Three hundred oars had dipped into the sea three hundred thousand times for a few drinking cups of blue glass. Humans seemed to love anything that reflected light, anything sparkling and iridescent. There were mirrors, polished metal, and another material as well, a transparent, gleaming skin they used to decorate all sorts of objects. Hermes watched with amusement as the young woman rolled a shimmering, close-fitting sheath of this stuff down the entire length of his increasingly animated and quite prominent friend and only then took the full pleasure of his company, although it was clear that no demigods were in the offing that way. Not even common mortals; nothing at all.

• • •

While they were having lunch, Aegina appeared ahead, so they were not all that far from Athens. They played a trick on me, thought Helga, and decided from then on to say "Athens Fool!" instead of

"April Fool!" and tell people what a lousy travel bureau it was. To restrain her anger, she concentrated on the pleasant prospect of seeing again the Corinth Canal, which had fascinated her on the way out. In the layers and fissures of its high walls she read an immense history of failed, fulfilled, or forsaken love, the story of the world's end. It wasn't hard; you just had to know where you were on the wall and then seek a way out, like a river at its source. She hoped the ship would pass through more slowly this time.

The blacksmith bent over her table and asked if she wanted to play Ping-Pong. The poor guy had no idea he was taking on the oft-crowned champion of Stendal's Locomotive Sports Club. He seemed to be seeking her out for some reason. Deep down she felt sorry for him. A decent man under some sort of pressure. She replied: "I'm resting up for the going-away party." She'd said it too quickly and had to repeat herself.

She wasn't looking forward to Stendal. No dark-skinned lover there, no sudden, intoxicating, gripping love. Instead that artificial birdcage at the toy store on Unity Street (still the old name, from a time when "unity" had only one meaning). The bird's recorded voice had been chirping the same thing over and over since February: "Hello! I know your name! I've got a present for you!" Then he would shake his tail, fall silent for a few moments, and repeat it. She'd grown frightened of it and avoided Unity Street. She wanted to leave Stendal as soon as possible.

To live in Santorin! In a house on a precipice with a view of the sunset, as the hostess and lover of a smoke-colored god from the earliest stages of mankind. All she had to do was learn Greek. *"Chronia polla"*—"Here's to many years"—that was the Easter greeting, the triumphal cry of resurrection. She'd celebrated another sort of resurrection, with the resurrected one himself, and he had indeed risen. She'd stolen jeans and a jacket from a farmhouse for him. There'd been no danger, because everyone was watching the midnight procession. Then they strolled through the city with the others, watching the procession and the people. The tabernacle was borne upon a white salver covered with flowers. Up in the tower, illuminated like a fish in an aquarium, a sexton tolled the bell. Small cannons were being fired, as they had been intermittently throughout the day. Perhaps they were meant to replace the earthquakes that accompany all true resurrections.

Helga leaned back and closed her eyes with a smile. A god, cunning, with excellent timing, dark. They understood each other without a common language. The sounds of their voices had sufficed, the melody of the tale. Helga talked incessantly, the more so since she saw how carefully he was listening. About how little love there'd been in her home life, though that was in the past. (She told him about Henri Beyle, a French soldier who, in 1807, spent a night of love with a certain Minette in 19 Schadewachten Straße, now Friendship Street, then chose the city's name as a pseudonym and became a famous novelist.) To the west of Stendal, she said, lay the midpoint of the world, in the village of Poppau bei Klötze. Actually it was only a large stone, but from it hung the mighty chains that bound the continents. He listened entranced, then spoke in Greek. She understood effortlessly that she was the most beautiful, wildest, most passionate, most enchanting woman—in short, one for whom he would gladly die, if gods could, and that she should hear how she made the blood pound in his ears. And indeed it was true.

Yes, ears. The black god was crazy about them. He kissed her ears over and over, the right one especially. He didn't care for her earrings, or the scarf she was wearing that Easter night. But there was nothing doing. Her instinct was to offer everything, to open up completely, whenever he wanted, as often as he wished—but not her right ear, without really knowing why.

Then she ran into the Frenchman Jean-Claude, who wanted her to come see something in the shop window of a small white building with a cupola near the church: an oil painting of the Grand Canal in Venice. Bridges, black gondolas, and on the balcony of a palazzo a calm naked figure with dark skin and bright eyes. Both a messenger and a message, but of what?

When she turned back to her companion, she found his jacket and jeans hanging across the handlebars of a bicycle near the window. He was gone. The Frenchman was still there, however, smiling at her. He wanted to go up to her room but had badly misjudged her. For her it was now a god or nothing.

She didn't believe it was finished. Naked he came, and now, shaking the dust from his feet, naked he went, Hermes, her lover from the cliff. Gods don't leave for long. They come and go as they wish. If she didn't despair and just kept on being cheerful, then he'd be back.

• • •

Back for the first time in a man's head again! Having paid a brief visit to the arbor vitae in the cerebellum, he was sitting beneath the vault of the cerebrum. This spot offered the best overview of the labyrinth of passages and channels, thought sources and memory depots into which he would soon venture, where even the most ingenious of gods occasionally lost their way. And he no longer knew what a normal brain was supposed to look like, nor did he know the man's language, so he couldn't orient himself with common concepts. Perhaps he should have chosen a child first, and not a *mathémeticien diplômé*, some sort of mathematical slave *délégué aux assurances*. Nevertheless, *Jean-Claude*, whom he now shared, so to speak, was on the ship with the young woman and was a grown man to boot. So no pleasure was beyond him. He could make sure that Jean-Claude kept a good eye on Helga. That was her name, *Helga*, as he'd discovered inside. At first he'd barely recognized Helga through Jean-Claude's eyes. They weren't very clear eyes, turned more often inward than outward.

Helga on the other hand was Hermes' type. Would she have stolen clothes for him otherwise? She risked giving something she didn't own but happily stole. That proved it.

Now he had to learn about the present-day world. He had to

see what Jean-Claude was seeing, learn the words he used and their broader context. Precisely because the *français* wasn't his type and couldn't think, let alone see, except conceptually, he was ideally suited for learning. When he came across a new concept, he tended to visualize it verbally rather than record it aurally, and that, too, was an advantage. As soon as Hermes knew a thing or two, he planned to have another go at the beautiful Helga.

Jean-Claude was lying on a deck chair of stretched cloth, staring at the seagulls as they glided along in the wake of the ship, their wings motionless.

The ship was huge and white, without a single sail, and scarcely swayed. A light trail of smoke came from a structure above the deck. Aeolus, protector of the winds, would no doubt be annoyed by this ship. Hephaestus must have built this floating fortress, for wherever one looked it bristled with wheels and metal, and the walls were dotted with iron studs. The ship's belly held a hot fire called *la machinerie,* something Prometheus surely never dreamed of the day he stole a tiny coal of fire from the forge of Hephaestus and smuggled it out to mankind in the hollow stem of a plant. He had only meant to offer them protection against wild animals.

There was no denying it—Hermes was biased against the ship. It moved by arrogant, unnatural laws, and unfortunately Poseidon seemed willing to put up with it. How easily he could suck ships down to his domain, with all their men, beasts, and treasures. But the god of the ocean and Hephaestus must have made a deal— they seemed to be getting along for a change. A mere metal skin divided Poseidon's cool and infinite empire from the force and flame of the god of fire. Hephaestus' power had seemingly increased if things were going that smoothly. No wonder—he was always making something (it was his form of eroticism), and unless someone stopped him, it was only a question of time till that unbridled demiurge was omnipresent through his artifacts alone. At any rate, Hermes mused, all I want is to stretch my limbs, take a look at what's going on, and command some respect again. No tiring fights with lovers of material power.

He wished only to wander along, a messenger with no message, taking things as they came, at ease with everything. Having descended dark-skinned from the cliff, he had no interest in a *carrière.* The word occurred so frequently in the Frenchman's brain that its meaning was clear. Too bad Jean-Claude spoke *français* and *anglais* but not Helga's native language. At some point when her ear was free he would have to switch from Jean-Claude to her. He preferred women's heads anyway. Except perhaps during truly intimate moments—and even then changing places added spice on occasion.

He would have to figure out the world in French—a good way to start, since it was a language unclouded by vagueness and mystery.

All right, then: these big new buildings were made of *beton,* not rock, and the streets were *bitume,* not lava. Another thing crucial to everyone's happiness, but especially Jean-Claude's, was *multiplication.* It meant rapid increments, faintly reminiscent of amassing wealth. It didn't depend on fertility, luck, or genealogy, however, but consisted of frantically increasing identical elements in a slavishly reproductive drill.

Jean-Claude had slept with a skillful and experienced prostitute on one of the islands, and now he was worried he might have a disease called *SIDA.* Hermes hadn't figured out yet what caused it. He did know, however, how much money was involved: one hundred dollars for the night. Based on the price of courtesans twenty-five centuries ago, that equaled three hundred obols or fifty drachmas or half a mina, about the price of a small, simple pearl necklace. A jug of wine, then, should cost about five dollars. Hermes didn't care much for arithmetic, but inside the head of a *mathématicien diplômé* it was child's play.

Learning how to move and manipulate was more difficult— turning on the lights, for example. When Jean-Claude entered a darkened room he would reach inside and feel beside the door, then touch or press a spot on the wall without looking, so Hermes could never tell what it was. Not even the name of this spot on the wall appeared. A god in a man's brain learned by means of phrases he found stored in fissures, gyri, and fossae beneath the skull's roof. He could register involuntary or thoughtless actions, but the vocabulary for them was missing when the subject came up. He would have to learn to control those actions as well, once he was traveling in his own form again. He had ample opportunity to witness how the leg-wear called *pantalon* were fastened (Jean-Claude kept looking down, and so he did as well, to make sure things were in order). He couldn't discover the principle behind it, however—the man pulled and it closed, he pulled again and it opened. The direction seemed crucial, as in other cases where something is done magically with the flip of the wrist (a tiny motion, but in one clear direction). Or take his feet: Jean-Claude wore white footwear of leather and cloth, with soles of soft, nonsticking resin. To close, you pressed down on the flaps. To open, you lifted the flaps with a ripping noise (nothing was damaged). Then there was a place where bodily waste first saw the light of day and was then chased noisily off to sea. First it was deposited in a white bowl. After you pressed on a metal handle, Poseidon's power would flow into the bowl from several openings, roaring and revolving like dancing maenads, and soon it would all break up and disappear. But Jean-Claude had no word for it, he didn't think of it, he didn't say it. It all took place so thoughtlessly! In other cases—on doors, for example—he found the right words: *closed, open.* The washbasin had handles on the pipes. If you turned them to the left, water came out; that was *eau.* If it didn't come out, it was *merde;* if it came after some time, it was *enfin.*

Jean-Claude found it hard to approach Helga because he didn't speak her language. And more important, she didn't care for him. The fact that Hermes kept shoving thoughts of Helga to the front of the mathematician's mind didn't help either. He forced him to seek her out and try a conversation in English. She said she wanted to read. Not a book, but the wall of the canal the ship was passing through. That, too, showed she was Hermes' type. She traced the plans that lived in rock and wood, trying to recognize in the contours of cliff and clay, in the sequences of veins and fissures, what lay in store for them and for herself, to see the future, not suspecting that Hermes languished not an arm's length from her in the ear of the mathematician. There was another difficulty. When a god lodged in another body, the mind of the host affected the guest's mood, as a home might, and the god influenced the host in turn. Although Jean-Claude was in love, his attitude toward Helga, and women in general, differed from that of Hermes, who didn't understand women but simply wanted them. Jean-Claude had a large, carefully arranged collection to which he constantly added new categories: round and slim, extra-long legs, pretty little neck, dark locks, blond curls. He thought he understood women because he had so many stored in the locker of his mind—he'd slept with very few. He considered it his duty to treat women properly. The key word for his type was *correct*. Which didn't prevent him from wearing socks to bed, woolly, scratchy ones. He had no idea how itchy feet, suffocating in the miasma of socks, could lay waste to a brain overnight. And things were bad enough anyway. Only a few images still rose from the past, and when they did they were static, they no longer shimmered and danced. The words *enfant* or *France* produced an oil painting of one of Jean-Claude's ancestors, called *le Connétable,* in a suit of armor, with an extensive meadow called a *parc* surrounding a large, turreted building in the distance. Little Jean-Claude used to play hide-and-seek there with his sister. While she was looking for him, he was pissing behind a bush, hoping she would catch him in the act. There were some images of this sort, but in general they were few and far between.

The gods find no effective instruments of change in dull minds. The spirit develops only in a convoluted brain, bright, observant, and sparkling with memories, one that can be directed toward discovery, toward full potential. Fortunately the overly correct *Français*

lay down to rest up for *la fête* that evening. Hermes slipped out of his
ear, donned the Frenchman's clothes, and went to Helga's cabin. But
she was resting too—she had closed her door and plugged her ears
so she could sleep. So he went up on deck, stretched out in a chair
next to the dozing fat man who spoke Helga's language, and
removed his clothes. He wanted to learn German. It was a robust
button ear like a bear's, with a slightly greasy outer canal and a
somewhat callous tympanic cavity. In his rush to get to the cerebrum, Hermes took a wrong turn at the pineal gland and stumbled
over a longitudinal sinus. When he arrived in the vault, intense
dreaming was in progress. A wave of memories and fantasies broke
over him and tumbled him forward to the hippocampus major.

He knew he needed to proceed cautiously in dreaming hosts,
but even so he was startled by the aural memories in progress:
ringing hammers, flying sparks, a deafening din, and in the midst of
it all the message THE FORGE MUST BE MASTERED! A blacksmith. Fortunately the dream was ended by a mighty hammer blow. The man
stretched and opened his eyes. Jean-Claude's clothes lay on the chair
beside him. Helga was just passing. He rushed to the outer ear.
Should he leap across? But once again her ears were blocked by an
insurmountable barrier, black this time. Each ear held a plug, joined
by a band beneath her chin, and music chirped faintly from them.
Hermes suspected the worst: someone else was already sitting in her
head. How else could music come out?

The other possibility was to slip out of the fat man's ear and
don Jean-Claude's clothes again. He chose that, although several
passengers watched in amazement. While he was still pulling on the
pantalon he was brusquely confronted by a man in white with a stiff
cap who asked something incomprehensible. He had no choice but
to abandon his pants and return to the ear. He found the name of his
interrogator: "officer," together with a large dose of negative feelings—the blacksmith didn't like that type at all. The officer looked
so dumbfounded that Hermes broke into a long, loud laugh, which
dizzied the blacksmith.

Helga, who had noticed nothing, was leaning against the ship's rail, her eyes closed. With a few tickles and tugs at the blacksmith's brain, Hermes managed to get the fat man up and over to the young woman. Since his host spoke neither *anglais* nor *français*, Hermes was hardly prepared to speak German—so for the moment there was no chance to have him say in German, "I'm Hermes." He left the choice of words up to the blacksmith and heard him say: "Want to hit a few?" having no idea what he meant. She opened her eyes and said: "I beg your pardon?" "Ping-Pong," replied the blacksmith, and produced a clear image of a small white ball. She shook her head with a smile and shut her eyes, returning to her chirping earplugs.

There Hermes sat in this smithy of a brain not even learning "German," except for "Have a beer." For a god with two thousand years to make up, the detour was too long. Hermes knew the stock this blacksmith came from, the typical "jolly innkeeper": good-natured, alert, and always ready for a practical joke, a man closer to Dionysus than to Hephaestus. But those traits had long since disappeared. He was like slaked lime; alacrity had waned with good nature, good nature with alacrity. It all had to do with a plague or illness called "work." He didn't know its origin, but he did sense that it destroyed the spirit, depriving mortals of freedom and leisure, retarding both the mind and the imagination. And a part of the blacksmith's mind was shut off, dungeon-like, separated from the rest of the mental apparatus; not quite a tumor, but something strange. Hermes couldn't figure it out. All he sensed was the smell of pitch and ashes rising from the region.

But now mental echoes of the concept "officer" were resurfacing from an earlier period. The blacksmith had been in the army but not in battle. He'd spent hours on end as a "lineman" with a long pole, clamping an endless black field cable to construction poles. Officers were there to make them work faster, and in some cases any reasonable man would have dropped a long pole on one, as did the blacksmith, who wound up in a dark "stockade," while the officer escaped with a "lump."

• • •

An office sparkling with glass and chrome, but an oilcan on the desk and stained overalls hanging from the back of the chair. A heavy man on the telephone, broad-faced, a smoldering Brazil in his rusty paw, rocks nervously, seems annoyed. Two golden crutches with strange, baroque curves lean close at hand against the desk. On closer inspection they prove to be shaped like slender young women.

He kicks the wastebasket. "It's not 'Yes,' it's 'Yes, sir, Mr. Consul' or 'Yes, indeed, great master.' And I've given orders that he's always to be referred to indirectly, never by name."

Leaning forward, he listens impatiently.

"In whose head? What's his name!"

He lifts his chin, ponders with bated breath, and watches the rising smoke.

"I know him. He was an apprentice with Münch in Freystadt. How recent is this information?"

He takes a slide rule from the pencil tray and attempts to stem his impatience by running through a few calculations. The tongue-like middle section of the rule isn't gliding smoothly enough for him, so he removes it from the groove to grease it, passing it through his hair. He has little choice, since the bald spot has spread: the only place his hair is thick is on the back of his head and above the ears. He yawns.

"Nonsense! How would he know the code? If I have anyone under control, it's the Cyclopes. Better on vacation than at the forge. Do you think I'd have freed the Cyllenian if he were dangerous? He's looking around a blacksmith's brain, fine. He won't find it that pleasant. He probably thinks our relay station is a tumor, and he wouldn't understand the Lemnian arrangement even if it were explained to him. He was and is Ptolemaic; the sun still revolves around the earth, for all he knows. Besides, we know he only understands individual cases. That's certain."

He's so angry that without warning he lifts his hand slightly and slams his fist hard on the desk; then he balances his cigar on the ashtray with a strangely gentle, almost tender touch.

"Thor, of all gods! He should stick to tennis, reach number one, and let it go at that. Those hysterical Germanic gods are even less reliable than our own pack. What's he doing on the ship? I sent someone long ago. Thor should exercise or sit at home on his moor and watch how prettily rotten wood sparkles. Now here's an order: the son of Maia is henceforth our main concern!"

The slide-rule tongue now glides easily; the man clamps the receiver between his ear and shoulder and goes back to his calculations. He manipulates the slide rule so rapidly, multiplies with such quick virtuosity, that the instrument heats up. He keeps pulling the tongue out of the slide rule, blowing on it, waving it in the air. Then he slams the receiver down so violently that it bounces off the cradle with a clatter. He lifts the extinguished cigar from the ashtray, relights it, and ruminates. How should he spend what's left of the evening? Porno? Have the artfully constructed artificial slave satisfied by the even more artfully constructed robot? Or cross over to the workshop, start a fire, lay the iron in it, take the hammer, stretch, compress, chisel off, insert rivets, set up dies, pick his nose, get those lazy Cyclopes in gear? Or a game of poker, at least ten hours' worth? The best would be all of them, in that order.

• • •

By now Hermes knew his way around the blacksmith's mind. Given precise images and sounds for metalwork, Hermes was at home in the craft before the sun set. He watched glowing iron, heard the bell tone beneath the hammer, knew how to handle forge and anvil. Perhaps he could hire himself out as a blacksmith. Then he would even stand under the protection of his old adversary.

There was still something uncanny about it. Thoughts weren't roaming freely, memories and desires weren't expanding fully in the blacksmith's inner forge. They were magnetized like metal, attract-

ing or repulsing each other like filings, according to some mysterious law. The result was chaos, not of a free, vibrant kind, but the
frightened sort, the chaos in the brain of a victim, a fateful readiness
to obey when someone whose assignment it was to do so spoke or
whispered. The blacksmith knew how to handle tools, but he was
one himself. It was unclear, however, what man or god had set him
in motion and was now using him. The blacksmith longed to dance
but knew he couldn't, so he indulged in too much beer before and
during a "party," remembering all the while that he had never
danced, not even in "Freystadt Oberpfalz."

Language: German. Strangely enough, the fat man understood
other Germans, but they had trouble understanding him. Since he
never thought about it, his guest never learned why. He could only
learn things a host actually said or had on the tip of his tongue.

At any rate, what Helga had said that Easter night could now be
deciphered. Hermes' memory was as divine as at his birth in the cave
on Mount Cyllene. Henceforth he knew about Henri Beyle's night of
love in Stendal, about the squawking bird in Unity Street, and that
the midpoint of the world lay in Poppau bei Klötze.

He had never been in the brain of such a thoroughly dissolute
body. Thoughts moved with difficulty in the belly-heavy head. The
reverberating echoes of that stomach blurred all thought, which was
continually focused on food or drink or, due to constant gas, the
next welcome fart, to say nothing of the pleasure of a belch that
would give any normal man a concussion. In technical matters the
blacksmith was quite alert, but even then he was thinking of his
stomach, which he had to care for and fill. When he needed to think,
he patted it. And conversely, the moment he stroked his round belly,
he started thinking—he was stimulating not his brain but rather the
entity around which all his thoughts revolved.

The man did an interesting thing with his mouth. He suckled
himself, not with milk but with smoke, drawing it from a thick,
brown phallus, which he tongued pleasurably. A new type of He-

phaestic self-gratification. Hermes assumed all metalworkers carried them in their mouths as a badge of recognition. He had no interest in learning how to set himself on fire. He couldn't in any case, for there were limits. Skills that were beneath a god's dignity were denied him: arts of avarice or hate, the thoughts of the eternally foolish—and now this embarrassing facial vulcanism. Jean-Claude's strange art of *multiplication* seemed in the same category; at any rate, Hermes was unable to master it.

A strange figure always sat somewhere near the blacksmith, watching him, a tall man, heavy but not plump, powerful looking, with shoulder-length blond hair, perhaps a Nordic demigod. His eyes, a pale clear blue, slanted slightly inward. The resulting gaze was penetrating; he squinted with ambition and concentration. His languid movements contrasted strongly with his rapid, sharp-tongued speech. What was it about the dull, brooding blacksmith that held the interest of this bird-eyed, pale-skinned he-man? He watched him constantly and kept trying to strike up a conversation with him. Finally he brought over a tall glass of water he called *vodka*. And that was the beginning of true hell.

At first it was only interesting: the water with the strange name descended into the blacksmith's chest like fire, setting his stomach and navel furiously and pleasantly ablaze as no wine had before. His perceptions became more acute, not of details perhaps (the blacksmith could hardly find his way to Poseidon's sluice and back), but for those truths that bind us together or tear us apart. After two glasses the blacksmith was certain that the blond, hawk-headed man had ulterior motives, so he swore at him until he stood up and walked away. But he continued drinking, as his enemy wished, bumping and barging into someone whenever he moved. He tried to explain his condition, but could only manage to stammer: "Scuse me, scuse me."

Since no one would talk to him now (Hermes watched with melancholy as Helga appeared in the background), the fat man was reading a "newspaper." But how he read, moving his head at every line! Was he trying to show he could read in spite of being drunk? Was he trying to conceal his state? No, it was something else. He was reading differently than he did when he was sober. Each word became an image in his mind, but at the word "taxes," such a powerful fountain of bad feeling arose that the blacksmith's soul dissolved in the flickering forge of his belly and shifted to destructive euphoria. *"Down with it all!"* he yelled. To keep from falling prey to his own wishes and committing suicide then and there, he tried to continue reading, the only thing that could save him. He swiveled his head line for line, in forced rhythm, forcing his eyes onward past any dangerous word that might singe them. Sitting in such a heavily fogged brain would frighten any god. This was a ship without a captain. But the damned blacksmith just sat there and drank. Hermes could hardly exit with all these people around. And there were more and more of them, gathering for *la fête*. A musician was sitting on the tiny stage with a big-bellied stringed instrument, while his colleagues were changing. With fierce determination, Hermes dived back into the muddled wishes and swaying thoughts of the blacksmith, but in vain. He raced to the cerebellum and made him sneeze, hoping to expel some of the fog. Finally he made him feel fatigue, got him swaying in the direction of his cabin—and forced him to choose the wrong door! For the first time, Hermes had piloted a host against his will to a place of his own choice. It was the cabin of one of the band members.

• • •

Music! That a simple scratching and scraping, plucking and puffing, could produce a universal mood, a joyful dance of the mind—even the gods found it awesome. Now that Hermes had entered the head of the "drummer," he had been dancing cautiously between the hippocampus major, the vault, and the arbor vitae, observing every touch and beat, each tone and harmony.

Strangely enough, it now appeared that humans considered higher notes cheerful, while using the lower ones to express sorrow and death. In the melodies he used to play on the lyre, high notes expressed isolation and loneliness, indifference or departure, while lower ones showed intimacy, warmth, joy. Someone had stood music on its head, and perhaps the world with it.

The musician whose right ear he had entered so happily under the roaring "shower" was named "Charles" and came from a town called "Sparta, Illinois." He kept a steady beat for the "band" but now and again threw in an unexpected variation, which was important. During the first few hours of the cruise, Hermes hadn't considered a musician, keeping an eye out instead for his own kind: thieves, merchants, orators. Musicians were considered disciples of Apollo. But the drummer's performance combined music and rhetoric, and some of his complex sequences required the assurance of a master thief. Hermes was comfortable inside the man and decided to help him. Charles was susceptible to divine whispering and could be guided from the middle ear. He could even be made to speak the god's German, so Hermes could use him to approach Helga. Charles for his part would be a virtuoso in no time, able to play anything in dreamy abandonment.

As they had from time immemorial, humans understood only half of most things, and not always the better half. The gods grasped an even smaller portion but could develop from it, scanty as it might be, a new whole of their own, which for a time would be considered perfection itself. When Hermes had absorbed what Charles knew about music, along with his musical ability, he saw possibilities that had been overlooked or never attempted because of their technical difficulty. And he could do something about it, since he had no equal as an accelerator of human brains. He improved circulation, created new shortcuts, and achieved by pure presence a speedier transference of electrical charges. No, he had forgotten nothing.

The people beneath the garlands were singing now. Charles and his friends played a song Hermes could easily decipher: "All You

Need Is Love." Although he viewed humans quite clear-sightedly, once they started singing they seemed to him calm and joyful, almost godlike, because for once they ceased trembling, stumbling, and stuttering.

• • •

Helga had never heard such a drum solo. She loved anyone who was truly gifted. Who made everything mesh! She loved all virtuosity. They sprang to their feet, cheering the inspired musician. Now he was standing beside her on the deck, good-looking and still perspiring, smiling at her. She felt a pleasant shock in the pit of her stomach, a tickling sensation, and her eyes tried in vain to find a place to rest on the horizon. The drummer revealed, in what was clearly the blacksmith's Oberpfalz dialect, that he was under the guidance of Hermes, was in fact Hermes himself, in a manner of speaking, and needed to talk with her. Could they find some quieter spot?

"I could have sworn you came to me as Jean-Claude."

"Could be. I've been in him. Connétable's great-grandson, all talk and no action."

"My god, just feel how my heart's pounding," she replied. He felt a spot where the beating of her heart was cushioned to the point of faintness, but she was right.

She gazed toward a ship at sea, a mass of sparkling light. Perhaps they were dancing there too, and if so, then surely with the gods. The world was teeming with them.

"Good, let's hit the road, then!" The drummer spent a long time in her cabin, talking. It took a while before she believed, for example, that his grandfather was Atlas and had been turned into a mountain because he looked at the head of Medusa. Sometimes sentences slipped in that weren't his but he wanted to try out anyway: "The forge must be mastered" or "We cast slabs" or "I hung the crane hook on the loops of the molds—does that mean anything to you?"

"Of course; my father is an executive in heavy-metal industry. But why don't you come out and show yourself as the Hermes I know?" asked Helga.

"And what would we do with Charles?" said Charles. She could see the problem. She wanted to show that she believed him completely. He was welcome to stay the night. Her only reservation was whether the Mondo Gold condoms she'd brought from home still offered reliable protection against the creation of little demigods.

But she found out that wildly inspired musicians weren't necessarily wild about her or inspired in bed. Things quickly turned to little more than a soft cuddle and sleepy exhaustion. Well, after all, an artist . . . But it wasn't quite enough for her, or for Hermes, sitting in his head.

The ship arrived in Venice. The band member rejoined his colleagues and packed his things. Helga wanted to stay with him to save money—rooms were expensive in Venice. And if he was hosting Hermes, he'd certainly catch on to things sometime.

But it wasn't a good morning. The drummer's luggage was rifled by an agent, then sniffed by a dog they'd fooled into thinking that hashish was something interesting. The band member was led away in handcuffs, with Hermes still inside. He gazed sadly at Helga—or was it hopefully? More likely the latter. Hermes in prison? That was a laugh!

She knew now that Hermes would always come to her, in the forms of various men, and perhaps not always the most suitable ones. But a variable god was better than none at all.

• • •

The head of Charles from Sparta, Illinois, was not a particularly good place to be. For one thing, it was permeated with fear, which crept in when they put the silver metal loops around his wrists. Now that same icy fear was paralyzing his entire brain. No matter how hard Hermes tried to keep the visual center and vocabulary in working order, his nestling and messaging were to no avail. Charles just sat there dully, eyes unfocused, brooding. The word "shit" was constantly floating about. It meant many things, and Hermes couldn't quite get the full sense of the word. Often it was a black clay the dogs and officers had discovered in small earthenware jars, but sometimes it was also the erotic misfortune of the previous night.

Hermes was not at all happy. The ancient methods the gods employed to control a powerful, high-spirited man's body seemed to have lost their effectiveness. How could he turn him into the greatest musician in the world, yet fail to exercise the least control over his lovemaking—he, Hermes, of all the gods? It was upsetting. The man seemed too concerned with the possibility of sudden fame as a musician to be turned on by Helga's desire. Of course, Hermes had considered exiting and taking care of things himself, but he abandoned the idea with a heavy heart: what sense would there be in making love in the presence of a god-forsaken man from Sparta, Illinois, who might well turn aggressive? Granted, it would be easy enough to throw him out—but then Helga would no longer be in the mood.

He didn't see much of the harbor, since Charles barely looked around. It smelled of burnt oil, the water was dirty, the buildings tall and made of "concrete." Soon he felt through Charles's eyes the gaze of a batlike creature high above the harbor. Perhaps it was a local spirit; they were by no means limited to mountain waterfalls or meadowland trees. There were Roman letters everywhere. STUCKYS stood on a building across the water, MARILENA on the bow of a huge white ship from the tip of which a blue-and-white cloth was waving in the wind—he had covered himself with one very much like it and only managed to attract even more attention. CARA-BINIERI was the name of the place where Charles had been taken. With what little sight remained to his host, Hermes could still read letters but could make no use of his prophetic abilities reading pebbles, cracks, textures.

He was liking Charles less and less. True, he wasn't as washed out a child of man as the blacksmith, but he'd turned into a megalomaniac, which didn't mean he wasn't frightened. On the contrary. Hermes knew his type. Alcibiades had been like that, in the presence of Zeus, of course—an entirely different order of greatness! He considered himself the greatest and acted like it, so he developed a large following and attained great power. But because it had all been feigned, as if by an actor, it was of only limited duration. One night, drunk like a hoplite after a victory, he went out and knocked the manly ornament off the column of none other than Hermes himself. Megalomaniacs generally fall surprisingly out of character, and always just before a conquest.

The officers, military puppets of Ares, with stiff faces and eternally jutting chins, began an *interrogatorio* in their language, which Charles recognized as an "interrogation" and then tried to continue in English.

Apparently Charles had digested neither the musical success nor the amorous failure of the previous night. At any rate, he said to the splendidly capped men of Ares: "I'm a famous artist, you know. I'm beyond your laws." That wasn't very smart, because they understood it. They rose, their chins thrust out even further, and shoved him into a small metal room. They slammed the door as loudly as possible, no doubt intending it to sound like an earthquake. Then there was the rattle of keys and the sound of receding footsteps—the whole thing was reminiscent of the Socrates affair. The difference was that Socrates knew how little he knew and in addition was well aware of what he was doing.

Hours passed. It was all the same to Hermes, but Charles suffered. Hermes tried in vain to get him to beat out a little music and stir up some good humor and mischief. A frightened musician—who ever heard of such a thing? There were people in the world who lacked courage and others who were only lazy but were using their laziness to save up strength for the right moment. They were the ones Hermes sided with, but Charles wasn't among them. He spent all his time making excuses. Hermes found that handy as far as learning a language went, but sooner or later he wanted out of this scared rabbit from Sparta, even if he was easier to control at night than in the daytime. Humans had turned hard of hearing when it came to the gods, that was clear enough. They wore wristwatches instead.

The door opened, and they led Charles down a passage and put him on a boat that buzzed like a hornet and stank like a tar torch. The fog was gone, along with the ship *Marilena*. The boat foamed along with unusual speed between a multitude of painted buildings and boats and ships, a painful blue light flashing at its bow, forcing everyone out of the way. Hermes was able to see buildings now and again, standing in water. The windows were outlined in white with green shutters, mostly closed. Rusty corrugated-metal skins covered the doors at the landing places, and a faded layer of paint peeled away from the walls. Once out of this head, he would be able to read them all.

Charles found himself sitting in another "interrogation," conducted by a fat man who was a specialist in matters of shit, with a chin like a small rear end. He was *Commissario Fibonacci,* or so the other polished caps called him among themselves. Charles noticed that the *commissario* liked young men and did his best to get him to like him as well, thinking only, How do I look, what does he think of me? It was getting too warm for Hermes in this fear-filled, complacent skull. He decided to leave his unworthy, uncontrollable host once and for all. He would have risked a direct leap into Fibonacci's ear, but he wore lavender buttons in both ears so he wouldn't understand the prisoners' answers. He would have been better off covering his eyes, which kept getting hung up on various pairs of trousers. Or at least covering his chin.

All right, here we go! That opened the *commissario*'s eyes. Two leaps in black nakedness across table and chairs, then one officer shoved against the other two, tumbling down. He got the door open—he'd learned a few things now. Air! Sky! Sun! But where to? To the midpoint of the world, that's it. Wait, first steal a pair of trousers and find some food. And look for Helga: she must still be in the city.

He'd have to read where.

VƐNICƐ

"What are you thinking about?" a child's voice said in Russian. Helga turned to see a small girl who was staying with her parents in the hotel. But since she hadn't heard them speak until then, it was the first Helga knew they were Russian. The breakfast room was relatively empty; the girl's parents hadn't yet arrived. Almost all visitors to Venice slept late, then groaned about the heat as they lost themselves in the narrow streets and tiny squares.

The child seemed to be waiting for an answer. Helga fumbled for what little Russian she knew: "Why do you ask, little one?"

"Because you keep smiling."

She realized it was true. Wasn't that fitting! Her father dead, a suicide: she'd learned about it at the post office on Rialto Bridge. He was already buried. She had been amusing herself on holiday in Greece and Santorin, was now lounging around Venice and smiling. When she got home they would ask her what had been so important about this island cruise, why had she left her poor old father alone. Surely she must have suspected . . .

"I'm smiling because I'm thinking of Hermes," she said to the child. Why invent a story when she already had one? She pronounced the god's name in German—Hermes had never come up in her Russian lessons.

"Tell me about Germs!"

"He's a god, a spirit from"—how did you say "Greece" in Russian?—"from the West. Will your parents be here soon?"

"In a while. I'm supposed to play till they come. What else?"

"Hermes was born in a cave on Mount Cyllene—that's in Europe. His mother was named Maia and his father was Zeus. The little one lay in his swaddling clothes, asleep in his cradle. When his parents went off for a minute or two to entertain themselves, he unwrapped himself, stood up, and found he could walk. He went to the entrance of the cave, where he met a tortoise and had a chat."

"Is that what you were smiling about?"

"No; it was something else. He made a balalaika out of the tortoise's shell. He made the strings from cow gut after stealing a herd of cattle from his brother Apollo. Then he played music on it."

"And what did Apollo do?"

"He was very angry, but the music was so beautiful that it calmed him. Then Hermes gave him the balalaika, and that was worth more than the cattle. So Apollo taught him how to read the future from pebbles."

"Have you seen Germs?"

"Yes. He's very handsome, his feet are beautiful, and he has a magic staff. Sometimes he's completely naked."

"And that's what made you smile!"

"Yes."

That's all she said, because the child's parents arrived. The little girl turned abruptly and ran to them.

Helga was almost out of money, and she'd lost her return ticket to Stendal. She was living in an inexpensive but not cheap hotel on the Campiello agli Incurabili. By midday it was already hot, which exacerbated the disgusting smell of her plastic luggage. Someday she would travel with an entire set of matched leather luggage, with two or three men in tow to carry them. But right now she lacked the most important thing of all. She certainly did not want to ask any German compatriots she might run into, always waiting for someone to provide them with a better life and complaining because no one did.

Must she return to Stendal? At this moment? Just to decorate the grave? She would do that only if she could take as long a detour as she wanted, by way of America or Athens, for example. Or stay in Venice until she found her god. She pulled the blinds down to dream about him.

Peggy Guggenheim, the millionaire, lived nearby. She could introduce herself to her as a hitherto unknown daughter of Hephaestus. "That sounds interesting!" Peggy would say. "Take a look at these paintings, your bed's over there, now come out onto the roof garden, we have lounge chairs and umbrellas and the champagne is ice cold—do you like oysters?" Peggy's guests would be sitting on the roof terrace, looking out over the Grand Canal. One of them would be a dark messenger who would rise joyfully, himself the message. A sign outside would read: CHIUSO PER RESTAURO. Then Peggy would go off to bed, and the other guests would depart. . . .

No, she couldn't get into the mood, couldn't get into the story. Her dead father kept resurfacing. With a "bored-out gas pistol" (whatever that was) in his hand and constantly changing final words: "You, of all people, my own daughter . . ." It was too much.

Since her mother's death, he'd rejected all love, including his daughter's. And she had loved him, in part because he was a genius. He modestly called himself a blacksmith, but he had been much more than that, even a father, in the end. If she had hated him as well as loved him, it was because he'd been incapable of returning her love.

She tried to imagine herself out of her own body, and it worked. She was Peggy, or had changed places with her. Peggy marched into the Pensione degli Incurabili with her famous retinue of dogs and was musing on art, while Helga reigned as the sole inhabitant of the palazzo. A gondola steered its way toward the landing dock, bearing a lonely, dark gentleman, smiling with outspread arms, a messenger. She would invite him to tea on the terrace, but first he would want to see the paintings. She would expound on the cubists, but he would kiss her instead. And he would say, "What I truly desire is your friendship, but the one does not exclude the other. Afterward I'll tell you what things are like inside Western heads—you might find that important—and I'll teach you to read the world as fluently as I do and to recognize the gods in the clouds." They would drink tea on the terrace and then break off to start all sorts of splendid nonsense with mortals and the world. They would read Venice and its clouds, and in every fissure and ligature they would find confirmed the love that drew them to each other like love-crazed siblings. "Hermes and Helga"? No, her first name didn't fit the story; it would have to be changed.

She reached behind her head and stretched, almost cozily. "Helle," that would be her name, Helle from Hellespont. If she were still alive today, she would certainly be a goddess.

And with that she fell asleep.

• • •

Since the gods and local spirits live eternally in our midst, they are theoretically in a position to correct many of the details of our traditional myths at any time. Of course, they don't give direct answers to public inquiries, but they leave various hints on occasion. How else would a novelist get the idea that Hephaestus, driven by a motive like jealousy or revenge, bound Hermes in Santorin and held him prisoner for two thousand years? Myths constantly evolve, and they are continued most actively by those directly involved. We owe this diagnosis to no less a figure than Dr. Zimmertür, the psychoanalyst, and not a day passes without further confirmation of his thesis.

In 1989 or 1990, an artist and banker from Istanbul by the name of Burak Doğu, while on a brief visit to Gallipoli and on a day devoted to the letter *H*, thanks to the encyclopedic lifestyle of his cousin, discovered an ancient Greek clay tablet between two large and long-untouched folios. It contained a hymn in praise of a hitherto unknown goddess. In classical times the city of Crithote lay on the shore of the Dardanelles across from Lampsakos. The hymn celebrates a beautiful goddess by the name of Helle, the secret daughter of Hephaestus and the cloud goddess Nephele, who was officially allied with the Boeotian king Athamas. Given her purely divine origin, Helle was clearly also a goddess and therefore immortal. Her anxious mother raised her as Athamas' daughter, along with her brother (in reality half-brother), Phrixus, since Hephaestus was interested in his children only if he could employ them in the smithy, and Nephele wanted to spare her children that fate. When Athamas cast her out, Helle and Phrixus were made miserable by Ino, the classically evil stepmother who replaced her. Zeus, however, ordered Hermes to supply a winged golden ram, on which they were to fly to Colchis. The ram was probably Hermes himself, or he was inside, enabling the ram to take off and fly. Unable to cling to his horns as her half-brother did, Helle fell from his back over the narrow straits between Crithote and Lampsakos while trying to clutch his wool coat, for golden fleece pulls out easily. According to myth, she drowned in the straits later named Hellespont. In fact she swam to shore and let Aeolus blow-dry her hair. Her father, Hephaestus, arrived from Lemnos and built a palace for her directly on the shore. Crithote was built upon its remains, and since its citizens still worshiped the goddess, they held a swim competition every four years in her honor. Helle probably lived in Crithote for many centuries, in widely varying female forms. The city was so blessed that it grew increasingly beautiful, until it was known simply as Callipolis, "the city of beauty," which eventually became Gallipoli. Here, in our own day, at one end of the street leading to the power station, a surveyor and treasure hunter from Çanaccale found a crystal vessel containing two locks of golden fleece. He kept this secret from all but his closest friends in Berlin. In his report, the section entitled "The Golden Fleece" is suspiciously brief, the discovery itself unmentioned.

• • •

Hermes was having problems navigating the city, as if it were his first time in a strange brain. It was a city built on the water, something unknown in his day, constructed on gigantic floats that had detached and were now gently floating away from the Venetian coast. Someday they would travel down the river Styx and bring new life to the Underworld—Persephone would be happy indeed! It was divine pleasure to read this city. Hermes found reading material wherever he looked: in cracked doorsills and shutters, rusty streaks, speckles, bright islands of peeling paint on the sides of buildings, or crocodile skin fashioned into purses and sold by blacks on the Campo San Stefano. The wrinkled skin of beggars too, of course (stout men never made good reading material, and the smooth skin of gods offered nothing at all, which was their distinguishing mark). He read wherever he could and learned of a brewing global misfortune. Zeus no longer ruled the world. Everything was turning inside out, the outside was dissolving, and "up" was turning into "down." It proclaimed the arrival of a final, irreversible end to everything, as he'd sensed at the garbage heap on Santorin, in spite of the large clump of thyme.

But he had not learned what he wanted most to know : Helga's whereabouts. He knew a great deal, but not enough.

He arrived that morning, departed from the police station around noon, and since he was still trouserless, slipped through a few ears into heads, Italian mostly but German and American as well, both men and women, although the latter often had their ears covered by loosely falling hair. By late afternoon he was speaking four languages so well that no one noticed his accent, and was moving among mortals like a fish in water, being a god. He managed to buy a good pair of trousers and a silk shirt without difficulty, having stolen almost five talents in lire, marks, and dollars from various wallets. In ancient Athens that would have amounted to a respectable dowry; today it approximated the price of a private apartment in a nice area of Milan, as he now knew. Stealing was so much fun—he was Hermes after all—that he also stole a shirt, pants, Roman sandals, a cowboy hat, and a bright-yellow plastic bucket to hold his money.

Anything for sale was as easy or easier to steal—"heavenly delight," for instance, which was green and repulsively sweet, yet trembled reverentially when divine lips approached. Anything was better than the pommes frites on the ship, rectangular yellow worms made of fat and muck.

He was surprised there were no slaves in evidence. It was inconceivable that all this wealth had been generated without them; they had to be somewhere. But he missed the smallest hint of them in any brain thus far. Perhaps they worked so far beneath the earth or at such a great distance that they had entirely disappeared from the consciousness of rich and free mortals. Another strange thing was that so few people wore hats, except for the gondoliers. There were lots of bald men with their heads mercilessly exposed to the sun. Hermes wasn't about to stay in such overheated attics any longer than necessary.

He traveled in passenger boats called vaporetti, and once in a gondola. He was now sitting in the head of a young Norwegian woman whose lover, or husband—they were on a "honeymoon"— didn't love her anymore because she didn't act or look like or sing as well as a certain *Gianna Nannini*. Hermes couldn't tell what sort of woman she was or whether she was adequate grounds for divorce. At any rate, they'd had a fight at the hotel. No, not a fight: they'd maintained a leaden silence, which was far worse. The next morning the man was gone, quite simply disappeared. She went to the railway station, *ferrovia*. She stared blankly ahead, her head the iciest spot Hermes had ever been in, freezing herself solid. He wasn't surprised. He'd experienced such things ten thousand times, and inwardly. As she disembarked she banged her knee on the side of the boat and started weeping. She pulled herself onto the dock, collapsed in a paroxysm of tears, while everyone tried to comfort her: it's only a little bump, your knee's all right, you can still move it. Others told her, "Just go ahead and cry, let it all out," having read books on the subject. Hermes knew she'd ultimately commit suicide, he could see her time had come, and that was more powerful than any god. Brains could be read too. But he didn't want to ruin her big scene by exiting from her ear in the midst of all these consoling idiots; it wouldn't have been fitting. He waited until she was in the train, then left discreetly. It was time: she had poison in her purse and didn't intend to reach Norway alive.

The railway station was constructed totally of cast iron, which was interesting. Cast iron was a form of multiplication. He gathered from the signs he read that Hephaestus ruled the world—who else had that much iron? He spoke Greek no longer but a mixture of many languages, and he wrote in the Roman alphabet. There were, however, some walls with letters that weren't Roman but looked instead like pictures to be read hermetically, fish and birds, like heralds of letters to come, brushed on with ingenuity, surely the drawings of rebellious young gods. He'd learn who before long.

Most of the young women seemed too slim to Hermes, simply too skinny, and they were tall now, too elongated. Maybe men liked those snaky shapes. The women were cool for the most part and in love with themselves to all appearances. They were always looking in mirrors, which wasn't hard to do, given the profusion of glass. When they were out with men they let themselves be kissed and caressed on the street, but they made eyes at any other man around, even in restaurants. It wasn't that way before—a good courtesan wasn't cheap, but she looked only at the one who was paying. And the source of all the boring music remained a mystery. Fifty instruments and the people playing them were squeezed into a small box on the wall.

A beautiful woman aware of her beauty was sitting on the vaporetto, talking with a girlfriend but touting her allure with every movement of her lips, every look, every gesture—doubtless because she'd noticed the increasingly bright gaze of Hermes. But she suddenly had to laugh at a little boy who tripped over her foot, steadied himself by grabbing her thigh, and stared at her with large round eyes. She glanced quickly at Hermes to see if he thought she was beautiful when she laughed.

Some things hadn't changed at all. If you wanted to attract a woman's attention, you stared admiringly at her homely friend, and soon not only the friend but the beauty as well would be staring back with interest. He'd set Aphrodite on fire for the first time around six thousand years before with that trick. At the moment, he had no intention of using it. He wanted only Helga. His investigations of cracked, streaked, and tangled signs had yet to yield anything definitive about her location—the only thing that would help now was polished marble. And for that he would have to enter a church as himself, clothed if possible.

As he crossed the Campo San Stefano, the African blacks hailed him, first in an unintelligible language and then in French, asking his name. "Paleos Kaimenos," he replied, which of course they didn't understand. They insisted he should be wearing shoes and a wristwatch—the reputation of Africans was important in their business. They had a hard enough time getting rid of their imitation purses from Hong Kong as it was.

"I'm not African. I was inside a volcano. You always look like this afterward," Hermes replied. They hesitated, then broke into laughter and let him move on. He liked all the buildings on San Marco Square except the church, which struck him as dangerously swollen. And there were too many stupid, greedy pigeons with stupid people feeding them. He did like watching the children startle the pigeons into flight. They were unchanged since Athens or Cnidos or Callipolis, having fun frightening the pigeons, or at least trying. In this case they were children from a country he'd never heard of called *Japon*. Hermes thought they were the cutest children he'd ever seen. Even so, he thought quickly, I have no special love for humans. He couldn't tell much about the children's parents, who hid their eyes behind small whirring objects. High above, a winged lion sat enthroned. In spite of all his flying experience, Hermes had never seen one before. And two stiff black men were standing on a tower, beating on an overturned pot with long-handled hammers— evidently a shrine to Hephaestus.

He liked the city, but most of the people were so ignorant he could learn nothing from them. They didn't know the difference between silk, wool, and cotton, how "radio" or "television" pro- duced sounds and images, or even what made an "automobile" move. It was a good thing that those glass tortoises with wheels were banned from the city—they'd just fall into the canals. They stood in the heat on the Piazzale Roma and didn't make a peep.

One thing was clear: he was involved in a complicated story. How did it go? After two thousand years chained to the wall of the volcano on Kaimeni, he had to find his way about again, learn new languages, figure out who the top god was and where he lived. He had tasks to perform, he mustn't go to Athens, someone was to lead him to his magic sandals, winged hat, and staff, he was to visit the midpoint of the world. Meanwhile he was in search of Helga and had to read the path to her. Not knowing his enemies, or where they lurked, he couldn't risk overusing his own divine but blackened form. And he had no idea how to reintroduce his cult when the gods had slipped so deeply into oblivion. No one he inhabited praised his name afterwards. They all considered it an unfortunate episode or a hallucination. And to add insult to injury, instead of saying, "I have Hermes," they said, "I think I have Alzheimer's." Who in the world was that?

The streaks and speckles of San Marco didn't tell him much,

which puzzled Hermes. The veins of marble, cut into flat planes and polished smooth, had always provided the right answer to any question. But now they carried messages of bravery, threats of eternal punishment, and warnings that were—quite clearly—about Hermes! He could see no more than that, even with his famed gaze, sharply focused, then broadening, which could always be counted on for total disclosure. It was probably the fault of his own clouded sight. The sweet odor of the sepulcher certainly contributed, rising from the sticky residue of incense beneath the arches and cupolas, intended for the gods, who were pictured everywhere but nowhere present. Most of them seemed to have suffered some terrible fate, pierced with arrows, burned, or nailed to wooden crosses. Even so, if they were gods they must still be alive. No matter how closely he looked, however, Hermes saw no family resemblance, though they must have descended from the gods he knew. A few of them had wings, but in the wrong place: not on their hats or sandals, but on their backs, like birds. He left the church, looking for a better one.

Across the Grand Canal, in another church, he found a fascinating painting of a young woman, perhaps a nymph like his mother, Maia. He was pleased to see that she was in better condition than the other gods. He'd already noticed her, even outside the church, on the walls of houses, mostly in small cages or as a statue under a tiny roof as in the Calle del Dose Da Ponte. She could be recognized by the stola she wore around her head and body and by the infant in her arms. This time the stola was green with a golden border, and the son was relatively large. He was standing on her thigh, as the child Dionysus stood on Hermes' hip in days of old. She held him with wonderfully beautiful hands, gazing down placidly from her throne with a barely noticeable twinkle in her eye, a tiny smile. A cunning storyteller who served up quite a tale about her child to the solemn old men surrounding her. And they believed every word.

She might be one of his great-granddaughters—at any rate, he wanted to get to know her. It wasn't erotic love; his feelings were entirely fraternal. With the exception of Athena, he'd never had a female comrade, just lovers of various sorts. But this young mother was clearly meant as a friend. She needed a companion, not a man. She shouldn't be alone, placid and calm, smiling that little smile to herself. She should be laughing aloud. Laughter had to be shared, and Hermes wanted to be the one to share it with her. She seemed to know all about men—that's why she found it so easy to tell them stories. Since she was far and away the most appealing goddess he'd seen, he had no doubt she was Gianna Nannini, the woman Norwegians left their brides for the morning after their honeymoon night.

• • •

The marble wasn't revealing anything anywhere. It was late afternoon, and somewhere high above the haze, Helios wheeled his solar carriage. Did he still see and know all? Surely not every detail in a city like this. There was no way Hermes could contact him without his hat and staff, so he was reduced to vague suppositions. He walked along the Fondamenta delle Zattere talking with the pigeons, each of whom had a half-worn, shell-encrusted piling to himself. They were complaining about the big cities in the west and south, where the smog was so thick you saw even less. They had never seen winged gods, or heard of them. Perhaps even Gianna Nannini and her little boy were a pure invention.

On the Campiello agli Incurabili he ran into a pack of strangely well-groomed and strikingly thin dogs. He watched them head for a small pensione and disappear inside. Did Hecate live there? And if so, was that the best she could do? A few houses on, voices emerged from a trattoria, speaking Etruscan with a Celtic accent. He turned and saw his first pair of local spirits. They were sitting, invisible to all but gods and other spirits, at a small table in front of the tavern, drinking wine. They held their glasses in their hands or claws, which rendered them invisible as well.

Male spirits generally had animal-like forms, while nymphs

appeared human. None of them could change appearance, or enter mortals. Unchanged over the centuries, they were recognized easily by gods. Hermes had already heard of the long-legged hairy chicken with four claws called Seuss, a former swamp and sea guardian in Venice. The other one, whom he didn't know, had the dark face of a spiky perch but a lovely voice, like the singsong of the Sirens. With his squat seal's body, he needed no chair, sitting instead on his neatly rolled and endlessly long tail.

Hermes sat down with them and, in response to their curious queries, told them who he was. Because he was visible, he had to order something. "Have an *ombra!*" Seuss suggested, and a small glass of wine arrived. "We sit out here in the sun when it's too hot for mortals and drink *ombras*—they're small enough that you can have several. We never pay, of course; we serve ourselves, invisibly."

"Taverns where local spirits gather generally don't make much money," murmured the other. "Even Harry's shuts down occasionally—that's making us think twice. We spread out around the city as best we can. By the way, I'm Orffi, but they call me Olivolo because I lived on an island by that name that disappeared. I was there before fishermen invented the barbed hook, my lord. And now? A local spirit cut off from the ambience I'm meant to serve—what a life! Another *ombra*, please!"

Hermes reordered while Seuss fetched wine for himself and Olivolo, who didn't want to bother rerolling his tail. Hermes took the opportunity to ask about "ambience," a word he'd never encountered. When the waiter had filled the only visible glass, the bottle had far less wine remaining than it should have. But things had been that way since time immemorial, and no one paid any attention.

"So you're free again, mighty Cyllenian," said Seuss. "I must say they did a good blacking job on you!" He dipped his beak in the glass, took a sip, and then lifted his head toward heaven to let the wine descend. "You won't have much fun. We don't know exactly what happened, but Olympians have little to say these days, or don't want to. Zeus is retired and lives in America. We don't know about the others. There's no top god anymore, just a manager. Around here they call him *Ingegnere Mulciebre,* but he's seldom here, he's almost always in Germany, where he's known only as the Consul. Either he's Vulcan himself, Hephaestus, or he's stolen everything from him. We don't know exactly and don't want to know."

"Why is he in Germany?"

"Because that's where the midpoint of the world is, in Poppau bei Klötze. . . . Shall we have another *ombra?*"

"I'm looking for a German woman named Helga," said Hermes, when the glasses were full again. "She's very pretty and graceful, with large ears, usually with earrings or music plugs in them."

"You'll have to ask Hezzenegker," Olivolo replied. "He's from there, from Bavaria. He joined up with the Romans at some point and got stuck in Venice. He's responsible for foreigners, as well as the Fondaco dei Tedeschi and letters to foreign lovers. He has a good memory for names."

"Where do I find him?" asked Hermes.

"Where we spend our nights, in the Scuola Materna-Elementare on the Giudecca. It's a wonderful building, stays nice and warm under the roof at night, and there's a southern view from the school library. We like it there. And there's no one but us, except for the troops of kids in the daytime. That's why we're sitting here now. Did you say your fugitive courtesan had her ears covered? Maybe she's a goddess trying to save you that trouble. You can't enter an immortal's ear, you know. You'd run up against a wall and bang your nose."

Later that evening they gathered with the other spirits at the Scuola Materna-Elementare. They'd taken the vaporetto, but Hermes had to make a few detours and spring across a few of the smaller canals, since a waiter and two pursers from the boat were hot after him. He could have tossed them a few banknotes from his money bucket, but that wouldn't have been sporting.

The house of the spirits shimmered in the evening sun, an inviting home for twilight, overgrown with greenery, and in the distance to the south loomed the Lido, a long, sandy island for strollers. The local spirits were somewhat strangely shaped and seemed fatigued. They were weakened by lack of respect and countless *ombras* and were basically bad-tempered, like all the local spirits in the world. Mortals were crowding them out, leaving them fewer and fewer places to sit, sleep, and haunt. Faced with an important god like Hermes, they were respectful and ready to serve.

Hezzenegker, a tall, thin, red-haired man with a mustache and a myriad of freckles on his pale face, seemed almost energetic. As with all active swamp spirits, his eyes glowed bluishly in the dark. His passion was to glide invisibly behind boats and ships at the end of a long rope, which he did quite well by means of his amazingly broad flippers, like a swan's but much bigger. He was proud of them. "I first grew them when I took over as a spirit here." He knew all about the Norwegian couple. He'd swept along in a few broad curves behind a customs boat that morning and been diverted: "I can't be everywhere!" He complained about the overload of duties he faced with so many foreigners around. "Some awaiting love letters, others death, a few expecting both. I handle their mail, but sometimes I'm late, through no fault of my own. This man Aschenbach, for example. He was in love with a boy named Tadzio, sort of a good-for-nothing, but he mistook him for you, Hermes! He died, of course, of forbidden love and Venice. He was barely dead when the letters started arriving, one after the other, all from Tadzio. I'm sitting on a whole stack of letters like that; the attic of the Materna-Elementare is full of them! Are you going to visit the Underworld again?"

But then Hermes learned something important. A German woman matching his description was living in the Casa Venier dei Leoni, a palazzo full of paintings, normally the city residence of Hecate, currently divine messenger between worlds, together with her cursed pack of dogs. But this time for some unknown reason she had moved to a pensione on the Campiello agli Incurabili. That was all Hermes needed to hear, and although the spirits invited him to spend the night and the place was comfortable, he took his leave. A few were already asleep, resting up for midnight. Olivolo inflated himself to a huge ball and ascended into the air until his long tail barely touched the floor. Seuss tied it to a bar of the jungle gym in the kindergarten with a neat sailor's knot. "He always sleeps up there," he said. "Olivolo has negative weight—around two cats below zero. When it comes time to wake him, you have to haul him in gently and wave an espresso under his nose." Then he yawned so widely with his giant beak that Hermes took a cautious step backward. "It's about that time for me too, Cyllenian. Watch out for blocked ears, noble god of mischief, and for bad-tempered Germans. Sooner or later you'll have to visit the Consul. Italians are the only people in the world who can get along with the Germans."

"Then I'm Italian," said Hermes. Seuss said nothing more. He'd closed his eyes and was fast asleep.

Hermes turned to go. While he'd been talking, a thief had taken all his money, and he hadn't noticed a thing. Hermes watched him disappear with the yellow bucket between two houses in the distance. He didn't even consider chasing him. He had to laugh: Either I'm Italian, or Italians are my type; it comes down to the same thing.

• • •

Glances were projectiles. They struck a glancing blow, at least those of a god. As his gondola arrived at San Marco from Giudecca, Hermes knew that Helga was standing somewhere on a roof, waiting for him. He couldn't see her yet, but it wasn't a matter of catching sight of her; he felt the same longing gaze from the Dutch-blue eyes he knew from the straits of Schmidt Cliff and the war memorial Taverna Mythos in Thera. But if she was indeed waiting for him, how had she known he was coming, and at this very moment?

Now they could begin softly, slowly, yielding and passionate again, as they had been in the hotel room in Thera. Charles, the drummer from Sparta, had been seriously interested in women (as opposed to Jean-Claude), but he had loved in a Spartan fashion, under pressure to prove his manhood. If you've got something to prove, you get it done as quickly as possible, and Charles had shown a speed with Helga that would have won him more applause on the drums. No matter how hard Hermes applied the brakes internally, he was soon confronted with a *fait accompli,* little more than a makeshift, hasty salute. It was clear that if he wanted any pleasure making love today, he would have to handle things personally.

He felt a fluttering in the pit of his stomach, like a string being plucked: a joyful timidity, the familiar shock of desire. What would it be like? His body was flexible enough now for the most daring positions of love. But would his renowned snake staff be able to perform at its usual high standard, given its current rampage—a cramped root curved to a horn by the restrictions of his trousers, raging for release. Good thing it didn't have a voice, or it would be roaring. Funny to feel such timidity. Like an all too young man, this old, worn, and blackened god.

Why was everything taking so long? He needed a galley with three hundred oarsmen. A half-dozen dips of the oars, and he would be standing before her. Poseidon, lord of the seas, stop teasing, release that poor gondola's keel! No boat in the world travels that slowly with a grown man plying the oar for pay. Free the keel, push a little instead: weren't you ever in love? I seem to recall a number of nymphs, more than a few, plunged into ruin by you, father of all downfalls.

Perhaps the gondolier wasn't from Venice but was sent instead by Hephaestus to delay him. He asked him a question in the blacksmith's language. The man replied that his name was Rinaldo and that he'd been born in Nürnberg. That was suspicious.

He realized he would have to handle Helga with care. Perhaps his passion had already frightened this delicate, austere Northern being. Perhaps she feared she might be thrown off track. If he could get in her right ear, he'd know for sure this time. He wanted to throw her off track, all right, but it would be fun only if she threw herself off as well.

• • •

She knew it must be Hermes. Why else would a lonely, dark man be sitting in a gondola? She didn't need a telescope. She'd seen or read that he would come by gondola; at any rate, she never doubted it. He was still a long way off—how slow those heavy black boats were! Another ten minutes at least. How calmly he was sitting, how patiently! A god, sure of his savagery. A god in the rapidity of his grasp, but blessed with an immortal's rich expanse of time. Hermes, a unique, admirable mixture of lust and intelligence, the rapacious god of twilight and street litter, the worst wild boar with the finest touch, a god among gods.

First of all she would kiss the scars on his arms and feet left by the chains, which meant he would have to take off his shirt and trousers. And the scars on his neck. He would touch her then, holding her head gently with one hand, turning her softly to kiss her shoulder, while his other hand brushed her nipples. A careful reconnaissance of the landscape of her skin: was everything there as anticipated? Was all in harmony with him, *him*, HIM, and completely? Oh, yes, completely! Every hollow, every furrow, and the round hood of his awakened snake was already feeling its way between the hemispheres, seeking its way into the slipperiness, while his teeth fastened on her neck between two kisses. She would turn to him with a smile, ignoring the quivering stem, kiss his nose and say: "Take your time, immortal one—how about a little music?" Go over to Peggy's walnut record player (made in 1957), bend over the records, and act as if it might be possible to find in this pile of staid classics the right background music for the longest, wildest, juiciest, and hottest copulation in modern, post-Lutheran history. The way she moved, the view from the rear, her graceful turn to the cabinet and to the record covers from which men gazed divinely, all that would further entice him. He would seize her in his arms, pull her roughly from the joyless music cabinet, and make her forget all about the classics. His hand would grasp her thigh, brush the curly pubic glade, turn her. She would sink with helpless desire and do her best to sink his veined swingle with the inevitability of a foundering yacht or a motorboat caught in the spray of the reef, like the one off Rügen, dancing more and more wearily, more and more awkwardly, until it descended at last to its final rest in the depths of the ocean. . . . Damn, that gondola was approaching slowly! More like drifting than moving along. The gondolier was spotting friends everywhere, from the Punta della Dogana to the Campo della Salute, and they were legion. He kept hailing them gaily, exchanging greetings, enjoying himself, in no hurry at all to arrive.

• • •

He'd never set foot in a gondola again! How could you call that transportation? In the meantime he'd mentally explored countless paths to the most glorious of pleasures, and if he wasn't careful he would arrive ahead of schedule.

But there on the dock at last stood Helga, her hand resting on the mooring pole. Oh, you divine ranks, how was he supposed to disembark without indecency, given the humped tent below his waist? Fortunately her appearance irritated him slightly and served as a distraction. She was wearing a stola, pulled over her head, green like Gianna Nannini's in the Chiesa dei Frari. The face was clearly Helga's, and the ears had the right shape; only the eyes weren't blue but were the brightest glowing brown of a mountain goat. Did she want him to think she was the young mother from the church?

"Welcome, god of love!"

"Hold on there," replied Hermes. "I'm the god of the phallus. Eros is the one who deals in ambience."

She didn't look particularly hot for love at the moment. More like a polite hostess, good-natured but reserved. He'd probably have to tour the dog goddess's collection of paintings with her first—an unwelcome delay. Or was she hiding her passion to make him work a little harder?

• • •

The bed was silk but narrow. If two people tried seriously to sleep in it, one was bound to lie awake, rise eventually, and go to lie down somewhere else. After two thousand years of rest in the crater, Hermes was in no need of sleep. But she was fast asleep, curled up like a cat. Or was she only pretending? What was her name, if not Helga? Where was she from, if not Stendal? She had large hands, a large nose, large ears. It wasn't every day you found them so charmingly united, with ears that large, yet pretty. If she were human, he thought, I'd take a look around in her head. But she wasn't; the entrance was barred; she was a goddess.

He would never have thought she was immortal. Now that she had revealed herself as a little-known "more or less Nordic" goddess, she was even more of a mystery. Why wouldn't she reveal her name? Why couldn't she speak English, when everyone else did? Why Russian, a language so foreign he had no idea where in the world it was spoken? Why did she ignite and enjoy storms of desire that simply blew away the erotic teachings of Aspasia, but refused before or after to say who she was? She was not allowed to lie. Gods were forbidden to give a false name once they had revealed their immortality. So she said nothing. She had his every step watched in Venice. Seuss was one of her spies, or in league with her, at any rate; as was the gay *commissario* with the lavender button in his ear, who wanted to see how much control Hermes maintained over humans when he was in their heads. But what was the point of it all? Love? Was she jealous of his maternal friend in green? The young mother wasn't called Gianna, he knew that now. She didn't even sing.

It smelled nice in here, almost like roses. It was the fragrance of a white blossom he knew well, "gardenia." Hermes glanced around, wondering where it could be. But the wonderful fragrance rose from a matching set of four high-quality leather suitcases.

His sleeping beauty stretched and woke, the large-nosed, pretty-eared one with no name. She opened one eye, recognized Hermes' shoulder, laid her head contentedly against it, and fell back asleep. It warmed his soul. No, I don't like humans in particular, but this is a goddess. One that needs sleep, and that's rare.

In the morning, as they strolled through the city, she wanted to hear all about his forays into human heads and how he connected words with the images that arose inside them. Apparently she herself wanted to nest in humans again and was totally out of practice. Or was she finding out for someone how much old Hermes could still manage? Had she lured him to Venice to keep him from Athens? Who was she and why was she so curious about him! Could he enter a woman's head? she asked. And how did he read the connections and progression of the world from clouds, lines in the sand, or peeling paint—although it was clear that she already knew how, even if she read a little too quickly. She always knew where to find herself in the drifts of signs; that was how divine spirits drew knowledge from chaos. She rebelled against the idea of reading lines of print as if they were messages in rust or in the dancing pebbles of a fountain's basin. Interpreting them was easy—all you had to do was strictly ignore what the writer wanted to say. She showed a quite undivine interest, however, in the ideas human authors were trying to develop in their manuscripts. He told her what he could read: he saw from *Il Gazzettino* that his companion was an emissary, and the colony of spots on a mirror in the restaurant revealed that she would tell him that very day her identity and intentions.

The day was far from boring. They studied the harbor and the clouds from the roof of a church. Then they ordered two *ombras* in the restaurant and managed to persuade the headwaiter, who was so dignified he could hardly move, to serve "heavenly delight" and try a few spoonfuls himself, upon which he suffered a fainting spell and sank into the middle of a flower arrangement. They continued amusing themselves with various nonsense, including a slightly lascivious dance they improvised all the way across the Campo Santa Margherita. This drew the attention of three carabinieri, who intervened energetically and soon found themselves missing, respectively, a cap, a pistol, and a pair of trousers. The couple placed these on the statue of a man whose considerable nudity was so emphasized by his fig leaf that they felt it should be covered. The goddess related all this, plus a few high spots from the night before, in rueful tones to a man in a woman's robe. He was sitting in a small box with violet curtains inside a church and sounded somewhat annoyed, because he thought she was boasting. At the erotic high point, he became agitated, which gave Hermes, who was sitting in his head, a great deal of pleasure. In the end the poor man was compelled to forgive her. That was his job after all, and he didn't know how else to react.

While reading, they came across more signs of what he had assumed were young gods. Hermes learned from his companion that they were mortals. He noted the expressions "graffiti," "writer," and "tagging." A "writer" was the Hermes-like antithesis of a carabiniere. Writers were annoyed by monotonous surfaces and used spray cans to leave wild, brightly colored traces behind, unique and clearly recognizable expressions of individual personalities. "Tagging" was signing on the wall the names they had chosen for themselves. One of them, who sprayed on images of fish and lightning bolts without signing his name, was known by his style alone.

• • •

Toward evening his goddess awoke and suggested they go up on the roof to catch the last rays of the setting sun. When they arrived on top, a dark storm was gathering. Hermes wanted to go back in, but she decided a storm was just the thing: she wanted to take cover in his arms.

It turned out she was using the storm to tell him the truth

about herself. During loud thunder the microphones and receivers of Hephaestus were temporarily silenced. And no other than Hephaestus had commissioned her to follow Hermes' first steps.

"Why did he send you?" asked Hermes. "And why did you agree?"

A bright flash of lightning crossed the sky. She waited for the thunderclap and whispered in his ear: "Because I'm Helle, from Hellespont. You probably don't remember me."

So she was Helle, daughter of Hephaestus and Nephele, goddess of fog. After her birth they pretended she was the daughter of the mortal king Athamas. That was the origin of the fairy tale about her deadly plunge into the straits. The thunder and lightning were nonstop now. Soon it would rain.

"I knew you only as a little girl."

"And I knew you only as a golden ram losing its hair."

He had always assumed Hephaestus' daughter had been hiding for three thousand years because she was ugly, deformed by her fall perhaps, as her father had been by his. Instead she was utterly beautiful, an immortal mixture of fog and fire, a goddess of passionate journeys and of falls that end happily. Strange that her father kept her so long in Callipolis; she seemed to have been a good daughter after all. What she went on to say—the storm was now raging happily—confirmed this. She was engaged to Thor, a Norwegian hammer god, but didn't spend much time with him. He played tennis and hated Ping-Pong.

Luckily the storm continued. They were soaked to the skin, but Hermes had learned a few things he couldn't have read anywhere: Zeus was living in America, in New Athens, Illinois, and whenever the New Athenians annoyed him, in Sparta, Illinois. He played golf daily in Saint Louis, Missouri. Nothing else interested him. Donar, the dull-witted Northerner, was in charge of thunder and lightning. Ares, who was so forgetful he hadn't changed his appearance for ages, lived as an ancient writer in Germany, studying plants and beetles. He'd discovered a hitherto unknown book-scorpion, which now bore his name. Wars seemed to manage without him. By virtue of Hephaestus' refined technology, wars were more impersonal but still as deadly as ever. Aphrodite had taken leave of beauty and lived for the most part as a man these days. Athena was still in Athens, giving passionate speeches and chain-smoking—that's right, smoking.

"Truly, goddess?" Hermes cried into the storm. "Athena in thrall to Hephaestus?"

"No. He has no power over her; she just likes to smoke. She was a minister for a time, but never in his service."

"And what is Apollo of Delphi doing?"

"He's permanently affronted, spends his time opening art exhibitions. Hephaestus has taken Justice from him and turned it over to the Lemnian media. Apollo's light has served its time. The Lemnian system will no doubt replace logic at some point; only limited resistance remains."

"From whom?"

"From Hypnos, Thanatos, Morpheus, the Muses, Dionysus the alcoholic—all your type, more or less. But they aren't always at their best, and the Lemnian system has them in its grip: drying-out tanks, psychiatry, protective custody, television institutes—I'm afraid you may experience all that too, Cyllenian."

"Do you oppose your father?"

"Not at all. On the contrary. What he's doing is good: he's creating peace. He's taken Thor's hammer and replaced it with strenuous sport, so he'll learn to live without it. The world doesn't depend on gods anymore, which is good."

"What about people who still want to worship the gods—Dionysus, say? Or Hermes, for example."

"For mortals who desire the divine he's created a generalized god who doesn't give him any logical or Lemnical difficulties, since he doesn't exist."

"He doesn't? That's an interesting way of looking at it, at least for a goddess . . . ," Hermes said thoughtfully.

Helle responded impatiently. "I mean he exists less. He is responsible for everything, which of course means for nothing at all. At any rate, mortals can't help you. There's no point fighting it or being bitter; you might as well recognize Hephaestus' splendid preeminence from the start. His system is error free, because all errors are built into it initially and then transformed into positive factors. You might as well cooperate."

"Why should I fight it?" asked Hermes. "I'm just an adventurer who wants to raise a little hell to keep from getting bored, that's all. I'll be glad to recognize anyone's superiority anytime."

It's doubtful that Helle believed him, but she pretended to. "It's not so bad if you're clever, and you are. Hephaestus doesn't have to know everything—about us, for example."

"The thunder has stopped—can't he hear us?"

"The sensors will be dead for half an hour. The problem hasn't been solved yet, and people are upset with Donar, so he makes even more noise. But otherwise everything is conceived and controlled with unbelievable intelligence, you'll see—again it pays to be smart. He's forgiven you for your affair with Aphrodite; otherwise you wouldn't be free. You could retrieve your sandals, hat, and staff, travel back and forth between this world and the Underworld accompanying dead souls, you could raise mortals of your choice to greatness and change entire countries and continents. I think he needs you. He wants you on his side. And the two of us would be free to do what we want."

He embraced her, protecting her from the passing storm, or one to come, and asked her craftily: "My sandals, hat, and staff— where do you think I'll find them?"

"They're in the Glyptothek in Munich—but you didn't hear it from me. A Bavarian king once ruled in Greece, and when he was deposed he took your things with him. He thought it was a costume and wanted it for a party called Fasching. The hat has a ding in it; otherwise everything's in good shape."

She noticed he was reading the clouds, asking questions not

meant for her. She said worriedly: "Hermes, I don't want you just in bed; I want you for a friend. I'm tired of heroes who take on too much, get humiliated, and wind up drunkards. Promise me you won't try to steal those things."

He felt uncomfortable about the whole affair. Having the daughter of Hephaestus for an enemy was an unpleasant prospect. But that was what she would be, once she learned the truth: that Athena was his friend, while what he felt for Helle was lust. He desired her tenderness, her talent for wild abandon, he loved her passionate tongue, her dancing bottom. Once she realized that, if he was trying to tarnish the glory of her beloved father . . .

"I'm the god of reversals, the sower of confusion, and the god of thieves, *aprés tous*." He spoke mildly, as if it were still open to discussion. "I'm the god of twilight and street litter—you're taking a chance when you ask me to promise anything or to keep those promises. . . . But keep calm; I'll read what I'm to do." He gazed into the black clouds, but he wasn't reading; he was brooding. Athena a smoker? It was hard to believe.

"What does *'aprés tous'* mean?" asked Helle.

• • •

There was no point in adding to the already innumerable photos of Venice. Since Helga had run out of film and had to watch her money, she hadn't brought her old Pentax along in the first place, leaving it instead in the side pocket of her smelly plastic suitcase at the hotel. After four days in Venice she was broke. She couldn't even buy the postcards she wanted at the Guggenheim palazzo, and borrowing from Peggy was out of the question, since she'd been dead for years. Could she get enough for her camera somewhere to pay her way to Munich? Her table-tennis friend lived there. She wouldn't be thrilled about lending her money again, but she would do it. Helga stepped onto a chair, pulled her suitcase halfway out of the wardrobe, and reached into the outer pocket for her camera. She was in for a surprise.

Along with the Pentax she found two thick, tightly tied bundles of hundred-dollar bills. Now don't fall off the chair! Knees trembling, she concentrated on climbing down carefully.

She felt a wave of gratitude. Not for the money, but for the fact that Charles, the drummer drug dealer, had stashed hot money in her suitcase, and not bars of hash or packets of heroin. That was thoughtful of him. Or of Hermes.

Shouldn't she at least give him some sign that she had it . . . ? She hung the camera around her neck in confusion, made her way to a police station, and explained that someone who had been jailed four days before left something at her place. Unfortunately she knew only his first name.

She saw a good deal of Venice that day from unusual perspectives: the police station, customs officials, the American consulate, a detention center. She couldn't find anyone who was willing or able to assume responsibility. Finally a police officer—who was not named Fibonacci or hard of hearing—knew of the case and asked her questions, first in English, then in German.

"What is your relationship to the prisoner, Signora Herdhitze?"

"We met on the ship. He came to . . . my cabin." She felt herself blushing and was annoyed. She'd known she would have to answer that question.

"Did he hide anything there, stick something in your suitcase?"

"No, but he left something—this camera. Could you put it with his things?" Helga shoved it across to him. He opened the case and examined it.

"No film; that's too bad. All right, signora, I'll take care of it."

She took her leave and walked back to the pensione, buying a nice-smelling leather suitcase on the way. She packed, paid her bill, stepped into a water taxi, and traveled across the laguna to the airport. Venice sank into the waters like Atlantis, leaving more stories behind than any other city in the world. And it could hardly have appeared more beautiful than it did as she looked back across the wake of the boat.

She could have flown to Athens. Instead she boarded a plane for Munich, for she was long since a prisoner of the story: if Hephaestus wouldn't allow Hermes to go to Athens, then there was nothing there for her either. And a story could not be simply annulled. She let herself be steered like a ship. She would have to change direction in large, sweeping curves now, until the course was set for Athens.

She tried to catch a quick, final glimpse of Venice, but the plane was already slicing smoothly into a cloud.

IV

THE CELTIC PERSPECTIVE

Hermes had never been particularly fond of temples, Ionic columns, the golden mean, or so-called classic profiles. Ideals and ideal proportions were Apollo's domain. But here he was, lost in melancholy on Munich's Königsplatz, circling a temple-like building that reminded him of Athens. If only he were in Greece, not caught here in the gears of Hephaestus! Still, the Glyptothek lay across the way, the museum of antiquities where his magic attributes were preserved. Once he had them and knew the tasks set for him, he'd head straight to Athena, his only friend. He'd been in Munich two days now, a guest in almost thirty different people, learning, noting the concepts and images that arose as they listened.

Strangers meeting on trains or in parking lots often found it hard to make conversation, but if they did manage to, they were soon discussing ethical priorities: should we protect human life at the cost of the environment; should we help as many people as possible or only those who deserve it; should we save trees and animals, or jobs and factories? Hermes enjoyed sowing confusion, constructing new arguments from what he heard, drawing pleasure from skeptical frowns. He also liked to inject sentences he'd heard elsewhere, like those from the graceful girl with beautiful teeth: "Hey, I'm cool! I'm no loser." The conversation had been about babies or AIDS. She didn't even realize she had beautiful teeth, and covered her mouth when she laughed. Or a young bodybuilder: "My ideal is a well-defined body." Some of his body parts still apparently lacked definition, since he bolted the moment a woman looked at him. He jerked off at home and felt guilty afterward. Then, as self-punishment, he worked out on machines, developing muscles not used since man learned to walk upright, except perhaps in the silver mines. A Berlin architect also said something he could use: "Let's face it—brothels in Vienna and Munich are still worth a visit, but in Berlin you do better in a quick-print shop."

At first he enjoyed parading about in his dark skin. Last night he'd visited a little cinema, where Charlie Chaplin was playing in *Modern Times,* hoping to learn more about current events. Afterward he went from pub to pub selling roses, looking for local spirits but finding none, nor any receptive mortals who might have spoken his name or even known it. He had so many questions. Questions were fun and worthwhile, but you didn't dare ask too many. He was bothered by the way people talked when he was his black self. They avoided meeting his eye, and when he asked questions or had something to say, they were polite but guarded. They seemed to understand what he was saying but acted as if he might not understand them, although his German vocabulary was already better than that of many native speakers. But that was the problem. Any foreigner speaking German so well seemed odd and had to be watched. Strangely enough, the people who showed no interest in him asked him the most questions.

So that night he started moving from head to head, examining concepts from the inside. The only time he encountered his name was in the annoying phrase "hermetically sealed," which had nothing at all to do with him, with receptivity for the unknown, with mischief and clever tricks. Instead it referred to a Ptolemaic mountebank and charlatan by the name of Hermes Trismegistos, who was known for making humans, barriers, and systems impenetrable. Trismegistos, the thrice-great quack, sealed things off, while he, Hermes, opened all paths. "Hermetic" had better take on another meaning soon, or he would be annoyed every time he heard it. Had Hephaestus thought up this insult?

Helle had disappeared without a trace after Venice. Was she jealous because he'd mentioned Athena? She'd have to make at least a brief visit to Stendal as "Helga" to handle the estate. Naturally she'd be back: he read it in the treetops, and it was only logical. After all, she was crazy about him.

He saw no distinguished gentlemen strolling with pretty young boys these days. That sort of love had apparently died out. He'd spent time in the head of a rich and respected doctor who averted his eyes and concentrated on his profession whenever he saw a good-looking young man. And that had been a neurosurgeon, who knew a great deal, for a mortal, about the structure of the brain. But he knew nothing of love. Hermes also saw the man's unfortunate wife, but he felt no desire to discover what things looked like inside her.

• • •

"Whatcha looking for?" asked the man at the counter.

"Guess!" replied Hermes.

"Well, I'm askin' because . . ."

"Right! Because I'm black."

"Not exactly. But it's closing time."

"I'm seeking refuge."

"Here? With us?"

"Sure. This is the antiquities museum, isn't it? I'm Hermes."

"Hermes? He's some sort of god."

"That's me. Where else would I go? I'll pay the entrance fee, if that's what you want. Don't worry. I'll leave afterward."

Since the man just stood there with his mouth open, Hermes put down five marks, tore a ticket off the long roll, and entered the exhibition hall. Immediately he spotted something familiar: a nude mirror bearer on a lion's back, with owls on her shoulders. Her smile was as beautiful as it had been back then, in the home of Sparta's most expensive courtesan. The mirror was splintered, leaving only cracks and spots of rust, reflecting nothing, which meant, however, that it could now be read. Hermes was certain it would reveal the location of his hat, sandals, and staff.

A female voice said: "Grüß Gott!"

He liked the greeting, even if it was grammatically suspect. It was common here in Bavaria and referred to the generalized god Helle had mentioned. But Hermes basked in the feeling that it must actually refer to him. He liked the variation, "Grüß dich, Gott," even more—and it was better German. The woman had a willing look and large breasts. Nothing to object to in that area.

"As god, I greet you too," he replied.

"I'm Nathalie. Nathalie Rittberger."

"Isn't Rittberger a jump? I know about it—jumping's my passion too," said Hermes, fiddling with the laces of his cape and sizing her up. But it was no easy ear. There were corkscrew curls hovering about, which made calculations difficult.

"My great-grandfather was a figure skater," said Nathalie, slightly embarrassed. "I play table tennis myself." Hermes postponed his leap for the moment, hoping to see her playing table tennis as soon as possible.

"Helga told me to show you the way, so come on! Your things aren't here anymore. The Wittelbachs have them in Nymphenburg."

The name Nymphenburg was so incongruous it pleased him. Nymphs would never allow themselves to be imprisoned in a burg; it was inconceivable. He followed her toward the exit. She looked for a taxi stand, but he held her back and opened a car door.

"You drive a Jaguar?"

"Sure; why not?"

"You must make good money." He saw she had no idea he was one of the gods. It seemed Helle hadn't told her everything.

"Not at all. I'm stealing the car—what do you take me for? I was on the road with an Italian pro today. I can even handle a Rolls. Hop in!"

As the Jaguar swept along Nymphenburger Straße, Nathalie swore she'd never been in any car like it before. Meanwhile she slipped into the familiar form of address with him. "What are you doing later?"

"Playing table tennis with you. My first time too. By the way, where can I find my things in this Nymphenburg?"

"In a glass case on the balcony, beside the sculptures. I'll take you there."

"Can't do it. I have to steal them. Regulations."

"Whose regulations?"

"Mine."

• • •

Hermes had already seen the castle that morning, through the eyes of a beautiful, long-necked woman named Rosangela, who had gone cycling there. Back home in Pasing, she took her bicycle up to the fifth floor and hung her sweat-soaked clothes on the handlebars. She was a poet and delivered a wild, aggressive recitative called "rap," a musico-rhetorical excess he found particularly appealing. Unfortunately she went to class at engineering school, where she drew one right angle after the other. He switched over to a teacher and escaped, but only as far as the WC, for a swig of whiskey from a hip flask—the man was bored silly with right angles too. Hermes wanted to get back to Rosangela's long neck and rap music that evening, once he'd played table tennis with the well-endowed Nathalie, but only if his wings and staff had failed to bring him to Helle. Spring was in the air, coming from the park behind the castle.

At the entrance, he asked Nathalie for her address, because she was going home to her little daughter. She refused to take the car, boarding the tram instead. Hermes entered the castle and discovered the glass case with his winged garb to the rear of the mezzanine, in a corner next to an empty pedestal. A label in faded script read: "Otto, Fasching 1844, Athens." A portrait of Otto hung on the wall: a nice-looking, good-natured boy in a king's robes, with scepter and crown. Hermes opened the case, placed the hat on his head, and slipped on the sandals. A whirl of female voices came from the next room, a girls' class. He tried to keep his thoughts clear, although the voices confused him. He didn't want anyone to see him flying away. But since he couldn't slip into anyone's ear right now and there was no other door to disappear through, he threw his cape under the glass case, leaped onto the empty pedestal, looked down, and froze in contraposto, his hand pointing portentously toward heaven. Only a statue could hold that pose for long. Unfortunately he'd left his staff in the glass case. Now the girls streamed in, and the teacher began telling them about Poseidon, referring to him as Neptune, and Ares, whom she called Mars.

Hermes was certain he looked like aged bronze and would even feel metallic if touched. They might notice, however, that he wasn't wearing a fig leaf where they were normally worn in Bavaria, the land of stripped fig trees. At the moment, a single leaf wouldn't have done the job, or stayed in place.

"What's with him, then?" one of the girls asked boldly. The shocked teacher ignored the question and rushed panic-stricken to the king's portrait on the wall. "Here," she said, speaking very quickly, "is our young Otto, shown as always in Greece, in his kingly robes. The staff is called a scepter; all kings carry them. And the crown," she said, "the crown . . ."

"What crown?"

None of the girls was looking at the portrait; only the teacher was. Realizing she was losing control, she pushed the small band of confused but slightly resistant girls out of the gallery. Hermes, the clairvoyant, saw she had only one thing in mind: lodging a strenuous complaint with the Bavarian Castle and Lake Commission as soon as possible.

Calmly descending, he seized his winged staff and cape, and took off through the window into the heavens above the city as if he had been doing it for months. Two millennia of imprisonment were over, forgotten, repealed.

• • •

Helle sat at the dining table, waiting for her father and the foundry master, Fudit. She didn't want to go over to the workshop area, since she knew her father didn't like talking with anyone when he was there, not even her. When the cook asked if he should serve the meal, she said no, went to the window, and looked over at the factory buildings. From a distance the ancient yellow brick monstrosities appeared like an industrial museum, but up close they resembled the ruins of an air attack.

Her father felt at home in Lauchhammer—he always enjoyed new beginnings. At the moment, there wasn't much work, but in a year or two he would be able to gaze out the window of his home in South Lauchhammer at new buildings and smokestacks across the way, and more smoke than all his volcanoes put together could ever produce. He loved mortals because they enabled him to maximize noise and fumes. He disliked forests, loved forest fires, and the only reason he visited Helle on her heavily wooded farm in France was for her goose liver pâté.

At first he had been unsure about moving his base of operations to the nation that coined the phrase "swords to plowshares." That made no sense to him as a blacksmith, since from a craftsman's point of view, swords demanded more exacting labor. He spent an entire dinner holding forth on damascene and inlays, threatening to throw any barbarian who disdained those arts into the depths of Tartarus. He had his idiosyncrasies, gods knew, but his system was magnificent, and he was constantly at work expanding it.

Here they came. Helle heard the clatter and stamp of crutches, then a brief conversation in the hall before the door opened. Master Fudit seemed to be apologizing for the fact that a few customers had deserted them because the telephones weren't working in the West.

When they entered, Helle approached her father with a smile, took his hand, and began their father-daughter dance. They circled easily, and he held the golden crutches high, grinning, lumbering like a bear in fresh snow, letting himself be gently turned. No one but his daughter was allowed to do this; he detested dancing and dancers like the plague. Breathing heavily, he sat down and leaned his all too strikingly shaped crutches beside him against the table. Helle sat to his right, because he heard better from that side. If Fudit had something to say, he shouted.

Pea soup and sausages. How could her father do that to himself? Food fit for starving mortals, not for the gods.

"All in good time!" he said. The men were trying to reach an understanding on "Reconstruction of the East" and the coming reunification. Fudit spoke at great length, offering a plethora of dire warnings and pessimistic opinions. According to him, a rude awakening was in store for everyone in a few years. Her father devoted himself to his food and let him talk. Then he answered with his mouth full: "If the fire doesn't glow, the solder won't flow!" Fudit gave a start. Had he known he was talking with the god who ran the world, he would have been shocked. As it was, he hid his irritation behind a respectful nod. "Absolutely, Herr Consul, that's clear!"

"Let's see, fresh pike and new potatoes," said Hephaestus. "The boniest fish in the sea. Just what I like." He proceeded with surgical skill, laying back the skin, probing here and there. Then he pulled a slide rule from his pocket and passed it through the hair above his right ear. "With a fish," he said, "you have to know where to start measuring." He held the slide rule up to the light and made a calculation, picked up his knife and fork again, and divided the fish triumphantly into three totally bone-free sections of precisely equal size.

The fish tasted better than the sausage, but it only served to awaken an even stronger longing for nectar and ambrosia. At mealtimes her father tried to convince himself and others that he loved mortals and belonged among them.

"Now, Helga, what did you want to say?" He called her Helga in front of anyone who didn't know they were gods. Fudit's presence at the table complicated their conversation slightly, since they had to speak in veiled terms. It worked because her father was excellent at decoding, but it was a strain.

"I've spoken with Herr von Kühl" (meaning Hermes) "and picked up a little information here and there" (she'd spied on him). "I think you're right to hire him" (it was right to set him free). "He seems steady enough, except for a few traits that come with the territory" (he's still a thief). "Even now, as far as his belongings are concerned" (he's stealing his hat, sandals, and staff while we're sitting here). "He has a lot of catching up to do: for example, he's dealing actively in autos, and he's spending a good deal of time in consultation—in a literal sense."

"An old schoolmate of mine," Hephaestus explained to Fudit, "who's been handling pipes and cigars but who's stagnated a bit in the meantime. God knows what he can do."

"I see," said Fudit, totally confused. He didn't seem to care much for the meal either; he probably missed vegetables and a salad. But the gods don't need vitamins, and Hephaestus detested them almost as passionately as he did meadows and forests.

"Which reminds me: I'm worried about our joint venture. We should call Cast Steel West before Herr Feldhoff leaves for lunch. Or ask for Herr Knittel; he usually stays at the office and eats yogurt."

Fudit folded his napkin. "I'll take care of it immediately."

When he was outside, Hephaestus said, "If he could at least play poker! They've forgotten everything. Forty years of socialism with nothing to show for it, while all we had to do was blink thirty times and we were three hundred million times richer. So what's the Cyllenian up to? He's stolen his wings and staff? Then for the moment we have no control him over him?"

"No, Papa."

"No problem. Do you think he'll be of any use?"

"He's still undefined. All he wants to do right now is have a good time and satisfy his curiosity. He can read destinies, but the modern world is still somewhat obscure to him. He has a delicate touch. A delicate way of picking the right moment for things."

"Can't understand a word you're saying. Did he bang you?"

"Wasn't that part of my assignment? I think he'd make a good manager or entertainer. But he doesn't have any interest in math."

Sliced turkey with mashed potatoes, beer on tap. He was a glutton, like her unlovable husband, Thor. When the gods went in for human food, they ate voraciously. No salad with this course either. Fudit hadn't returned. Hephaestus talked as he chewed.

"Hermes presents no danger. He can't multiply or divide, doesn't know what a copy machine is, hasn't a clue about the media. The Lemnian logic is divide and conquer, then multiply again and let it all work for you! A whole raft of mortals understands that, but scarcely any of the gods, and certainly not Hermes. It comes down to the question of whether we can use him at all. I think I'll send him to the Underworld—we're short on staff there."

"That would be a waste, Father. I think he can be a real star: he doesn't have to understand the big picture. Oh, by the way, he turned completely black in your volcano."

Hephaestus grinned and slapped his thigh. "Black! I like that. Hadn't thought of it. Never tried that before. Black!" He wolfed down the rest of the turkey, chasing it with half a liter of beer. "He's no mathematician," he said, "but he's like a knight in chess: no one else can make his move, not even the queen."

"And don't forget," Helle added, "Hermes is still highly regarded by the other gods—"

"Well, well. What have we here? Sugared pancake with apple-sauce." Pile it on, Helle thought, gazing at the golden yellow mound on his plate. She poked around on the bare china beside the pancake and lifted the almost empty fork to her mouth. Her father shoveled his food in greedily. A silence fell.

"You need stars," she resumed. "They give the masses a sense that they have a chance. . . ."

"And what if he joins the others and turns against me?"

"I can't believe you're worried about that. He's still a big baby, a snot-nosed kid, nothing more. He wants to play tricks and have a few good laughs, that's all; just right for the public."

Smacking his lips, Hephaestus pushed his plate aside, his face showing that things were going just as he wished. The cheese platter came swaying in.

"That's my daughter! Who else could see through me so easily?"

"Look, Hermes is more than either of us cares to admit. He's the antiworld you need. While he was pinned down in Santorin, the Hermetic impulse was just a slight disturbance. Now there's a chance that—"

Hephaestus suddenly turned impatient. "Hold it right there! I put a lot of effort into changing the meaning of the word 'hermetic'; it cost me centuries. I don't want to hear you—"

"Sorry, Papa, it just slipped out. It won't happen again. It's just that I think Hermes can restore a gleam of the divine to mischief and thievery. You want to do away with universal principles—you've told me why. You need him for what's to come. Otherwise the con men and the rich won't join in, and you'll be wondering what to do."

Hephaestus shoved the cheese platter over to her. "Have some! Cheese tops things off."

He tried to suppress a laugh but then broke out so heartily that he had to lean against the table. One of his crutches fell to the floor.

"You've fallen in love with him, you little scamp! I figured you would."

She nibbled crossly at a piece of Romadur. Her father wasn't the sort of god who showed his cards, even to his daughter, although he sneaked a look at other hands. He knew every mortal and god as if he'd forged them himself. Perhaps they were so transparent because they'd adapted themselves to the systematic order of his smithy.

"All right, then," said Hephaestus. "Tell him to go to Vienna, the Hermesvilla, exactly one week from now. I'm doing him an honor; I hope he realizes that. There are trees and bushes all over the place—I don't know how I'll stand it."

"I can't contact him," Helle replied. "He's in Munich, airborne, free as a bird or a fish. Not a single engineer, locksmith, or blacksmith is in touch with him, nor any local spirit we control. I know he's looking for me, but how do I let him know where I am?"

"Simple: we'll pique his curiosity. Count Leif is making a balloon ascent east of Munich, the greatest ever, as high as possible. Air traffic is being routed around him. The count will bring him to you, and you'll bring him to me!"

• • •

Hermes flew more slowly than a bird, which gave him greater leisure to select palaces and rooftops as vantage points. From the roof of a church he watched the majestic ballet of construction cranes, then looked back from one of the cranes at the sun-drenched splendor of the stone church, reading in the iridescent tiles of its roof what he might do next. A few buildings had new tiles produced by the computerized ovens of Hephaestus, baked to uniformity and revealing nothing. But older ones remained. His wings bore him aloft as always, even though Otto had ruffled them somewhat during the Athens Fasching, as the women had ruffled Otto. He gave up flying for a time and sat on the back of a motorcycle, but the cyclist's helmet prevented him from entering his ear to learn how to handle it. Unfortunately there were very few motorcycles—Hermes liked everything that was noisy and smelled, except volcanoes.

The ancient mysterious power of the staff rendered him invisible, at least to mortals. He could fly effortlessly through open windows and pass through closed doors. And slipping in and out of ears while he was naked was no longer a problem, since his hat, sandals, and staff shrank with him and could be taken along into heads, although he still had to find a place to leave his sack of clothes and booty each time.

Perched on the organ in a concert hall, he dangled his winged feet and listened to music in which magnificently murderous tones occasionally reigned, but with slow, formal beauty. A calm elderly gentleman kept time with a staff and prevented any confusion. Hermes liked the violinists best, because they moved in unison. When they came in, it looked like the wind in a meadow, all the stems swaying in rhythm. He also liked watching the audience listen to the music; they were so much more attractive then. When the symphony was over and the old man lowered his staff, Hermes raised his and momentarily put the whole audience to sleep. The musicians looked around uncertainly, waiting for applause. The conductor looked up at the organ, recognized Hermes with a wave of his staff, and grinned. He was clearly a god himself—not light on his feet, but certainly not Hephaestus, the blacksmith. His staff held magic powers of another sort.

During the piano concerto, Hermes heard a small peeping sound coming from the audience, like a baby bird but steadier. A man at the end of a row got up quickly and left the hall as quietly as possible. It was the neurosurgeon Hermes had seen earlier. He flew after him, saw him enter a police car, and passed through the front windshield. The car raced toward the clinic, its blue light flashing, its siren offering a harsh fanfare that Hermes could have done without. In the surgeon's head once more, Hermes looked forward to learning how to do brain surgery. The surgeon was not at all nervous; he concentrated calmly on his artistry, polishing his glasses. A famous politician had collapsed unconscious with a massive brain tumor that was pressing everything else against his skull. Hermes knew this problem firsthand from countless heads. A crowd of men and women with cameras and lighting equipment stood outside the clinic, practically blocking the police car, trying to get pictures of the doctor. But he didn't even look up; he just kept on polishing his glasses.

First there were figures to consult, charts with curves and values, along with X rays. A quick change into a green gown, then an eternity of hand washing. In the meantime, Hermes looked around the clinic, discovering a few people whose bodies and brains were ready to die but who were being kept alive by machines and tubes. One had been dead for some time, although no one had noticed. As escort of souls into the Underworld, he observed these things uneasily. He could only guide mortals to a dignified death from a state of life or sleep. This condition struck him as ambivalent.

Inside the operating room, which was an orgy of electronic technology, the patient was held fast in a sitting position, his body entirely covered with white cloth except for a shaved spot on his head. The skull had already been bored open by another doctor. Hermes was now looking into the opening through the polished lenses of his host. He was surprised at how brightly colored it was, mostly from the blood, which trickled intermittently. Up to now he'd known the human brain only in darkness.

Three hours later Hermes knew how to skillfully apply a scalpel to a well-developed tumor, knew the various grips, the names of all the instruments, each part of the brain, and all the assistants and nurses. He considered switching to the anesthetist to learn about anesthesiology, an important art but one that interested him only slightly. If he wanted to put someone to sleep, or into any other state, he could do it more easily with his staff. Removing a tumor, however, was beyond his power as a god, even if he did know his way around the brain better than any doctor. A tumor was an ineluctable destiny, and an operation was in fact an effrontery to the goddess Moira. In earlier times Hermes had taken the hand of those with this illness and, gently and at the appropriate time, led them down the path to the final ferry.

The politician escaped with his life, even, apparently, with his mind, though it remained to be seen whether or how quickly he would regain his power of speech. Unbelievable, how much Hephaestus had taught mortals. In spite of everything he'd suffered at the hands of the persnickety grouser, Hermes was beginning to admire him, and when he met him he would tell him so.

He visited Rosangela in Pasing, intending to work on his rap songs, but when he found her with a wiry, energetic-looking young man by the name of Mathias, Hermes decided to slip away and spend the night playing table tennis with Nathalie Rittberger. Then he saw that Rosangela's friend was pulling on a dark sweatsuit and throwing a heavy backpack over his shoulder, about to leave.

"No, you can't come! We do take women along sometimes, but they're professionals like us. It's too risky a business."

A thief! The gym shoes were further indication. He wanted to go along, help him pull off a major job, share his pleasure. He tried to get into his right ear, but Mathias was pulling on a stocking cap.

An hour later Hermes discovered he was no thief. He'd wondered about the paint specks on his gym shoes. Mathias was a "writer," one of the paint-spraying rebels he'd thought were young gods when he was in Venice. They loved trains and left their wild, interlacing letters and bright images on the walls all along the tracks, like dogs and cats leaving their scent. Mathias, his backpack filled with spray cans, met with six other writers that night in a small town east of Munich to spray-paint an entire train in a railway depot. The young men, all dressed in dark colors and with stocking caps, spoke softly or communicated by gestures. Guards who were supposed to be making rounds but were too lazy were watching television somewhere. For hours the only sound was the click of tiny steel balls inside the cans and the thin hiss of propellant. Hermes could see in the dark, but he was amazed at how beautifully the writers could spray-paint a train without light. The images extended onto the windows and beyond. A woman's face appeared, and a grinning gnome, but the true images were the letters with which they signed their self-chosen *noms de guerre.* The script reverted to shapes with lives of their own, bursting with impertinence and rendering their authors' names almost illegible. The letter egos, swollen with power, jostled one another, each trying to outdo the other, shoving their way forward, like real people. Hermes had no desire to reveal himself; it only would have disturbed them. But he also wished to spray his own name on a railroad car that would travel great distances, so that the world would once again connect "Hermes" with night, fog, mischief, and disorder. He stole three spray cans from Mathias's backpack and hid them behind a barrel.

The sound of a motor. A police car rocked its way across the railway yard, its spotlight probing the darkness for dark shapes. But the writers were prepared, calmly packing up their spray cans and disappearing into the night through holes they had made in the fence. The police didn't know the whereabouts of the holes, so they lost time, nor could they run as fast or as quietly as the rebels. Hermes was happy and decided to spray his name on one of the now unprotected police cars. He pulled out a can and set to work. It took a steady hand to spray the narrow outlines of the letters from the right distance. He'd noticed that the writers made curves by moving their entire bodies, not just their arms, as if they were engaged in a languid spray dance. It was some time before it occurred to Hermes that there was no point in writing his name in Greek, but as an image it worked, and the bright colors completely covered the word "police." Meanwhile the cops, out of breath and angry, had returned. When they discovered the present left for them, they didn't know whether to laugh or to swear. They did both, until they abruptly fell silent. An invisible hand was still working on the letters—the spray can also invisible, since it was in Hermes' hand, and the paint jet as well. The total image was nearing completion. For several minutes, Hermes heard only: "What is this?" "What's going on?" "What in the world?" No one thought of grabbing him or putting something between him and the car—they were too astonished. He continued working to the end, then stepped back a few feet to observe his artwork with satisfaction. He then rose into the air, dropping his spray cans, which immediately became visible, beside the car. The infuriated police yelled and raced in circles around the auto, one of them firing into the air.

Hermes flew toward the east, where rosy-fingered Eos announced the dawn. Now he wished to explore the countryside, rivers, forests, and springs. There must be nymphs or local spirits who could show him the way to the midpoint of the world. A cock crowed prematurely, a car drove toward a small village, weaving slightly after a long night, the dum-dum-dum drone of music emerging from its interior. The driver had turned the volume as loud as it would go, to keep from falling asleep.

Then Hermes saw something odd on the horizon: a ball the size of several houses rose against the reddening sky and continued upward. He gained altitude, looking for a suitable cloud or even overcast sky. Once he melted into a cloud, he could cover great distances in an instant (which meant he would find it easy going in Germany). Coming upon a nice, long fish of a cloud going in the right direction, he merged with it, saturating it. Moments later he emerged from the other end and floated down toward the mighty sphere that was now gleaming in the morning sun. It bore a sign with letters and numbers. A basket hung beneath it on ropes; it contained a sturdy, powerful man who repeatedly released a jet of flame upward with a blower, heating the air inside the giant hollow balloon. To learn more, Hermes made himself visible, swung over the rim into the basket, and said, "Good morning! I'm Hermes."

The man was expecting him. "Morning," he replied laconically. "I'm Count Leif. I'm supposed to stay with you until you're picked up. That's all I know, Herr Hermes."

"What's this 'Herr'? Just call me Hermes. Don't you believe in the gods?"

"Not before breakfast."

"Fine. Where are we headed, and what's for breakfast?" asked Hermes.

"Coming up," Count Leif replied solemnly. "And a balloonist drinks only champagne."

• • •

They sat waiting beneath the trees at a restaurant by the river. The village was named Truchtling.

"He'll come," said the count, lifting his glass.

Hermes gave a start. "What do you mean, 'he'?" He was expecting Helle.

"Some sort of woodsman. He'll take you to them."

Hermes ate hungrily. "Champagne and pickled pig's head—do they have this in every village inn?" he asked.

"Only in Truchtling."

The balloon had drifted eastward for three hours at high altitude in a light wind. Hermes tried in vain to explain his cloud-flight technique—he only knew it worked. He took his flying implements from his pockets and showed them as well. The pilot shook his head in doubt when he saw the tiny wings on his hat, sandals, and staff.

When a large lake came into view, Count Leif found a meadow without high-tension wires and brought the balloon down near the road. Soon thereafter a truck with four men appeared. They rolled up the heavy pile of canvas, packed and loaded the basket, cords, and blower, then drove Hermes and the pilot to the inn in Truchtling, for champagne.

Count Leif came from Brandenburg and was friendly but

laconic. He spoke only what he knew to be true, so his sentences tended to be brief. One of them was "If it's not one thing it's another!"

"Do you know who's picking me up?" Hermes asked.

"Here he comes!"

A fat, bald-headed man with a mustache was approaching. He was wearing what appeared to be wet and even mossy overalls of some artificial material, with no shirt, no socks, and threadbare rubber sandals. His face and hands were also wet, and water dripped from his mustache.

"A schnauzer mustache and overalls—that's him. Looks like he's been swimming," said Count Leif, rising. "Well, so long! Perhaps you can help me out sometime; never can tell what might happen in our line. . . ." He waved his hand and went inside to pay.

The fat man sat down in the vacated spot and looked Hermes over good-naturedly.

"Wull, lookee heyre, id's Hermes! An' in Truchtling uf all playces, didya effer here da like? 'Most as gud as da devil hisself." He introduced himself as Bedaius, a well-respected local lake and river spirit. He generally traveled as a fish, either a catfish or a wels: "A fine keddle a fish, fast or molassy, maykes no neffer mind ta me!" But he also enjoyed walking on land in human shape and spending the night at an inn. To do so he had to dress while still under water, so there was always a pair of mechanic's overalls lying ready for him on the slope of the riverbank.

"Da way Apollo cotched ya whun ya'd swiped 'is beasties, an' afterwards ya lay 'n yer mammy's lap, so he hadda let ya go agin—we gotta kick outta dat back den! We laffed oursels silly! . . . Fetch us a drinkee, dreembote!"

This last was aimed at the waitress—otherwise Hermes had trouble understanding anything he said.

Bedaius continued unperturbed: "Say, luv, yer as black assa bushmun—did da gimpy smith reely letya spend ta thousn yirs hangin' inna chimbley?" Hermes guessed that Hephaestus was the "smith" involved, but he hadn't understood the question at all. Without waiting for an answer, Bedaius ordered half a dozen white sausages and a pale ale. When he finally realized that Hermes could speak a sort of Munich student German, but not Bavarian, he tried to speak more carefully. The results were, to say the least, mixed.

"Ah'm sposed ta take ya ta da T'ree Blessid Wimmun. Idsa liddle daft, sinse dey lif onna mountain 'n' me inner wadder. Ah ken do id as a man, bud idsa pain! Onna way, ah'm sposed ta tell ya 'bout da wurld, how id's run, one a da t'ree wimmun tol' me. Sed ah was da right un, all right. May be so, sinse ah've got da Keltic slant on tings. 'N' da gimpy smith wus fed up wid de udders, da Romuns. Ah sed yeh, sinse ah didn' smel nudding. Bud inna oshun ah'm leff ad pease, no fact'ries, no irun, no graffi! Nun a dat dere stuff!"

Hermes didn't understand much of it, but he had the impression that Bedaius, under the camouflage of his corpulence, beer, dialect, and easygoing manner, was a passionate spirit. For the moment, he had to be patient and listen to his stories. He could understand why. After all, how often did an authentic Olympian come to Upper Bavaria? Bedaius said he'd met the "gimp" twice, the first time over three hundred years earlier, when he was building the first pipeline in the world, between Reichenhall and Traunstein, and then briefly in the Second World War, when he was south of Summring, building a munitions factory. On both occasions the conversations were brief, pointed, and vitriolic. And slightly over fourteen hundred years ago, two authentic saints dropped in, Irish they were, at Oberwirt in Keaming. Unfortunately he wasn't in time to engage them in conversation. It seems they'd spent most of their time quarreling anyway, each claiming to be a bigger sinner than the other. That sort of jealousy shows you've got a real saint on your hands, Bedaius said with a grin.

He'd arrived in this region with the Alones, a Celtic tribe, and turned into a fish because he loved the local lake. Being able to interact in visible form with mortals gave him a major advantage over most local spirits, and he knew mortals well. When the Romans ruled the area they built shrines to him as if he were a god. "Bud id wassnt respekt—nuttin buda tryck ta wipe us oud eysier, da swines!" He emptied his glass, trying to wash down the two-thousand-year-old lump still stuck in his throat. When Bedaius was excited he fell helplessly into pure dialect. Hermes realized he should have spent a few hours in some Bavarian farmer's head, but it was too late now. He shook the lake spirit's arm and insisted he speak standard German. Bedaius paused and then said with concentration: "Ah've god no munney. Ah meen, yur da god a thiefs, dun't ya haf eny? . . . Ah bin goin' on creddit fer ta t'ousand yers down dere, wid no trubble ad all. Bud on dat mountain nobuddy nose me. . . ."

"Here's plenty of money," Hermes replied, reaching in his backpack. "I took a look around a few banks."

• • •

At first Hermes meant to steal a car with a full tank from the gas station, but then he thought of a way to travel and learn Bavarian at the same time. He told Bedaius what to do. Bedaius offered an old farmer, who had just filled his mini, two hundred marks to drive him through the mountains for a day. Hermes meanwhile had rendered himself invisible and slipped into the farmer's head, where he managed to get him to agree. The trip was difficult because Bedaius was too big for the little car. He and the farmer were both nearsighted, and neither one knew the roads. The farmer wasn't old, he was ancient, and not very clearheaded. Unfortunately Bedaius wasn't of much help. They were on the road half a day, trying to find the meeting place. Hermes flew high in the air several times, trying to spot the mountain named Geigelstein, which Bedaius and the farmer, cursing and arguing with each other, described differently each time. Progress was made more difficult by the fact that the lake spirit and the old farmer insisted on stopping for sandwiches every three hours, a Bavarian trait that was historically connected with the rhythm of the Roman carthorses, which had to be rested and fed at similar intervals. The one great advantage of this practice was that after two hours Hermes was totally fluent in an old form of Bavarian dialect hardly spoken anymore, even in this region. He also learned what things had been like in 1916 at Verdun, how much money and food a tenant farmer received from the estate of the landowner, how to recognize the onset of hoof-and-mouth disease, how to drive a mini, and that a ninety-six-year-old man whose wife had died after seventy years of marriage longed firstly for death and secondly for sufficient beer, whiskey, and tobacco while he waited.

When they at last arrived, he exited from the farmer's head and slipped unobtrusively onto the scene. After Bedaius paid off the farmer and the mini disappeared behind a blue cloud of smoke, they started climbing, since there was no cable car. The Blessed Ones, who roamed the Alps as brown and black mountain goats called chamois, chose undeveloped peaks as their meeting places.

The local spirits were more numerous and less shy than in the lowlands. A few sat in the fissures of rocks as salamanders, their gazes awakening a clear echo in the wanderers. Goblins straddled the trees as thin dry branches, and two almost translucent spring nymphs, who called themselves fairies, spoke fluent Celtic and Langobard. Bedaius and Hermes stayed with them only a short time, since they had a lot they needed to discuss.

Bedaius proved to be a climber of great strength and endurance. In spite of his girth, he weighed relatively little, like all gods and spirits. He talked constantly without ever losing his breath, no doubt in part because he no longer had to try to speak "bookishly"—Hermes understood every word.

They discussed the state of the world, and in particular the deeds and position of Hephaestus.

At first he had been much like the other gods, a respected Olympian, although he was the most human of them all, and the slowest! That's why he loved iron, an armor hard enough to protect the slow, even though its weight slows them even more. For the same reason he became a master at manufacturing compensations for slow reflexes: clever animal traps that snapped shut, bows and cross-bows, cars and trucks.

Because he had so many human traits himself, he loved mankind even more than Prometheus, with whom he'd conspired to steal fire for mortals. No one robs Hephaestus' forge without his knowledge and consent.

Hermes found the lake spirit somewhat long-winded. He knew these things. He'd observed Hephaestus' dangerously warm friend-ship with a man named Archimedes long ago—until he had the Roman soldiers murder him: a typical tale of jealousy between mathematicians.

It was misfortune enough to love mortals, said Bedaius, for it led to disappointment. Hephaestus had also fallen in love with right angles, and that, too, proved problematic. As everyone knew, the Celts were the best blacksmiths in the world, but they paid no atten-tion to right angles, or at any rate didn't use them. They forged by eye and hand, and that was good enough. But among an infinity of angles, Hephaestus showed a rather embarrassing preference for the right angle, using it almost exclusively, partly because of an addic-tion to "multiplication," which worked perfectly with right angles. Multiplication resulted in rapid, blind increase simply by the filling in of rectangles. All care in construction, the loving addition of units after careful consideration, was totally lacking. This drunken drive for more was beneath a god's dignity, but Hephaestus couldn't stop playing a game that gave him such a sense of superiority over the ancient fertility gods.

Unfortunately he also invented the wheel, which could repeat a given operation each time it revolved—lift a hammer, for example, cover a certain distance, punch a die, or print a page. This made pos-sible the mass production of staple goods and led to the elimination of unique items.

Using this technique, Hephaestus produced and delivered whatever the gods wanted: tools, palaces, weapons. The quality of life had improved for mortals too, resulting in increased sacrifices to the gods and more splendid temples. Only gods such as Bedaius refused to go along, since a fish has no need of wheels and can live without right angles. A few others, Athena and Dionysus among them, viewed Hephaestus' mass production with gentle mockery, while failing to recognize its dangers. Multiplication was fine as far as the other gods were concerned, and without thinking much about it, they too attempted to learn the technique, with Ares taking the lead. But they weren't as proficient as Hephaestus, and before they realized it, he had gained superiority over them. He controlled them through their own desire for comfort.

One of the basic principles of the Celtic perspective was avoidance of all secular learning. For what, pray tell, was the result? All too soon even the ancient, traditional functions of the Olympians had been rendered obsolete, or replaced. And in order to weaken the gods even further, Hephaestus appropriated their worshipers, substituting the vulgar concept of a single, unambiguously good, universal god, who harmonized perfectly with multiplication. Individual human beings were now "equal in the sight of God," and a Christian was a Christian; one could use them to fill rectangles, creating a homogeneous Christian surface, which was exactly what they desired. With real human beings, say Greeks or Bavarians, that was inconceivable. It could happen only in a religion or in the army. With the introduction of the concept of homogeneous good, said Bedaius, all joy in differences disappeared, the best of all joys.

Hermes sensed with embarrassment that Bedaius loved mortals just as much as Hephaestus did. Who cared whether they were happy? There were far too many of them anyway, and few were worth thinking about.

Bedaius continued explaining monotheistic religion. It didn't always function well, but mankind had quickly adjusted to its absurdities. Because nothing was known about the life of the generalized god, he could be regarded as a god of chastity. For centuries people had been guilt-ridden the instant they gave in to their natural feelings. As a counterpart to this "loving" god, a purely evil "diabolos" had been invented, a creator and sower of confusion, called the "devil." He was black, limped, and lived in the fiery center of the earth, although he walked freely among mortals, seducing women and stealing souls. One of Hephaestus' cleverest tricks had been to combine himself and his ablest opponent, Hermes, in this antigod.

They climbed higher, the trees growing shorter, the rocks larger and more numerous. There was a menhir among them, a holy stone, no longer recognized by men grown deaf to the gods, but ringed by a powerful echo of the spirits. Directly across from the menhir stood a Christian cross, intended, Bedaius explained, to absorb some of the holiness of the spot, but the faces of the surrounding rocks wore an air of mockery. A glimpse of the future of the Alps could be read in the lichen on the stone, but Hermes was too absorbed in what Bedaius was saying. He had good reason to dislike Hephaestus, but he hesitated to agree with the lake spirit, although he found him rather appealing. The brooding rebel hidden behind that corpulence knew what sort of god Hermes had been and, because he was attracted to him, wished to warn him of the dangers he faced. Like all those who understood mortals, he knew how to judge the gods as well. He was convinced that something had gone wrong with the blacksmith and his system, and he possessed a sixth sense for the fine web of relationships, no great surprise in a catfish that had managed to avoid being netted for thousands of years. The weights he placed in any set of scales were solid. But where Hephaestus was concerned, it was difficult to separate what Bedaius knew for certain from what he had imagined in the depths of the lake. It could all be false, or at least outdated. Bedaius might even be a decoy and this strange outing on the Geigelstein a test, if not a trap.

Bedaius sensed Hermes' hesitation, but without affront. He switched the subject to tourism, one of the major plagues for all the local spirits.

A cross stood on the mountain peak, a sign of the sovereign authority of the single god created by Hephaestus, erected on even the smallest hill in order to intimidate the mountain spirits. But who feared intimidation not backed by action? Only mortals were impressed, Bedaius said. He took a dry bread roll from the top pocket of his overalls and turned it over a few times. "Ah'd redder hab a stake!" He was camouflaged again, a bit of folklore, a classic character evading the blacksmith's iron grip. Tyrants protect themselves against lean and hungry fanatics, not easygoing fat guys.

• • •

Hermes waited impatiently for the three goats who were to turn into women.

"Wull, dere takin' dere tyme agin!" said Bedaius, rolling his eyes. He was in a bad mood because the foehn was getting stronger, a warm wind that combed the thickest clouds into finer and finer strands, until it blew away the last remaining wisps. But it clouded the brains of longtime local inhabitants even more thickly, Bedaius clearly among them. No doubt his mood also suffered from the lack of a "sensibul sandwitch brake."

Time passed, and they still didn't appear.

The foehn produced wonderful musical arpeggios in the clouds. Within them Hermes read an astonishing turn in his destiny in the coming days.

Bedaius claimed the Blessed Ones were responsible for the foehn, but Hermes pointed out that the winds were created by Aeolus alone, who thickened or dispersed the clouds of the globe as he saw fit. Evidently the Bavarians knew nothing about Aeolus' destruction of the Persian fleet, which saved Athens from Xerxes. Bedaius fell silent momentarily, as if caught. All right, then: at any rate, it was the Three Blessed Women who prevented suicide in the mountains. Given the narrow valleys barely touched by the sun, there were many who grew tired of life, and mountain climbers unaware of their own self-destructive urges. The Blessed Ones were just what they needed, although they didn't always arrive in time. And they sang so beautifully they brought tears to your eyes: "La Montanara," for instance, or "Chum, chum, chum, my dear!" With his ragged bass, he tried to demonstrate how beautifully they sang. Hermes quickly cut him off by asking how he planned to get back to his lake.

"How? Lika fish—slip inta da streem 'n' hed on doun! Odsbods, ah'v 'ad enuf a dese wimmun!"

But now they heard them approaching, their hooves rat-tatting like an elaborate riff on the drums.

"Dose gotes ar priddy fansy wid dere feets," said Bedaius, "hoppin' arund lika pallet dans!"

The three goats stood staring with bright brown eyes. So these were chamois. When transformed into women, they wore robes like the young mother Mary in Venice. They didn't appear to be in a singing mood. They were Ambeth, Wilbeth, and Querbeth. Two of them approached Bedaius and started chatting with him, while the third, Querbeth, was, as expected, none other than Helle. A lightning exchange of glances: she could see that he could see that she was trying to see if he knew about the minor betrayal of her father. She knew that Bedaius opposed Hephaestus—did Hermes know she knew? To break this off, she embraced Hermes and drew him behind the rocks, partly because she wanted to have him to herself.

"I'm just a temporary substitute," she said. "The Blessed Ones are missing their third member. The real Querbeth moved to the low mountain range and made off with a guy named Rübezahl. That's the way it goes. By the way, before I forget: you no longer need to journey to the midpoint of the world. My father will join you at the Hermesvilla in Vienna as your guest. Aeolus will cloud the sky over tonight all across Austria, so you should make good time."

Hermesvilla . . . it sounded promising, but odd somehow. He was anything but a god of real estate.

• • •

Helga decided to stick with Trostberg Hospital. How did she know if there were any better? It could be assumed that the Charité had more to offer than anything in Stendal. For all she knew, Trostberg might be the Mecca of Western surgery!

She had forgotten, going into a curve, that a bike with a sidecar handled differently. If her head had been ripped off, as was often the case with bikers, they couldn't have done much on either side of the border, beyond the Iser or here in Trostberg. It would have all been over. She'd come out of it OK—tibia broken but not shattered, prolapse of the abductor hallucis, with no traverse paralysis, a dislocated jaw, cerebral blood clots, but her brain was still functioning, with occasional lapses. A week after the operation, she asked the nurse for her suitcase and was confused to find Navigation brand soap on a washstand in the West, although she'd placed it there herself.

Postponing her return trip to Stendal was no great loss. But she had meant to take the bike to Greece. She could forget that now. Athens Fool! Too bad about the nice old magneto-sidecar combination. From Munich to Höllthal on the Alz River she'd done fine, and the one beer couldn't have been the problem. She felt a rush of joy as the words "magneto" and "Höllthal" came back to her. Her brain was recovering. She wouldn't have to relearn anything. She could concentrate on the new.

She started with a new language, Bavarian. Several feet of the Bavarian author Ludwig Thoma stood on the bookshelves of the hospital library. The bed opposite her was occupied by a Bavarian woman named Notburga from Truchtling, and on the bed next to her lay a woman named Kreszentia, a peasant from Öden. Helga listened to them with interest, even while she was still coming out of anesthesia. The rhythm and melody of their speech pleased her, with its familiar Russian *r*.

Bavarian originated in the age when hunters and gatherers invented agriculture. It was circumspect, clear, and without ornamentation. You could spot a windbag immediately in Bavaria; he made a fool of himself by the way he used his own language. Through an unusual combination of words and silence, the language expressed feelings, and particularly gradations of mistrust and rejection, with greater precision and more accuracy than the most fluent High German. Imitating the sounds of the language, however, required a throat and jaw in excellent working order.

MANAGƐR AN▷ MAGICIAN

In the summer of 1990, a few people began arranging stones in small pyramids, first at crossroads in the mountains, then on balconies and in public parks, on favorite tables, even on concert grands. The purpose was as unclear as the phrase "Hit the road with Hermes," which continued to spread mysteriously. Some people, mostly those who read books, discussed him with a note of ex-pectancy: quite different expectancies, of course, since few things are as diverse as readers. There were those who thought he would enliven culture through the rediscovery of genius; others saw an important role for him in pedagogy, since he was a rascal and could understand rascals better than their teachers. Intellectuals believed his smooth, crafty style of lying would deliver them once and for all from the ironclad pillars of ideology. The passionate hoped for illuminating rapture and a new community of the inspired. Eccentrics, artists, and adventurers longed for increased mischief and the strength to follow their own drummer with even greater dedication. The poor wished for the lasting enlightenment of the rich, the rich for a rehabilitation of instinctual capitalist aggression: Hermes alone could free the world from the worst vice of all, an overly considerate attitude toward the poor. Philosophers and business consultants were switching roles—hardly noticeable since both groups had long since declared the need for increased chaos and disorder, even destruction. They saw Hermes as Lucifer, a primal force of derangement, a bringer of light. At a conference in Berlin, a French philosopher proclaimed that change was in the air, an open sea in sight. We were skating on thin ice, but at least we were no longer frozen fast. The combination of displacement, propulsion, and piloting called "navigation" was possible once more. It was a matter of unleashing a new Hermes from the right, opposing so-called progress, particularly technological. Skill had long since turned to skilled overkill, and what had once seemed fate was proving simply fatuous. Unfortunately the word-play in this argument was too much for the German left, who found the lecture suspiciously trendy and characterized it contemptuously as "Heideggerian hip-hop," unworthy of Hermes. Their Hermes was a leftist.

Increased curiosity, communication, silence, speed, caution . . . each participant in the growing Hermes discussion had his or her own idea about the world's problems and a special notion of the coming salvation, sharing only the desire to "hit the road." Some started a corporation called Project Myth, Inc., to develop a salvation and passion story for heathens, something they sorely lacked. Others founded Action Eternal Life, in which immortality was achieved simply by concentrating on the concept. Yet another group opened the World Transformation Office. In their conference room in Bad Gottleuba stood a small bronze Hermes in contraposto, his right hand gesturing eastward.

"Things are in a beautiful mess!" said Ignaz Knidlberger, who specialized in problems of the overly beautiful, in an interview. "It's time for the sower of confusion to appear personally, or things will lose all coherence." And Henry Pictor wrote from Pirgos-Santorin to the editor of a Hamburg weekly: "May I respond briefly to the review of my new Hermes poems. Hermes is on the wing again, though editors don't seem to realize it. He'll soon reunite all mankind. Then we can dispense with miserable *ersatz* products, traffic jams, alcoholism, and, to my great joy, weekly literary supplements. With all best wishes!"

• • •

Hermesvilla? It was large for a villa, more like a palatial hotel or a sanatorium, but they didn't seem to be expecting any visitors, and certainly not a god. The doors were locked, the blinds lowered, and a sign read: SPECIAL EXHIBITION CLOSED TODAY.

Hephaestus had presumably arrived, since he was organized and always on time. Hermes decided to let him wait a bit.

The park behind the villa was called the Lainzer Zoological Gardens, and the people strolling in the rainy weather were probably Austrians. He'd traveled rapidly by cloud, but it wasn't quite as pleasant on the ground. The rain had just started up again. He didn't think it would be fair to steal an umbrella from a Viennese burgher. They'd already suffered enough from generations of rain.

One of the two deactivated Blessed Ones said all bad things came from Vienna. She probably meant the government. The Viennese, even when they seemed morose, were surprisingly friendly when you talked to them, and if they didn't like blacks, they simply said so. Anytime Hermes asked a question, he could count on hearing the phrase "On the whole, actually . . ." He was never sure what it meant, and the words elicited no clear image. It seemed tied to the pessimistic conviction that things were not, and never would be, entirely as they could or should be.

He still hadn't figured out what bound people together, now that the gods were barely perceptible in their lives. When they raised the question themselves, the word "human" kept reappearing in various forms. It sounded good, but when you examined it closely it meant nothing at all. What kept people from cold-bloodedly killing one another these days, for money, or out of boredom, or to settle an old score? He was struck by how often they dreamed of it and how seldom they tried it. He'd ask Hephaestus; he would know.

After moving about invisibly for some time, Hermes wanted more practice in human form before meeting that notorious lover of mortals, Hephaestus. He was visible now, wearing the opera tails of a branch bank manager from Mariahilf. Unfortunately the banker smoked strong cigars, and his coat had been hanging on the balcony with good reason. Moreover, the pants were too big and the top hat was too small. But that didn't bother Hermes. He considered Charlie Chaplin a kindred soul, and stole a watch and chain to resemble the lovable tramp even more closely. He carried his other things over his shoulder, tied in a bundle.

The clouds were pushing their way toward the Lainzer Zoological Gardens. It wasn't raining now; it was pouring.

He thought back on the mountains, the cliff, and Helle. He was homesick and wanted to return to Athens as soon as possible—and to see once more the nude Aphrodite of Knidos, the most beautiful of all statues.

Making love on Mount Geigelstein did not begin to compare with Venice. The presence of an audience didn't stop Hermes, but he didn't like performing for them. He couldn't shake the feeling that Helle wanted to show the other women it was indeed Hermes who was screwing her. Even though he understood her pride, he still felt he was being put on show.

After making love they were thirsty and drank milk from a vessel in the shape of a cow, a form of cup he knew from Attica. Then, to get away from the others, he taught her how to use the clouds to fly. Sometimes she emerged from the wrong end of a cloud. "You have to know which part of yourself to enlarge," he told her, "your head or your feet. You'll travel in the direction of the largest part of your body and away from your smaller end." She could do it now. He wondered why she talked so much about death. What did death mean to her? Did she want to be the new guide of souls to the Underworld? That required greater callousness than she possessed, and on occasion greater cunning. Souls were always finding reasons to postpone the trip.

The one thing Hermes couldn't understand was why Helle never stayed with him but instead would leave abruptly and without warning. Of course, she never mentioned their next meeting, and his gift of prophecy and reading random signs seemed of little help. He didn't want to carry around an appointment book like the neurosurgeon, but he would have liked something to look forward to.

He had no trouble, however, understanding her ploy with Bedaius. She was torn between the desires to be faithful to her father and to betray him. She'd used the local spirit as an intermediary to warn Hermes without having to oppose Hephaestus herself. There was little chance, however, that this had escaped the omnipresent smith's notice. Perhaps this was her warning to her father that she was beginning to resist him.

He had let Hephaestus wait long enough. His delayed entry would lose its effect if he came in waterlogged, his coat and hat dripping. He walked to the villa and looked in—the ability to see through lowered blinds is part of a god's basic equipment. Yes, there he sat at the table, as powerful and ugly as ever, smoking a cigar, his golden crutches beside him. And grinning. Because of course he could see through blinds too.

• • •

"There he is, Hermes Ithyphallikos, the fastest skirt-chaser among the gods!"

"Is that you, the missing fathead? Where have you been—did you fall in a hole? You hammering old skinflint, I can't believe it! Let's have a sniff . . . it's you, all right! I may have lost a little speed, but once I was in Santorin it didn't take me long to find out about deodorant. You've missed some of the great wonders of the world, my highly honored half-brother."

"What language shall we use, you smooth consoler of widows? There are no Greek words for some things I need to say. Would Bedaius' Bavarian suit you?"

"Not if we have to talk about you, mighty machine merchant! I don't know the word for 'jerkoff' in Bavarian."

"We'll speak High German, then, and you can be the topic. So you want to take me on, do you? Good! I've been looking forward to it. Do you know what three times three is? Ever heard of mathematics?"

"Of course, since I know mathematicians. They know how to count, but you can count on them getting things wrong. They take a piss in the park and hope a woman will see them and think it's clever. And they do it at night, when it's raining. I feel sorry for mathematicians. I try to help them out now and then."

"You've got a typical peasant's mentality, can't get beyond simple addition. Without multiplication you can't even say 'three people.' "

"Nor do I care to. What's one horse and one pig?"

"Two mammals."

"That's meaningless! 'Two mammals' could just as easily be one mounted rider."

"So it could." Hephaestus yawned.

"But that would be wrong, since it's a butcher's apprentice on the back of a fleeing sow. What do you call that?"

"Granted. An equation with several unknowns is obviously unexplored territory as far as you're concerned. But I assume you've built up your cult. Are the sacrificial fires burning steadily again?"

"They sure are! In fact, it's getting to be a problem. Have you heard of 'smog'? About the 'greenhouse effect'? You ought to get out of the house more."

This was too much for Hephaestus. He broke out laughing and pounded his hand on the table.

Well, it's just as well he can laugh, thought Hermes. Who knows what he might do instead—perhaps turn Vienna into a new Pompeii. He smiled politely and waited for the god of the volcano to settle down.

"Next thing you know"—Hephaestus panted—"if I don't watch out, he'll be trying to steal my fog!" He wiped away tears of laughter. "Haven't you had enough yet, you insolent puppy? You're black enough!" He started laughing again, this time slapping his thigh.

"Go easy on that leg!" said Hermes. "You might hurt yourself. Seems to me you're the one who hasn't had enough. Good thing you don't have a hammer around."

Hephaestus turned serious. "Still the same old scamp. I'm glad to see it—shows I was right to take you out of circulation. As we say nowadays, you're a devil. But I've got god on my side, a mighty, all-embracing god. You'll get to know him."

"Zeus help me! Have we started believing our own lies? Each of us has whatever he's invented on his side. You're lucky this supreme being of yours is only an idea, otherwise that giant baby might crowd you out."

"He's not such a bad idea, and he's moved things toward righteousness. Take a look around. With just one god in control, a god of—"

"—of jealousy and self-satisfaction."

"Nonsense! A god of fire!"

"That seems unlikely. The art of starting fires is my invention," said Hermes. "All you did was industrialize it and harness Prometheus, you old imp. You're getting a little forgetful!"

"Hermes, I'm asking you to work with me."

"Work? Now what's that supposed to mean?" asked Hermes. "I was supposed to meet Helle here. Have you seen her?"

"She wanted to come," Hephaestus replied indignantly. "She's probably still in the park."

"It's raining."

"She has an umbrella."

"And the other gods? Let's hear about them, otherwise I'm going to get bored. Why is Athena still hanging around Athens? Why did you want to keep me away from there?"

"I'll have to go back a ways to explain that: everything in its proper order." Hephaestus pulled out his slide rule, oiled it on his hair, and proceeded nimbly through a lengthy calculation.

"Haven't you heard of calculators?" asked Hermes. "They run on batteries. And they move the decimal point without bothering your fat head, or even your oily hair."

For the first time, Hephaestus gave him a friendly smile. "You admire me. I know a backhanded compliment when I see one. How was the brain surgery?"

"Magnificent," Hermes replied, caught by surprise. "And you're right: I meant it as praise."

"That's a basis we can continue on."

Two hours later they were sitting one floor higher, in the Empress Salon. A few portraits of her were hanging on the walls. She was dark-haired and slim and suffered from depression. She starved herself sick and learned Greek to escape the world.

"She longed for me, and I was in chains," said Hermes to Hephaestus. "That's what she died of—see what you've done!"

Hephaestus said nothing but instead offered Hermes a cigar, which he ignored. Hermes rose, took hold of the chandelier, and set it swinging with a strong pull, then stepped to the window and looked out.

"All right," he said. "Describe your system. I trust it won't take long."

He hadn't learned much about the other gods, and all he knew of Athena was that she was using one of his names at the moment. Hephaestus wasn't interested in families; they no longer had a role to play, his own least of all. A few of the gods served as his representatives or spies: Pan, for example, who advised him on questions of mood and emotion, and Hecate, who served as a messenger and, in exceptional cases, guided dying souls to their fate.

Apollo was supposed to be protecting the arts, but he was so disgusted by their commercialization (after all, he was once the god of justice) that he handled his duties sloppily and was often absent. The once mighty god from Delos lounged around in grand hotels, watching television with a jaundiced eye. The light of knowledge and craft was encountered less and less often in the arts, while the number of panels and conferences that for a suitable fee bemoaned the decline of art grew.

Hephaestus had renounced divine power, as Demeter once had, but for a much longer time. He now lived as a mortal, proud of controlling everything entirely by means of his system: "You may be able to cast spells, but I can organize." His technology, he claimed, was superior to magic because it could be multiplied at will. But Hermes imagined he probably still resorted to a few easy tricks now and then, or did he truly have the technological means to listen in on conversations whenever metal was nearby? Through the iron table legs in beer gardens, the steel of the mini, the screws in the cross on the mountain peak—Hephaestus had listened as he talked with Bedaius, and since most adults have coins in their pockets or at least fillings in their teeth, he could listen whenever he wanted.

"It doesn't work with metals manufactured prior to 1977," the god of the forge explained. "The special substance that makes the whole eavesdropping operation possible hadn't been invented yet."

"What's Gianna Nannini saying at this moment?" asked Hermes. "Is she singing? I'd love to hear her."

"We can do that, but only over the central computing system. As I said, I don't do magic."

Then there were those who carried out orders as part of the control system. His devoted assistants the Cyclopes had gradually infiltrated all the metal industries, including hardware stores, automobile factories, steel and iron works, foundries, press shops, and die mills. Science, politics, and journalism were strangely helpless in dealing with Hephaestus, for without an adequate supply of iron their brains wouldn't function. He laughed at Bedaius' criticism: "The age of fish and breathing with gills is over. I use outmoded characters like him only because they're good for tourism."

His "Lemnian" system, Hephaestus explained, was by far the best path to just behavior.

"Yes, I know, using right angles," Hermes interjected, wanting to show he wasn't totally ignorant. It's also a matter, said Hephaestus, of individual rights and ensuring the rule of law (no other angles allowed, thought Hermes). The way Zeus and Apollo helped individual mortals achieve justice was imperfect even back then; now it was totally useless. "There are, at the moment," he announced after a brief but intense flurry of calculations, "7,185,452,300 humans, and in one minute there'll be twelve more. A god who doesn't understand multiplication might as well pack it up." No one, under Hephaestus, lived in misery or fear, and his system was the best of all possible ways to ensure that. Hermes gently shook his head. Surely multiplication was necessary only because mankind had multiplied too greatly—and whose fault was that? But all he said was: "Misery doesn't mean much to me. I'm more interested in indolence and debauchery."

Hephaestus leaped up angrily and pounded his crutch on the table. "Pay attention till I'm finished! No use trying to find a weak spot in my system; it's totally consistent."

But Hermes persisted. "If it's so totally consistent, why did you build in an East-West opposition?"

"That's past history. I had something else in mind with that originally, but it degenerated into a porno story that no longer excited anyone. You don't need to know about that."

At the moment, he was explaining managed labor, one of the most important features of his wonderful system. What had once been solely the domain of slaves had become common property, thanks to him. Now it was a misfortune to be without work, and not solely because of the money. Self-fulfillment was impossible if you didn't have a job, he said, and so it was a necessary human right. Hermes was stunned. He understood something about money, because you could steal it. But work? He thought back on all the human heads he had occupied, but he didn't remember much to do with "work." The drummer, the neurosurgeon, the rap singer, the graffiti artist, had all been artists; that was what made them happy. All the others complained about their jobs. He had never encountered anyone, employee or slave, who regarded work as "self-fulfillment," so the concept remained unclear to him. But it hardly mattered, since he had no intention of coming near work, except perhaps as a ruse, for fun.

As Bedaius had indicated, multiplication was a key factor in all this. It provided more jobs, more money, more power, more people, more needs, more popularity. A good family name meant nothing; he'd seen that with Jean-Claude. What counted was being a majority stockholder, running companies, sitting on parliamentary committees, writing articles, and above all getting on television. Success was measured not by achievement but by the rapid mechanical and electronic spread of the second rate. Well, why not, thought Hermes. I'll just learn the rules of the game; I don't have to follow them. If you don't believe in multiplication, it can't control you. I'll stay outside the system, find my own followers, and play practical jokes with them, or make them rich and famous, depending on how I feel. I'll hold my own masquerade and change things in small ways. Wherever I am, the system will seem slightly askew, and my white-hot brother will be banging his crutch on his desk. He'll want to send me back to Palea Kaimeni, so I'll have to be careful not to give him an excuse by getting involved with Aphrodite again. If she's still his wife, that is . . .

"Tell me, my dear brother, are you still married to Aphrodite?"

"Yes . . . but she's doing her own thing now."

"My, how new."

"No, this is something else! Somewhere along the line she got tired of eternal beauty and attracting men all the time, so she slipped into men's roles. At the moment, she's called Knidlberger and runs a therapy center for women who are too beautiful. In Thera—but you didn't meet her. I made sure of that."

"And Dionysus?"

"Visited Santorin one hundred and fifty years ago as a German artist and stayed on. He's an Englishman today, calls himself Pictor, drinks as much as ever, and writes letters or hymns, depending on his condition."

"Dionysus drinks at home? That's a bad sign: things must not be going well."

"We don't need him—he'd be drinking, anyway."

"How's that thoughtless hit man Eros doing?"

"He works well and follows orders. Every affair he starts leads to a job, directly or indirectly, and the world of advertising couldn't get along without him. I reward him handsomely."

"One more thing: do you love mortals as much as ever?"

"On the whole, actually, yes. There are a lot of them now, so there must be more geniuses and more men who are just."

Hermes had heard enough. "Let's not fight, dear brother. Let me visit Athena; don't give me any trouble. She's my only friend."

"Don't rush things," Hephaestus interrupted sharply. "We'll talk about it another time. That's all I have to say."

Disconcerted, Hermes fell silent. Why was the blacksmith afraid to let them meet? What was the story with Athena? Hephaestus reached for his crutches and stood up. "The car is here. Now you can see one of my jewels here in Vienna, an old forge, the local center of Lemnian control and Lemnology. You'll see how things are run."

"Does this Hermesvilla belong to me?"

"No; that's just its name. But if there's ever anything you'd like to have without stealing it, just let me know. I can always wangle it somehow."

"You impersonate a mortal wherever you go—what name is in your passport? I assume it's not Hephaestus."

"People call me Consul Herdhitze, the Cyclopes call me thrice-great master, my first name's not worth mentioning. My passport? I have a thousand passports, and none of them is fake."

They stepped into an early-model Rolls-Royce. "The only car for me," said Hephaestus. "You can't find a right angle anywhere in other makes." The chauffeur was wearing regulation sunglasses but had only a single eye, in the middle of his forehead. Since he wore a billed cap, no one noticed.

"So where do you live?" asked Hermes as they drove along. "Mortals tend to stay in one place."

"Why live anywhere? I have offices and workshops. I don't need sleep any more than you do. I don't imitate the mortals in all respects."

"What do you do for fun? What do you spent your money on?"

"I like money while it's still in the form of labor. Here we are at the forge—come on in. . . . I want to hear Gianna Nannini sing too. They tell me she sounds like a rasp in the hands of a master craftsman."

• • •

"Well now, I know a few of these tools from my Oberpfalz blacksmith," said Hermes, taking pleasure in comparing the images stored in his mind with the objects in the workshop. He recited the names as he pointed: "Quenching tank, bellows, sledgehammer, hardy, chisel, punch."

Two hairy Cyclopes heard him and turned around in surprise.

"Not bad." Hephaestus nodded appreciatively. "That sett hammer is ancient. I used it to forge the hinges for the doors of Notre Dame. A long time ago." He sighed. "The goldsmith's shop is through here. You won't know many of these tools."

"Sure I do. Screw gauge. Chasing hammer. Ring gauge. And that's an Archimedes drill, isn't it? As a boy, my blacksmith dreamed of making women's earrings. And of dancing in Freystadt."

"Your system of gathering information seems to work well, even if it is slow. Now take a look at mine. Let's take the elevator."

From the street, the building looked like an old, comfortable home for ordinary citizens. There was a conference room on the ground floor. Hephaestus' realm began beneath the actual basement, known only to him and the Cyclopes. The electronic center was in the first subbasement, the archives in the second, and the forge in the third. The elevator looked ancient, as if made of forged iron. It was used by the tenants but reserved for Hephaestus when he wanted to descend into the depths. Hermes noticed a sign: "Caution! Please keep children in the rear!" Someone had altered it to read: "Caution! Please kick children in the rear!" He must have followers in Vienna, perhaps even graffiti artists, the sort Hephaestus didn't like.

"There seem to be some Hermetics here," said Hermes, and was surprised to see Hephaestus wince. "Do they know the greeting 'Koinos Hermés'?"

"Yes, but not with your name. It's 'Gimme five.' "

The data center was a relatively narrow but seemingly endless hall with moving walkways in both directions. As they traveled along the chain of supercomputers, Hephaestus was greeted respectfully from every side. "Good afternoon, thrice-great master! Greetings, great one!" The Cyclopes were allowed to use the familiar form with him, since to them he was the master, not the consul.

"The Cyclopes work well with monitors: they don't need depth perception. When they were in the blacksmith shop it was always problematic—they kept hitting their thumbs." Hephaestus' voice, when he spoke in the system's center, took on a new, deeper, and more sonorous tone, effortlessly filling the endless hall.

On the moving walkway across from them, a slim female figure in black drew near. She stood gracefully, motionless as a statue, staring at them. A beautiful woman. Hermes tried to peek over the side at her legs, but her full-length black evening dress with three pleated flounces revealed nothing but a slender elegance. It was cut wide at the top so that only the outermost curve of the shoulders was covered, and they appeared broad against the narrow waist, with a gauzy material encasing the entire length of her arms. Was the dress silk or tulle? He would ask her when she drew close enough. She wore her hair loose and gazed steadily ahead with a strange lassitude. By Zeus, it was Helle! She looked stubbornly past him. Had she been crying?

"There she is!" said Hephaestus. "Hey, what's the matter?"

Hermes jumped over the side, landed on the moving walkway, and caught up with her in a few steps.

"What a beautiful dress! Is it silk or tulle?"

She folded her arms at her waist and looked away.

"What a stupid question," she said quietly. "Go away and play."

"What's the matter?"

Now she turned around. "It wasn't hard to eavesdrop on the conversation you had at the Hermesvilla. I've had it up to here with you!" She held her hand up to the spot on her wonderful neck where she'd had it with him, right under her chin.

Hermes said nothing, trying to think what she could be talking about. Meanwhile Hephaestus was moving beside them on the other walkway. He could change its direction and speed whenever he wanted. Helle saw him but continued without pause: "Athena? Your only friend? And I'm just good in bed? Go to her, then! What are you waiting for? Don't let me stop you!"

"He can't visit Athens—I've told him that," said Hephaestus.

"You keep out of this!" Hermes interjected. "Fathers don't understand these things." He had the impression that Helle was angry about something else as she whispered in Hephaestus' ear.

Now they reached the end of the moving walkway, and Helle tripped over her long dress. She would have fallen if Hermes hadn't caught her, transforming her carefully maintained haughtiness into rage.

"You traitor! Don't you think I saw how you eyed the other Blessed Ones? And you were frank enough at the villa—not with me, of course. You think because you're Hermes I'll just lie around waiting for you. All you care about is proving your manliness daily. Real talks are for men only. You think because you're a god you don't need to show me any respect or court me." She forced back tears of pure anger and regained her voice. "You thought all you had to do was wait and I'd come running, because I'm crazy about you. Well, you're wrong, Mr. Clairvoyant! No, don't try to follow me, it's over, I don't ever want to see you again! I'd be better off with any other god."

Her flowing gown disappeared through the door. Hermes shrugged and stepped back onto the moving walkway, where Hephaestus had been waiting. The blacksmith grinned and shook his head.

"Just like a woman—fire and fog. She'll be right outside. After all, she needs a little manly protection when she's that angry at men. We'll just take our time."

Hermes was too disturbed and surprised to say anything. But it didn't seem right to run after Helle. She was right about one thing: there were other women and he was interested in them. What sort of a god did she take him for?

"She'll need some time," he said to Hephaestus. "I can wait awhile myself, as you know. In some cases for eternity."

They had finally reached Hephaestus' original goal. "This is the holy of holies. Here's where I determine the future of the continents. It would be senseless to establish a fixed and final, unchanging system; the whole thing has to remain a process that moves forward slowly enough that mankind won't notice the return of the old. The problem is human limitations: they're too impatient, since, relatively speaking, they die so soon after they're born."

They stayed the entire afternoon and evening. Helle was for-gotten. Hephaestus showed Hermes devices so cleverly constructed and so intelligent that he was thoroughly taken with them: for example, the gravity computer. With its help the master of the earth could maintain contact with other bosses millions of light-years away.

"It functions by means of minute shifts in the position of huge satellites, using a binary code," said Hephaestus. "Each change in the universal gravitational system is registered immediately, so we don't have to rely on light, which is far too slow."

Hermes didn't understand a word. He was beginning to admire Hephaestus more than he cared to admit. If it was all a big lie, then Hephaestus was a better liar than he was. And that was something he had to respect.

"Zeus never suspected there were other worlds, and Helios still believes the sun he shoves along is the only one there is. None of the other gods understand these things, not even Athena. Over the last few decades I've discovered things and made others possible that I couldn't have imagined a thousand years ago."

He explained to Hermes the rejection of the mechanistic worldview and linear thinking, how the computer had proved mathematically that reality was totally unpredictable. "I'm close to being able to calculate chaos itself, down to the last digit in an infi-nite series. That will make everything possible, including squaring the circle."

Hermes tried hard to follow what Hephaestus was saying. One thing was certain: Bedaius' description of the Hephaestic system was several centuries out of date—he didn't have a clue about these new and exciting ideas. It was now possible to raise humans who were as beautiful as they were bright, and provide eternal life for at least a lucky few. Fear, physical force, the universal antierotic scarecrow god, even work—everything that ruined people's moods and bored the real gods would no longer be necessary.

Among the impressive rows of computers stood an old-fashioned box with note cards sticking out, like the ones Hermes had seen in libraries. "This is where I keep my enemies," Hephaestus explained. "Anyone who ever opposed me is under surveillance; I keep track of them." Here and there brightly colored markers attached to the greasy, dog-eared cards indicated the names of particularly zealous enemies. Hermes pulled out a card covered on both sides with a practiced Acropolis shorthand. To Hermes' questioning glance, Hephaestus replied: "François Villon. One of your type, long dead. I'll have to clean house sometime." He tore up the card.

When they stepped from the old Viennese building onto the street again, darkness had fallen, and Helle was nowhere to be seen. Hermes would think about it some other time; right now his mind was on his half-brother's arts.

"So what shall we do now?" asked Hephaestus. "Do you know how to play poker?"

"No."

"Fine; some other time, then. I'm the best poker player in the world. A lot of poker knowledge went into the Lemnian system, so I always win. I'll show you how to play sometime, even though you don't have the talent for it. It's played for money, and winning depends on having a system, not luck."

"Wouldn't luck help, even with a system?"

"Luck is a superstition, but a useful one."

They stepped into the car, and the Cyclops cut into the flow of the traffic so abruptly that brakes squealed and horns blared.

"You're right—he can't judge distances."

"I'll tell you what part you can play in my system. You can be the Zeitgeist! That's one of my most demanding posts, and you don't have to do any math at all. You needn't struggle to build up a cult; you'll have something better—a fan club! . . . Would you like some vodka?"

"No, thanks; last time was enough. . . . What would I do as the Zeitgeist?"

"Since you're Hermes, just be yourself. But not the same old

Hermes you used to be. You'll play the part, so to speak, pretend you're Hermes, the god of clever inventions, commercial adventures, of theft, your callous eye cast on mankind, sower of confusion, the god of mischievous pleasure and practical jokes—everything you're known for and a few things you're not. Your name will be known worldwide, you'll be the god on everyone's mind, your miserable existence will be a thing of the past. Of course, you'll have to give up a few things. We don't need divine messengers, with all the electronic devices we have. Hecate has to exercise her dogs from time to time, that's all. And please don't guide any souls into Hades: it's overcrowded already."

"What happens to the soul these days?" Hermes threw in.

"Nothing. We have all we need."

Hermes thought a moment and smiled.

"I'm too curious to say no," he said, "but I insist on two conditions. You've got to eliminate AIDS; it's too hard on my type. And I get to go to Athens as often as I want, for as long as I want."

"Agreed on both counts, once the probationary period is over," answered Hephaestus. "Five years. Then your wishes will be granted."

"A probationary period for Hermes? Don't make me laugh!"

"It's a probationary period for me as well. Either of us can back out at any time. And five years is nothing to beings like us, right? I have to convince you first that my system works. Believe me, it's an honest offer."

Hermes didn't like that last sentence; it lacked style. Whenever Hermes himself lied, he avoided such statements. And he wasn't about to believe Hephaestus. He had always lied; why should he stop now?

"All right, then; during the probationary period I'll hold something back as well: I'll play the Zeitgeist, but not as Hermes."

"That won't do! That would debase the whole operation. You have to appear on television personally, not as some mime with a little man in his ear. There's enough of that already."

"But, my dear brother, what's five years? Now show me what you know about poker!"

• • •

An appointment book came with the job. He knew now that "work" meant having to keep appointments. At certain scheduled times he was to be in the head of one of the two moderators chosen to incorporate the Zeitgeist in their broadcasts, Nadine and George. Sometimes adventurers have to put up with an initial period of boredom. He was curious to see what would happen if he went along. Work as curiosity. He checked over his appointments.

Session with George at the station to learn how radio works. "Against Sexual Repression, For Sexual Freedom"—sounds totally boring; we have to do better than that. Freedom's not something you ask for; you take it by force. And you're constantly playing with fire.

The director: if he manages two ideas at the same time on some subject, he gets goose bumps overestimating himself. Working lunch with Pan. My own son, but look how he turned out! One of Hephaestus' managers, with special shoes for his goat feet, fancy tie, capped teeth, exuding an air of fake self-confidence.

A moderator is supposedly "moderate"—they'll be in for a surprise with me in their skulls. Pan says not to say anything embarrassing. What's wrong with a little embarrassment? Moral hypocrites are embarrassed by amorality. I'll improvise amorally on George or Nadine's eardrum, as embarrassingly as I can. They have no idea who they're dealing with. Everything the public finds in bad taste, contemptible, and hateful will be worked into the broadcasts. It'll be more fun that way. Just what are "Nazis"? Fly off for three hours in the afternoon, do some girl watching, have a go with one of them, maybe the announcer. Everything fast-paced, you don't have to wait long for anything. Men with jobs don't have time for lovers. But I don't have to sleep at night.

Nadine and George are easily controlled, repeating every word I whisper, pronouncing my name correctly, announcing my imminent arrival. The Zeitgeist is a collective effort composed entirely of words, flowing directly from these people out into the world.

Broadcasting slogans for three programs. Provocation is people calling up afterward: "What's wrong with hate? It's better than being afraid." "You don't get a hard-on if you're just friends." Annoying the feminists—a noble occupation. Session with a politician. Luckily he's an alcoholic; at least he gets out among the people.

Radio broadcast in progress. Title: "Nothing to Hold on To." Its sole message confusion. A television show entitled "Ribwort." Opening shot a stand of ribwort along the road, rippling in the wind against a blue sky—why not chamomile or balm mint? Rosangela with her rap, Mathias spray painting, Nadine insulting everyone. A great success.

Mottoes, slogans, catchphrases. The country needs new punch lines, sinical and cynical.

"Don't wait for a better life, take it."

"What shall it profit a man if he shall lose his fear and gain a world of boredom?"

"Man is the only animal that robs his own species."

Yes, wake up, you knotheads, with your phrenological duty bumps, your faces mired in respectability. Everyone, East and West, listen to me, stop trying to force your own inanities on each other. Hephaestus recommends developing a separate network for private broadcasts. He'll take care of the licensing. The first few titles: "The Zeitgeist: Up Close and Personal," "Renaissance," "Morning Breeze" (a pornographic alternative to aerobics). On the whole, radio is better suited to this than television. Making mischief requires a thinking audience, even insulting them successfully. But Hephaestus says to reach as many people as possible, as directly as possible, that's the only way to get through to "mankind." Hephaestus is the inventor of the ironclad market share.

• • •

The first broadcasts were a huge success. George and Nadine, with Hermes whispering in their ear, praised him and announced his imminent arrival. An almost hysterical Hermes cult arose. Now people greeted one another in his honor: "Hermes be with you," "How's tricks?," "Gimme five," "Stay cool."

But did he have what he wanted? At least he didn't have time to think about it.

He picked up phrases and coined others as he went. He no longer prepared for broadcasts, just thought up pranks. There were two sorts of workers: those whose work was increasingly marked by laziness, and yet was done well, and those whose work multiplied, was done more and more ineffectively, and finally did them in. Hermetics belonged to the former group, but they often failed to get the job in the first place, because the people hiring them were more impressed by those who killed themselves working, even if they failed to do the job. They recognized them as kindred souls.

One popular quote: "Unemployment is no problem. Most people can do without work. What they need is a salary."

He developed slogans as he learned and inserted them as tinder in the brains of his Zeitgeist hosts to set the age on fire. But could market share offer a real substitute for the feeling of being revered?

The fun things were most peripheral: Getting people in various office canteens singing on the same day. Watching video clips and producing them himself. Viewing ads or posters, which he often preferred to full-length films. Playing jokes—releasing viruses into cyberspace. Spraying graffiti at night; confusing pretty salesgirls who normally kept their feet on the ground (that Spanish salesgirl in the jewelry store!). Studying all sorts of sexual perversions, in people's heads and in his own. Rap, drums, dancing—learning something new every day. He had to, because he got bored within a few hours. The first time he tried tennis he beat the number two player, the next day number one, and wasn't seen again on the courts. Running back and forth for two hours to score a victory wasn't worth the effort. He remained true to the pleasures of motion in a single direction: roller-skating, skateboarding, water-skiing, sailing, horseback riding. Not bicycling. What was the point of pumping along, ruining your knees? Driving a car was more fun, but only if you were going over one hundred twenty miles an hour on the autobahn in heavy fog—after all, nothing could happen to him.

He could tell he'd be restless in another week or two; it was already setting in. If Hephaestus exiled him again, he'd better be sure he had fun in the meantime. *"Nadie te puede quitar lo bailado,"* the salesgirl whispered to him in their night of love: "No one can take from you what you've danced." It was a good slogan for the Zeit-geist, better than "Eat, drink, and be merry!"

He knew his way around now. Fine entertainment could be recognized by its tendency to corrupt morals.

"Yesss! That's right! Down with the tyranny of values!" cried the director, and got goose bumps. Impertinence was suddenly the sole content and trademark of private television. Even serious programs were no longer morally straightforward. The religious program "The Path to the True Community" included the question: "What precisely is the objection to injustice if it results in greater peace?" The script came from the Lemnian Research and Writing Center. Hermes noticed that Hephaestus was doing all he could to plow up the world. It looked like he was getting bored too.

He ran into Apollo in Bayreuth, still playing the graying con-ductor and hearing himself called "maestro." Inwardly focused, his chin lifted, deep lines around his mouth, he obviously loved the role. He didn't seem particularly pleased to see Hermes on the loose. He turned away without a word. What was his problem? Since he spent all his time in hotels, channel surfing, he'd probably seen "The Zeit-geist: Up Close and Personal." He may have been offended by the claim that the overblown judicial system was so costly only the cor-rupt could afford justice. Hermes knew that wouldn't please the Delian—but surely he was overreacting. Or was it something else?

Helle had disappeared. Hephaestus claimed to have ordered a search for her, but he might have been lying. Hermes flew to Venice on a low-pressure system covering the whole of Europe. He searched through the Guggenheim museum in vain, made a visit to the Blessed Ones, and found only the two real members of the trio. He gave them a brief note for Helle, which remained unanswered. The next day he donned his sandals and hat, ascended through the clouds, and asked Helios, who merely shook his head in silence, apparently on Helle's side. Hermes floated back down and landed with some difficulty—when you asked Helios a question you were blinded by the light, whether or not he answered.

• • •

Helga Herdhitze enjoyed Vienna in autumn. She was in the right mood for it too. Everything seemed to be dying or contemplating death, but she had escaped, could stand and walk, was learning. And she was outraged by the West she had once idolized, an anger that stirred her so greatly she was actually thankful for it. Free enterprise, self-fulfillment! Arrogant cartoon characters who were actually mice, ducking for cover. The West consisted of countless variations of "Thou shalt not . . . !" and of pompous asses preaching to others about the things they shouldn't do.

She had appeared in court and showed her teeth, then returned to her hotel room to weep over what she had lost. Even clearing out the apartment in Stendal had an aftereffect. Her cousin had moved into the rooms, but Helga was still busy disposing of the blacksmith shop. Good tools that were salable, rusty ones to be thrown away, oilcloth notebooks filled with figures, an open box with dried-out cigars, brand name Speechless.

Big-talking predators from the West were busy in Stendal. One of these animals had tried to recruit her for a sect, a conspiracy bent on success. They moved through life in "zeta condition" and were totally ruthless.

Winckelmann's head had disappeared into the copper beech for the time being, because no one felt called upon to prop up the lower branches. The Magnet department store had been taken over by a new former owner. Scores of handguns in the window. More people than just her father were interested in murdering someone, either themselves or each other.

Ahead of her: the coming winter. A furnished room with a view of Leo Perutz Lane if she leaned out. A job as a secretary/interpreter in an Austrian-Yugoslavian trading, or rather holding, company. Evening exercises for neck pain.

The right man was nowhere in sight. She'd managed to avoid an office messenger whose veins stood out on his neck as if he were screaming—not, unfortunately, a rock singer or a hothead, but a weight lifter. She had coffee with an old bookseller in Hietzing, who taught her poker. Her father could have done that, but he had warned her it wasn't a game for women.

Politically, reunification, or "accession," was once more in the offing. Initially, love flowed in both directions, then it ceased to be mutual. Love tended to die out when it was no longer returned, a type of negative escalation. The result was disappointment on both sides, but not great enough to rank as tragedy. The bookseller said, "It's simply the continuation of high-stakes credit by other means." The Viennese were angry, without giving anyone cause for anger, which made it difficult to talk with them.

Once on the road of learning, she had no choice but to continue. She had to get her knowledge of genetic research up to speed. What was "neurotransmitter" in Serbo-Croatian?

Love could go to the devil. She didn't want the messenger with the bulging veins, and she'd given up on Hermes, for all practical purposes. He wasn't around enough; besides, she wanted a man with something at stake, not a god who didn't have to risk a thing. It's true he was the god of bold ventures, but the paradox was that nothing truly serious, like death or illness, could touch him.

She expected Charles to reappear. After all, she still owed him twelve thousand dollars, and her name and Stendal address were inside the Pentax case.

In the Old Blacksmith there was a public forum on "identity." She raised her hand when the audience was invited to participate and announced that identity was a journey, not a location. The local residents didn't bother to argue with her. They could tell she was from the East—she sounded strange.

• • •

Within a few days, graffiti art had been legalized, and whole trains were now being spray-painted for a fee. The artists weren't happy, but they accepted the money.

Hermes was particularly interested in erotic "perversions" that had not yet been assimilated and domesticated, ones that were still capable of arousing alarm and indignation. They were often playful reversals of power relationships, which was part of his job as "Diabolos," the sower of confusion. Sometimes it was truly entertaining. The powerful office chief played a submissive slave, the harried dental assistant took on the role of an ill-tempered and nasty noblewoman. Because the Hephaestic world refused to distinguish between the playful and the serious, all games that trifled with power were thought of as "perverse." That was one of their canonized inanities.

The only thing that upset him about perverts not yet accepted as "normal," but still considered monsters, was that this upset them. They lived irreproachable lives in an attempt to avoid even self-suspicion. Hermes knew sadists who joined leagues dedicated to denying parole to violent criminals. Others held honorary offices in nursing homes, or posted letters filled with vile threats of murder and rape but covered with Christmas seals. The moment he raised this issue on "Ribwort," however, their public image improved, which upset him even more.

To his annoyance, Hermes discovered that everything he

broadcast in an attempt to reinvigorate and defend social amorality was accepted as amiably as could be and tied up with a pretty bow of sympathetic understanding, if not actually given a ribbon of honor. He felt trapped and suffocated by a goodwill that found anything acceptable but lacked respect. They appreciated Hermes, as they said, because of his refreshingly cool demeanor. That was fine with him—he'd soon have them shivering!

He attacked friendship. "At least your enemies fight when they take something from you. Your friends think they have an automatic right to your time, money, and concern. Avoid friends!" The public agreed.

He offered a program of practical exercises on how to be heartless, how to tell employees they were fired, for example, without feeling bad about it. He tested psychopharmaceuticals with a reputation for ameliorating the life of the working class. Hermes had George reveal before the camera that the drugs were actually used to numb pity, tenderness, and compassion in order to facilitate business. They made people feel less ashamed of what they said and did. He demanded that they be made available without prescription. They were of greater benefit to those who sold them than to those who took them, and after all, what counted was good business. The public found the show thought-provoking and highly interesting, with a certain amount of necessary hyperbole, of course, but leading the way toward a more profound discussion of the basic issues.

He mocked the concepts "man" and "mankind." To call someone "a real man" simply meant he was a leper, a cretin, or a criminal. Applause, congratulations on a provocative program, but no sign of anyone provoked.

He suggested it was time to abandon the notion of solidarity and leave the poor of the world to themselves and their criminal gangs, which was the best form of self-help. And let's hear no more hypocritical prayer-wheel calls for birth control. The Pope was right: "Since we've stopped trying to improve the material conditions of the poor, which shows we're thinking clearly, we don't have to worry whether there are a few million more or less of them." Protest, finally! But only from a few clever con men, who wanted to maintain their "humane" reputations along with their slightly suspect sources of income. As well as a few anonymous letters of agreement: "Thanks for the breath of fresh air! With best wishes, A Realistic Taxpayer."

Hermes tried heating things up a little: "Once, man was a perfectible being; today the question is how to eliminate him." Rumors his license might be revoked, concerned foot shuffling on the part of lawmakers, but no attempt to stop the shows. They were handled another way, called brilliant and controversial, the moderators treated as stars. Hermes was a household name.

That's more than most gods could achieve in two weeks, Hephaestus pointed out. He congratulated him and ordered champagne. They were sitting in leather chairs by the hotel bar.

"Everything's going great," Hephaestus said.

"I don't know ... it's not like it was. I'm an institution, nothing more; worse, in fact. I'm a show. No one loves me. At least not for myself or because I incorporate part of life. No one thinks of that."

"Television's rubbing off on you: your prose is getting a little overblown. What more do you want? Everyone knows who you are, you're on everyone's mind, they're engaging you in dialogue ..."

"There's something wrong. I'll figure out what it is."

"You're not busy enough! Put in a personal appearance as your own black self, run a few companies, produce something. Do you want to own the station? I'll throw in a sex shop. What do you say?"

"Two or three steel factories, please." Hermes grinned.

"No way—that's my field. But you could go anywhere you wanted as a business consultant. The people who idolize you are entrepreneurs and managers; all you need is a consulting firm. Talk about anything you wish: rate changes, communication networks, creativity, ethics or antiethics for managers, any nonsense you want—you'll come up with something. I'll be in the background, making sure that everything turns out right and that your clients flourish. How's that for an offer?"

"Why expend so much energy on me? For two thousand years you allowed me to slowly go deaf and dumb—"

"Can't a god make a mistake?"

"If I go into the consulting business, do I have to smoke cigars?" Hermes drawled.

"I'm afraid you can't get around it. It radiates calm and breadth of vision. I know all sorts of women who are wild about cigar smokers."

"I know, like the ones after you all the time, my poor brother Vulcan. You can hardly move for all the women throwing themselves at your feet."

Hephaestus had trained himself to respond to Hermes' wisecracks with a neutral grunt. Unasked, he began to tell how to select a good cigar, how to handle it, light it, smoke it. Hermes could see he would soon be a functioning part of the system, like Pan. Hephaestus guessed what he was thinking.

"Of course, we don't have to smoke the same brand. I'll smoke Brazilian and you can smoke Havanas."

Hermes concentrated on his train of thought, unconsciously allowing his cigar to be lit. Was he capitulating in order to grasp his situation more clearly?

The smoke curled upward, constantly reshaped as men and gods moved and breathed in incalculable ways. It rose, drifting through the room, forming pancakes and flat fish above the bar, wrapping about a woman's bare shoulders, twisting among the bottles on the wall. Suddenly Hermes understood why a person smoked cigars: to produce a shape, a figure of unpredictable, elegant movements. He was its author, although he only sat and puffed and blew. Hephaestus, author and multiplier of the world's smoke.

Hermes placed his cigar on the ashtray. "I'll have to talk it over with Apollo. . . ."

"Better not. There's an oracle, the last one issued at Delphi, dealing with you and Apollo. You don't know about it, but he does. Stay away from the Delian, Hermes."

"I never believed in oracles. Anything of significance was usually faked. Perhaps you'll tell me what it's all about? . . . It doesn't take an oracle to know that multiplication is not for me. If I multiply myself, I cease to exist. My name is widespread—and turns common. I was more of a god chained on Palea Kaimeni than I am now. So, my good brother, I hereby withdraw from radio and TV and return to magic. If I'm involved with mortals, it will be one at a time. I'll be on foot from now on, a god of simple addition, unmathematical, like life itself!"

With that Hermes rose and headed for the exit. The revolving door caught for a moment—the god of the forge had thrown one of his crutches after him.

"You'll be sorry," Hephaestus yelled. "I'll be keeping a file on you, understand? You don't have a chance against me!"

VI

THE PATH TO THE WRETCHED

Helle could undertake nothing against her father without Hermes' help. No further resistance could be expected from the other gods, and she couldn't hide her own growing opposition to Hephaestus much longer. Why had Hermes played along with him, against the direct advice of Bedaius and her own indirect counsel? Why had he disappointed both the mortals and the gods who were already on his side, who had placed their hopes in him? How could he forget his dignity for a game and fall for the offers of an adversary who wished only to render him impotent?

But perhaps she was also angry because Hermes hadn't held her back in Vienna, hadn't even tried to follow her. She was in love and he wasn't. There was no way to force a person to love; that's why there was a god of requited love. But he had been cast into the eternal darkness of Tartarus by Hephaestus.

Hermes had forgotten her. Her feelings stirred again. No, he couldn't possibly have forgotten her. And accepting something impossible made no sense.

But she was sure of one thing. As long as Hermes employed his eloquence to entertain an anonymous public of millions instead of courting one individual woman, herself, she had no intention of seeing him again.

Helle picked up her motorbike in Truchtling, where a knowledgeable old innkeeper had repaired it. There were no unnecessary questions, since she looked like Helga and paid the bill. That afternoon she headed toward Sachsen, where her father was vacationing. That's what he called driving for miles from North Lauchhammer to Finsterwalde through the barren countryside, past rusty pipes and dead electricity lines, until he reached the moonscape of a former brown-coal strip mine, where he sat for hours working on various calculations, smoking all the while, planning projects for the East that—a necessary prerequisite—would be visible from the moon to the naked eye. In fact, work was not yet under way here; everything was falling apart; buildings without roofs or windows stood in the rain. Hephaestus was glad to see her, having forgotten about her in all the smoke he was generating while planning the "Eastern Development." He was in a good mood, like all closet depressives the moment reality seems more depressing than their inner state. He told her how angry he was with Hermes, the most ungrateful idiot in the history of men and gods. He would take him out of circulation as he had before. Helle held her breath and listened to the story of Hermes' abrupt departure and how he had searched for her in the mountains.

"If you're involved with him again it won't be on my account, and if you help him you'll share his fate. I can't use anyone who's not totally on my side."

Helle nodded gravely, embraced him, and left. Moments later she was riding the motorbike off into the night toward Stendal. If Hermes was looking for her, he would surely try Helga's home.

What could he be up to? No doubt he was constantly changing

hosts in order to escape Hephaestus, who would imprison him or send him straight to Tartarus. Hephaestus would have to take away his staff first, since it opened any door. Hermes was so careless that ought to be easy.

There was heavy traffic on the autobahn that night. The highway gleamed with red brake lights all the way to the horizon. Anger was still the dominant emotion among drivers. It was always others who were slowing things up. The first fog banks appeared, but the moment the congestion cleared, cars accelerated to top speed in spite of the poor visibility. Then more fog, un unexpected dip in the road, the sound of cars crashing into one another until it seemed endless, the cries of the injured. Once again the others were at fault, since they either ran into someone from behind or were struck from the rear because they had stopped. Except where displaced by pain and mortal fear, the anger grew. The glow of burning autos was both enveloped and expanded by the fog, giving the illusion of a huge mountain cave illuminated by a somber fire. The goddess of passionate journeys was stuck in a traffic jam. She got off her bike, grabbed the first-aid kit, and went to attend to the injured. Although she wasn't all that interested in individual human beings, she did what she had to, partly to disguise her true nature, but primarily to practice what she'd learned. First aid was a part of travel, and that made her the best first-aid technician on the continent, better than any of the other gods.

When she returned to her motorbike after several hours and left the autobahn for the forest, the fog seemed even thicker. Her divine instinct guided her along the timber tracks most likely to lead to better roads and highways. Roaring through forests of fog and trees, Helle suddenly perceived, in the sidecar next to her, the naked form of a woman formed entirely of fog. She tested her with a touch. Yes, she knew that warm, damp hair. Nephele, the plump goddess of fog. Helle stopped, turned off the motor, and quickly embraced her mother, knowing she was always in a hurry to disperse.

"Welcome, Mother. Do you know how the story continues?"

"Who knows exactly? You can't expect me to. You might ask the author, but I think he doesn't always know himself."

"What author?"

"The god no one knows, the one who claims all copyrights."

"I assume you're here for a reason, Mother?"

"Yes, I spoke to the triune muse in a fog bank on Parnassus. The god of impertinence won't fall in love until Anteros is free again, and the two of you must free him. That's the prophecy. Be happy, my child."

A final damp, warm breeze, and she disappeared into the night. Nephele could change locations far more quickly than Hermes; at that very moment she might be haze above the Mississippi or a wall of fog in the Urals. Helle started the motor and rode through the woods to a point beyond the traffic jam, rejoined the empty autobahn, and headed for Stendal.

Free Anteros! The two of them! Anteros was in the Underworld, and getting there was no easy matter. First of all she had to find Hermes. She expected someone, probably a woman, would be staying in Stendal, or soon turn up there, and reveal herself as Hermes.

She waited in vain for two days, even visiting the "Midpoint of the World," a large, heavy stone in the middle of a frogless frog pond, encircled with rusty chains. If this midpoint was a testimony to the state of the world, it was certainly accurate. Hermes may have stopped here, but if so he had quickly flown on. She returned to Stendal.

It wasn't much fun waiting for him in a town where everyone knew her as Helga Herdhitze and called her by that horrible name. She wished she were back in the year 1807, when she was still called Minette and bedded down at 19 Schadewachten Straße with the future Stendhal, then an officer in the Napoleonic occupation forces. It's true a type of advance squadron from the West was in evidence now as well, but you could search with a magnifying glass for a man like Stendhal. Times had changed. Now she had to hide her divinity by playing a woman out of work, sitting around in the corridors of the unemployment office. After four days she'd had enough. She resigned herself to traveling to Haute-Vienne, even though Hermes knew nothing of her country estate, Saint Hilaire, and would never seek her there. For the moment she needed the greatest possible contrast to the employment office in Stendal.

As she was stepping into the railway carriage, a police officer approached her. "Do you know a man by the name of Charles, a musician, and a pusher on the side? You do? Then it's you we're looking for. Follow me, please." A pleasant shock ran through Helle. But instead of following him, she stopped and said: "No, that won't do. Kneel down, you cretin, I have something to say to you!"

"But, madam, that will attract attention. As a policeman—"

"It's meant to attract attention. I hope it gets your attention too! Either you kneel or you won't get a word out of me."

The threat had barely left her lips when the policeman knelt before her on both knees.

"Good. First you're going to write me a letter, proper, respectful, and well-expressed! Put in a little effort for me, Don Juan. Address it to Madame Elle at La Lande de Saint Hilaire, Haute-Vienne. If you look up Hezzenegker in Venice he may—I stress *may*—pass on my response."

Meanwhile a crowd had gathered and were whispering back and forth about the meaning of the little scene before them. Probably something to do with sex. But on the job? Intolerable! It would never have happened before the changeover. Oh, yes it would have, someone said; they always do what they're told.

"And now be a dear and give me a hand with my luggage," said Helle. "But first you may as well get off your knees. . . ."

She headed for the train, he hurried over to her luggage. After heaving the big suitcase onto the rack above her seat, he turned to her, at a loss: "Madam, unfortunately I don't know who Hezzenegker is! Perhaps you're confusing me with someone else. All I know is that I love you and I'll follow you to the death."

Death? What was that supposed to mean? That tipped off Helle that it couldn't be Hermes. He was just an ordinary policeman who sensed the goddess in her. She was annoyed with herself for the mistake. She replied irritably, "No, stay here. You'll get my answer general delivery. What's your name?"

"Kleinert, Ralf-Egon, police captain."

"Fine. Just be patient, Ralf-Egon."

Back on the platform, he stood with his hand to his cap in farewell as the train pulled away. She was too disappointed to wave back.

She stayed in La Lande de Saint Hilaire for a long time. Although she didn't forget Hermes, at some point she began learning to live without him. He faded away.

Or so she hoped.

• • •

Hermes knew that in the heady hours after his initial release, he had made serious errors. His divine moral coolness had resulted in a performance that was superficially amusing but profoundly ignoble. Increasingly, from boredom or destructiveness, he had defended pure immorality, which did little to refresh him and was by no means divine.

By human reckoning the year was 1993. Two thousand one hundred and ninety years had passed since he had first been chained inside Palea Kaimeni, and three since he was freed. He felt he had to begin all over again, as he had in the Cyllenean cave, or even long before, at the stage when he was still simply a Phallus in the retinue of the great goddess, at most a concept of male divinity.

But what were mistakes? He had long since learned that if the rules of the game could be reversed, a mistake could be turned into victory. His specialty was turning things to his own advantage. And on the whole he was more cheerful and positive than during his television days as the Zeitgeist. Yes, his good name had suffered, and his television shows, now totally god-forsaken, made things worse.

But now he had his chance. He knew the world and his adversary Hephaestus. As god of the twilight he could make himself invisible and was master of the art of clever and efficient self-miniaturization. He'd spent a year in a small town as a bookstore assistant, serving the three-breasted goddess whose symbol jutted into the street over the shop's entrance. He recognized her as the great goddess of old. Since he didn't have to remove a book from the shelf to read it but simply touched its spine with his staff, he knew almost everything there was to learn from books, with the exception of Hephaestus' mathematics, which he still detested. Having played the Zeitgeist for a time, he now turned his attention to those books that incorporated the opposite of the Zeitgeist, and they were by no means the worst sellers. Someday, he thought, I actually will be the Zeitgeist. I'll be the one who defines it, not Hephaestus and the media. Then mischief won't be godless, not just filth, meanness, crime, malice, depravity, but under my guidance it will bring delight and knowledge, even happiness. Not that I'm overly interested in mortals (except for beautiful women), but I don't want Hermes underestimated and dismissed.

Hephaestus tried to track him down, of course, to take back the staff, hat, and sandals. But Hephaestus, too, had made mistakes, by revealing his methods. Hermes avoided metal and even carried a metal detector at times so he could check quickly for eavesdropping equipment, moving away from the detector itself. He had noticed that almost everyone who bought jelly or brawn in this country was an informal associate of Hephaestus, and that every joint-nourishing foodstuff was carefully protected against theft. But how could that stop someone who not only was invisible but could fly? Of course, the god of the forge had the other gods and goddesses watched closely, because he assumed that Hermes would try to get in touch with them. But Hephaestus underestimated him, for Hermes nevertheless managed to contact a few immortals. For example, Till Eulenspiegel, who knew why Athena was under house arrest in Athens. Hephaestus could not curb her spirit. She was a divine representative of invention and handicraft, and could not be coerced or compromised. All he could do was isolate her. And Robin Hood, hidden in a ram in Yorkshire, revealed the final Delphic oracle, which predicted that things would go worse for the world if Hermes and Apollo made common cause. "Worse for whom?" Hermes asked.

For a time he tried to recruit a few children in his name, for they were born Hermetics. Unpredictable, unselfconscious, totally visual, they were burning with unabashed curiosity. Unfortunately they later lost these positive characteristics, having too few conceptual aids to carry them over into adult life. But Hermes managed to make them more independent. In school they copied from others or let others copy from them, and they would even swipe something occasionally, then let others steal from them, with Hermetic pleasure. In this way they learned to control the game of life, to give and take without fanfare, only to forget what they had learned under the pressure of a straitlaced decorum, ending up either overly accommodating or totally lawless.

At any rate, children were always a good hiding place. They seldom had metal on them, unless they were having their teeth straightened. Of course, he had to prevent them from wearing jeans, because of the keen-eared rivets. Once he was inside their heads, it was easy to convince them that jeans scratched unbearably. In London he taught a little girl named Margaret to sing "The Ballad of Villon and Big Margot" in perfect French, something she couldn't possibly have learned anywhere. She lived in a large house at the edge of a park, with refined, extraordinarily prudish parents. When she sang the chorus, "in the bordello where we live," everyone who knew French was bowled over. Before long she was on television. Hephaestus got wind of it and sought to watch over her so he could grab his adversary.

Hermes had a hard time finding his type of people. Although they possessed curiosity, intuitive accuracy, courage, and the desire to change themselves and others, they were socially unacceptable. They seldom held public office, nor were they engineers or businessmen. Instead they drifted through the world as soul singers, writers, skiers, prostitutes, designers, and con men. The worst of it was that their all-too-active curiosity, considered "shameless harassment" by the system, tended toward brutality at times, because they had been god-forsaken for so long. Hermetics were all too often violent or alcoholic; they filled the prisons. Occasionally they managed some crude form of revolution, but more often the revolutions failed, and they were themselves destroyed. Responsible for terrible deeds, they enveloped the globe in war. Hermes came to realize that Hephaestus used particularly god-forsaken Hermetics for his plans. He needed a certain level of destruction to produce something new.

In the old days Hermes, like all the other gods, dealt with the richest and happiest of mortals, and when appropriate, he made many others rich and happy as well, so that they recognized him and prayed to him in gratitude. But he could see that times had changed. Growing rich these days was accomplished without divine aid, solely by means of the system. The rich weren't particularly happy either, just analytical and morose. So Hermes was unable to find or place his people among the elite. Whenever he found them, they took too much delight in blind destruction.

Inside the head of a gifted fourteen-year-old he was teaching to play the guitar, he found himself surrounded by a gang of drunken, howling adolescents about to set fire to an apartment building housing dark-skinned foreigners. They thought it would be fun, but at the same time they believed they were acting within a framework, fulfilling a task. They defined themselves, albeit drunkenly, as political activists, with no real idea what that meant.

Not that Hermes felt constrained to hinder the deaths of any particular mortals. But this annoyed him. He could teach the young man to play the guitar divinely but could not grant him the cunning and self-confidence to divert others toward less destructive acts. A few unfriendly pinches on the nerves in his brain gave his host such a splitting headache that all he wanted was to go home to bed. Then Hermes slipped out of his ear and within ten seconds had stolen every lighter and match from the gang, as well as their gasoline cans. A fight broke out. The teenagers were beating each other up, and he made sure each one received a full share of the punishment. Then he made himself visible in dark nakedness and asked, "Had enough?"

"Where'd he come from?" someone asked in shock. They rushed forward to grab Hermes, who raised his staff and forced them painfully to their knees. They were too surprised to cry out.

"Who in hell are you?" one asked.

"The god of foreigners and long journeys. When I was born I killed a well-intentioned tortoise, and a few years later a suspicious Argus of the many eyes. Don't even try it—just beat it!" They realized he was releasing them and took off running as fast as they could.

When twilight, his personal hour, and mischief and furtive action, his calling, were reduced to something as miserable as arson, it was time to step in. But he couldn't be everywhere at once. The temple of Artemis at Ephesus would not have burned down if he had straightened out Herostat's mind instead of spending the night with the all too wise Aristotle's young wife.

It dawned on him that Hephaestus not only knew how to deal with the deaf ear turned to the gods by mortals but in many cases turned it to his own advantage through his control of the media and the news. He understood more clearly why Apollo and the others had retired. But now Hermes was back. Things could only get better, or at least more fun.

It's true he'd started off on the wrong foot, as Hephaestus desired. His mistake had brought things to a boil, but it also clarified the situation. Delirium of a sort had flared up in several places since his television shows, so it must already have been smoldering. It was not, however, the sort of visionary and sensitive passion that could be guided by the gods but was instead the offspring of emptiness and indifference. The mania of malevolent Hermetics was opposed by the self-righteous rage of those who thought of themselves as "proper." "Do not do unto others what you would not have done unto you." This golden rule of inaction produced little in the way of pleasure, resulting only in the eternally raised finger of the inactive. They, too, were spiritually listless and could have been set in motion with a few simple words. They needed Apollo, the god of light, of enlightenment, of justice.

He visited all the grand hotels and finally found Apollo at the Holy Inn in Barcelona. He was sitting alone, drinking black coffee and reading newspapers all day with a bored expression, this once mighty god, like Hephaestus and Hermes the son of Zeus! He had the typical high forehead of a philosopher. Cares and concentration had engraved a lattice of wrinkles on his brow, the cross borne by a deep thinker. He was easy to observe, since he looked up from his newspapers only when he went to his room to watch television.

Hermes approached Apollo dressed in a stolen waiter's outfit and carrying a tray of coffee.

"I don't want to talk to you," Apollo said, switching the remote control to some cultural program he didn't want to miss.

"Do you believe the oracle . . . what does it say exactly? That we should stay away from each other?"

"If I don't believe in the Delphic oracle, who will? We're not supposed to be together: it will bring bad luck to the entire cosmos."

"As a reader, I find the opposite more likely."

"Please leave."

"Something strange has happened to Justice. It no longer creates further justice, as it once did, but creates only the desire to destroy. That annoys even me. No one is happy but the blacksmith—out of pure vanity, of course, because it lets him show he can develop a strategy out of dregs. . . ."

"Go away. I can't stand lectures! All I care about is art."

"Good. Then I've got something for you as a parting gift, a rap number. Don't worry, everything rhymes."

Hermes sang to the astonished Apollo, in increasingly aggressive rhythms, exactly what he thought of him and his refined reserve. And how his people, the Hermetics, didn't have a chance against the Apollonians Apollo had abandoned. They had degenerated into headmasters who thought all would be right with the world as long as there were headmasters.

Apollo seemed to be concentrating solely on aesthetics, his noble brow wrinkling into tiny crosses at the daring verbal combinations and departures from standard metrics, but he couldn't help noticing Hermes' accusations.

When the rap was over, he said, "You've been pretty busy stirring things up since you returned. . . ."

"Yes, you're right. . . . Unfortunately I have to go," Hermes replied without any apparent reason, and he laid the staff across his eyes and disappeared. He knew Hephaestus' men would be showing up at any minute to seize him or to take his things. He'd sung what he had to say. Now he needed to find Zeus as quickly as possible, for without his power nothing could be done.

He wasn't looking for Helle at the moment. She was surely constrained by her relationship to Hephaestus, and he must be watching her every move. After all, she hadn't just been in love but had been a spy and decoy for her father from the very start. Hermes thought longingly of her body, but he had to keep his wits about him until he had found a way to rob Hephaestus of his power in a great poker game. For that was clearly his weak point: megalomania. The blacksmith with his oiled slide rule thought he was the best poker player in the world.

· · ·

From the airplane, America seemed a play of light. Meandering watery arteries, lakes, rivers, and swamps glistened and sparkled in the afternoon sun.

But what was "afternoon" here? The flight across the Atlantic had been extremely uncomfortable. He'd never realized how dependent he was on the regular return of darkness to feel at ease. The plane had departed Berlin in the morning, they were in Paris at noon, and now it was afternoon in Saint Louis—eleven hours later.

His host, who read novels for the entire flight, was a professor of German from Washington University in Saint Louis. His upper story was well furnished, and he thought in German. Hermes looked around for heads that might have better prepared him for America, but everyone else was listening to music or watching the in-flight film.

Now he was flying under his own power, but grumpily, back and forth over Saint Louis, wearing sunglasses because it wasn't getting dark. He wasn't tired, but his eyes hadn't adjusted. America seemed to him an all-too-brightly lit night. The advantage was he could look for Zeus immediately at the Forest Park golf course. It was somewhat difficult, because the players were all riding landgoing carts and stepped out only to hit the ball. When he finally met two golfers on foot, he asked after a particularly powerful, bearded, middle-aged gentleman who was said to play this course often.

"Bearded? Yes, he's a retired sound-track man from Hollywood, I think," said one. "We call him Jovy. He hits the balls like thunder, and they always fly too far. You can't walk along Skinker Boulevard over there without stepping on one. He even hit a gas station attendant in East Saint Louis, but he wasn't hurt seriously, thank god."

"Then he must use a lot of balls. Does he buy any certain brand?" asked Hermes, who had an idea how to find Zeus.

The man turned to his companion. "What brand does old Jovy use—do you have any idea?"

"Titleist, Maxfli—Renegade recently," said the other, without batting an eye. "But he's nowhere near the place they wind up."

Neither of them had seen him that day, but that didn't prove anything. Hermes asked some boys who were repairing a bicycle on the park path whether they'd seen a strong old man with a beard. "Sure," they said, and told him how to get to the zoo—he'd find him sitting there at a little table, talking to himself and others. But the man sitting there murmuring was a cleverly designed automaton named Charles Darwin. Every ten minutes he would stand as if lifted by a crane and deliver a lecture on the origin of the species. He was a great favorite with the kids. When they got tired of waiting for him to stand, they chanted, "Come on, come on, talk!" until he recalled his duty.

Apparently "jet lag" affected mortals less than gods, precisely because the gods required no sleep. Mortals adjusted within three days by a strategy of forced wakefulness and carefully timed sleep, but not Hermes. You couldn't pull the wool over his eyes about night and day simply by changing locations. He was and remained a Greek god, wherever he was. He wondered how Zeus dealt with it. It was probably worst moving from continent to continent. Hermes vowed never to spend more than two hours in a plane again unless it was on the ground or flying in circles.

Hermes stole a few tubes of the right brand of golf balls in a sports shop and set out. He flew over downtown Saint Louis again, floated through a huge inverted ∩ on the Mississippi River, and then looked for the longest cloud he could find to fly to New Athens, Illinois. Too bad Hannibal wasn't on the way, where Mark Twain was born. He'd read his books as an apostle of the three-breasted goddess, and not just by touching them on the spine with his staff but in pure admiration, slowly, after the fashion of mortals.

New Athens turned out to be a small town on the Kaskaskia River, consisting of white wooden houses decorated with TV antennae and American flags. In the center of town stood a war memorial and an outdoor basketball court. A large number of unemployed miners lived in New Athens, and when they weren't fishing or painting their homes, they were sitting in Marilyn's Restaurant, eating catfish and french fries, and consuming vast quantities of soft drinks filled with ice. An archery contest was in progress in the back rooms, unfortunately without Zeus. Hermes looked on from various heads for a time, then let the one man win who knew his name and connected it with Greece, admittedly without knowing its exact location.

But they all knew Jove, who wasn't in town that day. They thought he might be in Sparta, ten miles away, where he went sometimes. Has a young thing there, someone said under his breath, and everyone laughed. They showed him Jove's house, an old white mansion with columns and empty flowerpots by the entrance and a nice view of the water tower and the police station. Hermes wondered that Zeus would live in such a place, just because of its name. He must be suffering from nostalgia.

He flew over an extensive mining area with bobbing water pumps. Hephaestus had undermined the whole region. His coal trains, called Illinois Central, were so long they needed four diesel engines to pull them and still moved at a slow walk. Sparta was a somewhat larger city to the southeast. It was supposedly evening, but to him it seemed like a particularly dark morning.

The jewel of the town was the fire station, which looked like a car dealership. Behind the large plate-glass windows stood fire engines gleaming with chrome, and two noble plaster greyhounds were seated before the entrance, their noses stretched longingly upward to catch the smell of smoke.

"Pardon me," he said to a pretty red-haired woman who was just entering her house. "Could you give me drink?" She stared at him and replied, "My god, what's someone like you doing in Sparta?" Her name was Nelly and she had three children but no husband. Fortunately the children were sleeping. After reflecting a moment she took him in, offered him a type of brawn, a glass of ice water, apparently one of the American sacraments, and forty television channels. By these and other means she managed to get him up and going. He asked her about Charles the drummer. Yes, she knew him; they had even gone to school together, long before his European adventures.

"He learned a lot there. Now he plays in a nightclub called Just Jazz in Atlanta."

In retrospect, Hermes recalled his two days with Charles almost gratefully. The ones who came after him had been much worse. He decided to look him up.

He asked about Zeus. Did she know him! He was the father of her three children. After Hermes revealed that he was a god, she wrote down Zeus' current address, in Atlanta, on a slip of paper. At least that's where Zeus said he was. He lived in a small Greek temple atop a skyscraper on Peachtree Street.

On the so-called morning of the next day, Hermes left freckled-faced Nelly, who would gladly have held him a little longer, and headed southeast. Fortunately the sky was overcast. In Atlanta he slipped into the small rooftop temple. No Zeus. There were in fact two temples, but he wasn't in either one. In spite of his luke-warm attitude toward the Hephaestic system, Hermes was beginning to find it a bore that gods weren't listed in the phone book and didn't even have phones. Where to look now?

He decided to return to Saint Louis and wait for Zeus at the golf course. But because he still wanted to see Charles, he postponed his departure, strolling instead through the streets of Atlanta, watching people. Whether it was Saint Louis, New Athens, Sparta, or here, no one seemed to want to walk anywhere, and no one thought anything about it. Was it dishonorable, or dangerous? People who loved to walk bought expensive electronic treadmills or "stair climbers," walking in place at home until they were dripping with sweat.

One nice thing about this country was that his dark skin didn't excite any attention. It was fine to be taken for an African or African-American, and far easier to keep his mouth shut than to explain what a smoked European god was.

When he ran into local spirits, they were American Indians. They didn't drink *ombras* but drank something stronger, and they harbored a strong, two-hundred-year-old scorn for their white conquerors. Hermes sensed what a powerful effect it must be over time for the local spirits to dislike the population. And the whites had no spirits of their own, except, for the moment, freedom and democracy. They just hadn't been in this land long enough.

That so-called evening, he went to the club in Tula Street, met Charles, and took a look in his head to see how things were going. Same old story, not much of a lover. But there was a woman who was sticking by him now. He'd practiced hard but hadn't been able to progress beyond what Hermes taught him on the ship. Hermes wanted to help him a little more, just for fun. Around midnight (which was simply a darkened noon), Charles played so masterfully that several famous black musicians and a white woman came on the stage to congratulate him. As Hermes saw the woman through Charles's eyes, he felt a shock of pleasure. It was Helle. She wanted to give the Sparta, Illinois, man what Helga Herdhitze owed him, and she did, an envelope with twelve thousand dollars. Hermes exited from Charles, got his things, put them on, and made himself visible. Helle wasn't surprised. But he could tell she was happy, even though she tried not to show it. "You're being careless," she said, and whispered a warning. She was so beautiful that he watched her speechlessly without listening. His first impression: she has ears just like mine. His next thought was to hit the road, bed her somewhere in Tula Street, tauten her nipples, and dip Grindel's club in the valley of the wellspring. Of course, he didn't phrase his request in exactly those terms. Nevertheless, she said: "Nothing doing, my friend!" She didn't want him now. First of all he would have to write her a nice, well-structured, and above all respectful letter and wait for her answer. Yes, wait. She would be at the Washington Athletic Club in Seattle soon. And since he was apparently listening now, she warned him about Hephaestus' agents, who were supposedly hot on his trail. The U.S.A. wasn't such a bad cover, since all the air conditioners set on high made it hard for anyone to eavesdrop. Zeus wasn't there: every few centuries he visited his brother Hades. Wherever he turned up he was surrounded by spies. And another thing: Hermes should avoid Seattle. The city was a Hephaestic center. You couldn't hide anything for long there, not the tiniest mouse or the least criticism of the Lemnian system.

Then she suddenly fell silent, gave him a hug and a kiss, and disappeared.

• • •

Hephaestus was sitting at a telescope behind a curtain on the top floor of the Washington Athletic Club. It was nine o'clock in the morning, he'd had breakfast, and the cinema, his cinema, wouldn't open until ten. He tried to spot interesting rooms in the Seattle Hilton across the way, with couples making love or at least naked women. It was a childish pastime, since he possessed the technology to look into any room in the world whenever he wished. But voyeurism requires a certain element of ritual to provide real pleasure, a ritual that in his case was a few centuries old. Nothing interesting today, worse luck, nor in the Sheraton on the other side.

He turned back to the table, took a sip of ice water, and thought how else he might pass the time until the first show at the Omnidome. He reached into the inner pocket of his jacket and pulled out the worn and yellowed transparent plastic sleeve containing both the authentic oracle and the fake one. Rereading both, and considering their various interpretations, was always worthwhile. Around a quarter to ten, the telephone rang and announced that the car was waiting. Hephaestus went to the elevator. He arrived at the fish market at precisely ten o'clock and stumped his way over to the Aquarium Cinema on his crutches. Since he was in Seattle, he planned to start the day with his newest film, directed in secret, with scenes of the eruption of Mount Saint Helens on May 18, 1980.

The managers of the Omnidome didn't care for him. They tolerated him only because he was a steady customer. He couldn't keep from smoking and coughing throughout the performance, like a miniature volcano. He paid with an emerald card that couldn't be run through the machine but had to be entered by hand, which pleased him. There were only five emerald credit cards in the entire world, and he owned them all.

His eyes sparkled again as he watched the thick smoke billow from the crater, lava flowing down the slopes, trees crisping in a fraction of a second, rocks as big as houses flying high into the air. The footage had been filmed from a fireproof helicopter by an equally fireproof Cyclops, who unfortunately had poor depth perception, so that shots were occasionally out of focus.

But erupting volcanoes and earthquakes were long since the amusement of a bygone day for Hephaestus, since the earth provided few modern examples of truly imposing devastation comparable to Strongyli or Krakatoa, although he did what he could to help them along from below. He planned to satisfy his destructive urge another way, while making the greatest film of all time—even if no one would be around to watch it.

He noticed that the twentieth showing of today's film wasn't as exciting as the first. When he reached the end of his cigar, he hobbled out and had his chauffeur order the helicopter to the fish market.

He looked peevishly at the mortals around him. No, there was little change in this dull-witted, stubborn race since the days of the fish market in Athens. What had they done with the knowledge he'd given them? They weren't worthy of his efforts. They would never have figured out how to build the Colossus of Rhodes, to manufacture refined steel using nitrogen in goose droppings, to construct the Saint Louis bridge out of chromium steel. None of them would ever have existed without him—he didn't know where to start or stop with examples. He had loved mortals at first, but they hadn't loved him. The only thanks he got for his gifts was an increasing hostility toward technology. And how did they repay his brilliant reduction of the gods to a single "Numero Uno"? With mysticism, saints, angels, the cult of the Virgin Mary, and, above all, Jesus Christ, that altruistic superstar. Yes, he'd gone along, building even their most patent nonsense into his Lemnian system. But there was no way to improve this race: they were too much in love with obscurity and the lies of history; they kept recycling the same old myths, sillier and more poorly told each time around.

He turned away in disgust, walked to the helicopter that had landed on the pier, and climbed in. "Take me to Mount Rainier," he ordered. He wanted to be four thousand meters above all the fish markets in the world, where he could breathe in clarity. The lonely giant of a mountain grew larger before them, its summit gilded by the afternoon sun.

His film would tell the only true story: how and why mortals were unworthy. It would show the final, ultimate explosion of the world of men and gods. It took enormous ingenuity to bring about universal death, but it lay within his power. He'd almost managed it with the cold war; the atomic weapons were ready, and there were those prepared to blindly press the buttons. The East-West method had eventually failed, but now there was something better.

They landed at the edge of the old crater. Hephaestus pulled on a heated quilted suit and dismissed the helicopter for half an hour. Alone on the volcano, he would think through his plans—his plans for final annihilation. He lit his new cigar awkwardly, because of the gloves, and let the smoke rings float upward in the cold air.

The perfect completion of any project was death. All deeds arose from death and returned toward it. He could never have managed the whole of this tremendous task had he not known that he was working successfully toward his own death and that he would take everyone with him, mortals and gods alike. He hated both, as he hated himself. For over five hundred years he had been longing for what immortals could only dream of: his own death.

He had finally figured out how to enlist mankind in this goal. His new method seemed paradoxical but had the marks of genius.

As long as human beings enjoyed living, hoping, loving, they were incapable of drawing the consequences of the logic that led inevitably toward death, even if they were accustomed to its initial stages.

Hermes would have been extremely useful, had he been unwittingly co-opted. But it could be done without him. Nothing would go wrong; death was certain.

He heard the helicopter again in the distance. The cigar butt sizzled out in the snow. Hephaestus danced the little bear dance he used to do with his daughter, then stopped and looked at his tracks. No, he hadn't failed yet, although apocalypse was approaching more slowly than he had planned. Just as an eruption of Mount Rainier would destroy these traces, so mankind would melt away, and with them, finally, the gods. He restrained a sudden impulse to let Mount Rainier erupt in a day or so just for fun, thinking of the Omnidome Cinema in Seattle.

When he returned to the club, Helle was there. He was suspicious, for there was reason to believe she'd been in touch with Hermes. But he kept his thoughts to himself, chatted briefly with her, and went to his room to make some phone calls. He sat for a while, brooding. He was scarcely back in Seattle's haze, and doubt was already setting in. Was he interpreting the true oracle correctly? He pulled out the transparent sleeve again and stared at the text.

"If Mount Cyllene and Delos Isle unite, an age will dawn in which affliction is unknown." Cyllene was clearly a reference to Hermes and the mischief he caused. Delos, the floating isle of light and measure, was Apollo's home. If they could somehow merge their talents, if Hermes could achieve Apollo's balance, if Apollo learned the benefits of impertinence, it would mean the dawn of a new age, with two results: his own Age of Iron would end, and the world would not. He had tried to keep Hermes and Apollo apart with the fake oracle. But was it false enough?

"If Mount Cyllene and Delos Isle unite, an age will dawn in

which affliction reigns." Could the revised wording have somehow endangered his plan? He reviewed each possible interpretation with misgiving, torturing himself. He had succeeded in driving a wedge between Hermes and Apollo, but just how effective was it?

A view of the cliff of Palea Kaimeni, painted by Dionysus in the previous century while passing as an artist named Max Schmidt, hung on the wall. The rigid body of Hermes, chained to the rock, was clearly visible to the initiate. Hephaestus bit his lip. Was he starting to make mistakes? Should he have left him there?

• • •

The main advantage of the *Esperanza,* a thirty-year-old tub that pitched and rolled terribly, was that it contained only pre-1977 metal and traveled so slowly that Helle and Hermes readjusted easily to European time. Since they spent most of their time in their cabin, celebrating their reunion, day and night meant little to them anyhow. Only a storm on the third day managed to attract their attention momentarily. Poseidon, father of shipwrecks, apparently wanted to have some fun with the *Esperanza* but hesitated, out of a sense of tact, to feed it to the fish while immortals were engaged in love play. Hermes and Helle, taking full advantage of the rolling motion of the ship, made sure that Poseidon never found the right moment. Helle was open as only a goddess could be, moved by a letter she kept with her but showed to no one. Hermes' loving words were for her eyes alone, and certainly not for publication.

After the storm, they each talked about America. To Hermes it seemed a land that one could love, in spite of the harshly bright nights. And they laughed at the stories of their hiding places over the past years, and their idiotic searches. Once they descended from Olympus, the gods lost their way more easily than mortals and were harder to find as well. In an overpopulated world bursting with technology, the gift of second sight didn't serve the gods as well as it once had.

"I thought you could answer any question by reading fractal patterns."

"Can you?"

"I always enjoyed it. . . ."

"It was a bold claim that we could read rust or ashes or coffee grounds," said Hermes, "but it was useful."

"Now you're exaggerating. I actually can read. I see the faces of friends and enemies alike in the grain of wood."

"My prophecies were made to impress young women—a glance into the future always predicted they would reach the pinnacle of pleasure with me. I think chaos theory was developed for much the same purpose."

"You're horrible," she said, and blew a warm storm into his ear, which he fended off with a low laugh. "But now we've got to get serious."

He had yet to grasp the true reason for the world's disarray, she explained. As long as Eros acted alone, he aroused disappointment and disdain with each new love he provoked. But Anteros, the god of requited love, was languishing in Tartarus, and so unhappiness increased each day around the world. Christians, for example, suffered precisely because they were always talking about love. If their own love found too slow a response, they considered it an insult to their religion. That's why they resorted to force so often over the last two thousand years.

"We've got to free Anteros. You managed it with Orpheus and Eurydice—do it again!"

"Why is he being punished?"

"He wanted Zeus to make Hephaestus abandon his craft. He had just invented gunpowder and the canon. When Zeus refused, he tried to convince Apollo to rise up against him."

"And what's he doing down there?"

"'Who knows? He's a prince in Hades' realm—on exhibit, so to speak."

"Fine; let's free him, then. I like the idea of causing a little mischief. The plan's dangerous enough that we'll need some luck. Our magic won't work in the Underworld. We may wind up in Tartarus ourselves."

"But if we don't, we've won."

"Not entirely. Zeus has to pardon him, Hades has to free him, and Hephaestus mustn't notice for as long as possible, since it's a challenge to his sovereignty. If he does find out, we have to prevent him from blowing up his whole shop around our ears, and the ears of mankind too. It won't be easy, but at least it won't be boring."

As they talked, Hermes became increasingly excited, because Helle's theory about Anteros and the importance of his absence squared with his own observations. Cyllenians and Delians—his followers and those of Apollo—had grown to hate each other because their love was not returned. Now he saw the reason for this persistent hate: the missing divine vitamin, requited love.

"Since when have you started talking about 'followers'?"

"From the time I realized they have no chance against the Apollonian guardians of law and order without me. Even their lack of fear is a disadvantage. They live in wretchedness, hate, and despair. Many of them commit terrible acts. They dream of 'hitting the road' but are incapable of doing so. Wherever the wretched are, there, too, are my followers. And my opportunity."

Helle reacted as any woman does when her man talks too long: she caressed him, doing her best to get his full attention. She wants to shut me up, he thought.

• • •

They were standing on the snow-covered banks of a river once called Aornis and couldn't find the rear entrance to the Underworld. Everything was so different—or were they at the wrong river? Had the tunnel to the fields of asphodels been filled in? What they needed was a good map to the divine territories. They knew that Hades' empire was beneath Macedonia and Greece. But where were the entrances?

"Let's fly on to Sparta and enter from the Tainaros side," said Helle. Hermes, ignoring her suggestion, studied the frayed 1961 automobile map—it was now 1994—and repressed the urge to comment on the choice of winter for a visit to the Underworld.

"It's probably somewhere in the next valley," he said. "Let's fly!"

He carefully knocked the snow from his flying sandals, set his winged hat aright, and lifted Helle in his arms. He rose in the air and crossed a forested mountain range, flying close to the tops of the trees so he wouldn't miss any cave entrances. Suddenly he felt a blow on his right calf, followed by the sound of a gun. He landed in the trees, shook the pain off into a snow-covered bush, and joined Helle in examining the bullet hole in his leg.

"We've got to fly invisibly from now on," he said, and touched the wound with his staff, whereupon it disappeared. "But I don't understand why they're shooting at us."

"That's war," said Helle. "I've seen a lot of it. They lie around and get bored, then shoot at anything that moves."

Hermes laid his staff across their brows, rendering them both invisible, and flew with Helle across the mountain chain. In the woods below, foxes were tearing at a dead man. And in a clearing, they saw a road leading to five barracks behind a barbed-wire fence. A number of men stood in the middle of an open square, in a strange military formation. They weren't soldiers but were ragged figures, thin as rails, who were being forced to stand outside in the freezing cold as some sort of punishment. A few had collapsed and were lying unconscious or dead in the snow.

Thunder rumbled through the river valley. The thunder of cannons, as Helle knew. A city appeared. Was it finally Aorna? They would have to ask. Hermes landed next to some sort of sentry station. Soldiers in camouflage stood near a high iron gate, with their hands on their gun butts. Their unshaven faces were bloated by alcohol. It seemed as though Ares had lost interest: his fighting puppets were in poor repair. What language did they speak? Hermes and Helle made themselves visible behind one of the trucks and stepped forward.

"What's the name of this city?" Hermes asked in English. The martial scarecrows instantly raised their weapons. Helle motioned to him to let her speak. She repeated the question in Russian. The faces relaxed a bit, but the weapons remained trained on them. The information was: "No information. Your papers, please!"

"I think they're too dumb. Let's pass on through," Hermes said in German. But the tin soldiers wouldn't let them. They released the safety catches on their machine guns.

"Stop right there!" one said in German, apparently the ranking officer in charge of the patrol.

Hermes paused only out of curiosity. "What are you guarding here?" he asked.

"Yes, what are we guarding?" The officer grinned and turned to the others, urging them to join in the fun. But not all of them understood German. "We're working toward an ideal!"

"And what is that?"

"The definition of Mankind. We're defining what it means to be human."

"On which side of this barrier?"

"We can handle both sides," the officer answered impatiently. "You're under arrest. How did you get here? This area is hermetically sealed."

Hermes smiled in annoyance. "Hermetically? You have no right to use that term, you midget. I'm declaring the area hermetically unsealed!" He raised his staff, and the iron gate began to soften, melting like smoke. It stood in the air a few moments as if confused, then collapsed. Hermes pursed his lips and blew away what still remained. He lifted his staff again, and the stubble-faced androids sank to their knees.

"That was 'hermetic,' " he said, stuffing a two-dollar bill into the mouth of the officer, whose jaw, hermetically unsealed, was hanging open. "For the toll."

They wasted no further words. A gigantic shaggy dog of horrific aspect sprang at them, its long, sharp teeth bared, its open throat shimmering bluely. Before Hermes could kill it, there was a whistle and the dog disappeared. Two dollars apparently closed mouths around here.

They walked into the city, which offered a dismal sight. Rafters stood against the sky like skeletons, huge holes gaped in brick walls, few people were on the streets. Walking was difficult; there were old shell craters everywhere, treacherous, covered with snow and ice, causing even the gods to stumble. Gods could shake off pain, but they suffered from cold like any mortal. In a bullet-riddled building, a few people were warming themselves around a smoky fire composed of damp roof beams. Hermes and Helle made themselves invisible so they could disrobe and warm themselves. Not all of the people were in rags or emaciated, but they all seemed dull and hopeless, even the children. They moved about mechanically, paying no attention to one another. A woman was putting on nail polish, at least retaining the memory of former hopes. An old man, held upright by a threadbare leather coat, sat talking quietly to himself, groaning and striking his forehead every few seconds.

A few of them looked up as men carrying stretchers rushed by, carrying wounded persons into the back area of a building that was still standing. Men with torn limbs whimpered, and now and again a bleeding, twitching muscle could be seen hanging over the edge of a stretcher. Hermes motioned to Helle that he was going to investigate. Inside the building, which smelled like a cattle stall, were two operating tables. They could be recognized by the flashlights tied together and hanging above them, and because they were dripping with blood. Hermes was surprised, because he knew from his time in Munich how much technology was necessary to operate successfully. Here they were even short on thread to sew up wounds. Were those two wielding the scalpels doctors? Strangely enough, Hermes couldn't slip into either head, even though he was naked. Had his magic lost its strength?

The patients screamed and moaned, for there were no anesthetics. They bit down on wooden dowels as their limbs were amputated. Hermes couldn't understand why Hephaestus allowed scenes that were so offensive to divine eyes and ears. Wasn't the state welfare system his great achievement? Or did he deliberately instigate this torture?

"Why does your father permit this?" Hermes asked.

"I think that with all his steel and Latin, he's still right back where he started," Helle replied. "But he blames it on humans. He says they're too dumb, and I think he welcomes anything that supports that view."

Hermes laid his staff across the eyes of a woman whose smashed foot was being amputated, trying to anesthetize her, but it had no effect.

"I think we may have already arrived," he said when they were by the fire again.

"Well, you're not on the beach!" a voice croaked. It belonged to an old woman who crouched on the floor. "At least put something on. We mustn't lose all dignity!"

Hermes and Helle now realized that they'd been visible all the time. They hurriedly donned their still damp clothes.

Again Hermes noticed the old man who was hitting himself in the head. "What's wrong with him?" he asked the woman.

"He's in despair. He would gladly have died before seeing all this, but he's healthy and will have to watch even more. He can't take it. Where are you from?"

She sprinkled a few drops from a little bottle into a crease on the back of her hand. Her lips continued to move. She was counting.

"We're European gods, looking for the city Aorna on the river Aornis. There's supposed to be a tunnel there to the asphodel fields. . . ."

The woman had finished counting. She licked the medicine from the back of her clawlike hand. "So you're European gods. Well, we don't like them here. Not anymore! What are you doing, taking pictures?"

"We need to talk to Hades, the god of the Underworld," answered Helle. "We want his permission to take Anteros, the god of requited love, back with us."

"Requited love? Here? You're certainly in the right place. You're crazy!" She crowed so shrilly that a few other people wearily lifted their heads.

They walked out, bewildered. So the Underworld was now aboveground, like the bed of a strip mine: that was something new. Now where? Finding that they could no longer fly, they walked instead through the city, which vibrated with the whistles and explosions of heavy shells. They were like mortals, and the mortals here were dead, shadows in the realm of the dead, mechanically repeating their actions over and over, wading in and out of mud trenches, creeping back and forth through holes in walls, crossing a bridge on the sole remaining girder, carefully, step by step, in mortal danger, to exchange a few beans for a used battery. "We're defining what it means to be human." The officer's words echoed after them. Perhaps he was Charon, the ferryman, in a new disguise, and the dog none other than Cerberus.

"If we've arrived," Hermes said, "he will have long since noticed. And I won't call him 'Hades,' but 'the Rich One' or 'the Good Counselor.' I've had some experience with him. All we can do is wait until he shows himself. There are things to see and do here."

They noticed a few people trying to drag a beam from the ruins of a building for firewood and joined in, pulling along with them, because they, too, were freezing. Helle picked up a splinter, but fortunately the staff still healed gods' wounds, at least minor ones.

Suddenly they heard a chirping voice from a section of brick wall still standing: "Come over here, Hermes! Here I am—the bat above you." There she hung, upside down, in true bat fashion. Her instructions, she said, were to lead Hermes and his companion to the "Rich Prince."

"Detach me carefully from the beam and stick me under your cape," she said. "I'll guide you as we go."

An hour later the devastated city lay far behind. They came to a hill with a ruined castle.

"Let me out here," the bat spirit chirped. "Go straight ahead to the former ladies' quarters, through the gate, and to the door with 'Identity 2' written on it. The guard is expecting you; there'll be no questions. Then go down the spiral staircase. The descent will take about an hour. The Rich One will be awaiting you at the entrance to Tartarus."

She spread her startlingly long wings, bid good-bye with a shrill whistle, and took to the air to find a new roost among the stones in the wall.

The air that arose from the spiral stairwell was worse than the dark and narrow steps leading down. Hades did everything he could to make the shadowlives of those in exile unbearable, including providing an infernal stench.

When they arrived at the bottom, it was almost pitch dark. A tiny glimmer of light came from the eyes of the god of the dead, the Rich One, who sat waiting for them in a sedan chair. Hermes recognized him immediately.

"Greetings, Hermes—I know you well. And who is this?"

"I'm pleased to see you, richest of all the gods! This is your grandniece Helle, daughter of Hephaestus and Nephele."

"Hephaestus? Of all the gods! He won my minerals in a poker game."

"All of them?"

"Yes, but I only gave him about a fourth. He had the pleasure of winning, and I had the pleasure of keeping."

"Helle's not on his side."

"Let's forget Hephaestus! Something important must have

brought you here. I'm not interested in what's happening above. Hephaestus has ensnared you with his metal: I know that much from Zeus, and that's all I need to know."

"Listen," said Hermes. "We need your advice. Things aren't difficult just for mortals; they're difficult for the gods as well."

"How things go for either you or mortals has always left me cold. Earth is no affair of mine."

"But Hephaestus is interfering with your rights. He's taking your minerals; he's brought the asphodel fields to the surface and turned them into a bloody laboratory. He'll wind up taking Tartarus too."

"He hasn't brought anything to the surface. He's buried his own affairs more deeply—for a time. We have a contract. And he won't come near Tartarus, any more than he would the Isle of Happiness. Zeus won't allow such nonsense."

"Unfortunately he allows anything these days. Otherwise we wouldn't be here."

Helle slapped her forehead. "Gods above! I know what Hephaestus is up to. He wants to die!"

"That can't be," said Hades. "He'd have to reduce the world to cinders."

"A laboratory! The word made me think. That's why wars keep getting worse. He's rehearsing for the apocalypse."

"It doesn't matter. We're used to heat. The Underworld won't burn."

"Don't be so sure," Hermes interjected. "If there are no more mortals, it may cease to exist. Remember, it's never been tried!"

"Dead people enter the Underworld; where else would they go? And they exist there as shades, which means they exist! No; I'm not interested. And how do you know I don't want to die too? Now tell me why you're here."

"Perhaps you recall that naughty little boy Eros, who kindles love in mortals but doesn't care if it's reciprocated, awakening more despair and disappointment than he does devotion. In the end, each person destroys the one he loves. They need Anteros. We're asking you to release him for a time."

"For the general good of mankind? Never! That interests me even less. By the way, Anteros has gone blind as the Titans in the darkness. Without a guide, he'd be helpless up there."

Hermes started to argue, but Helle took him by the arm.

"It's not for mankind," she blurted out. "It's . . . for the two of us. It's true. I talked Hermes into coming here. I love him, but he doesn't love me. He desires me, and he's polite. He sent me the most beautiful letter ever written, but unfortunately filled with lies. Without Anteros I'll die of unhappiness. I'm the one who needs him."

Hermes had to admire her. It was a sharp-minded diplomatic strategy. Hades could scarcely refuse a personal favor, and putting it this way allowed him to stick by his general principle of indifference about life. Hermes hid his admiration and nodded hesitantly, as if he were struggling with himself.

"All right," he said. "As long as it's out. It's a private affair."

"I sometimes close an eye in the case of private affairs. . . ."

The god of the dead in fact closed both eyes while he thought things over, and since they were the only source of light, Hermes and Helle waited for a time in total darkness.

"Well," he resumed, "I'm not one for granting favors and playing the obliging host. What's in it for me if I do you this favor? You haven't brought me anything!"

"Oh, yes we have, wisest of all counselors," Hermes said quickly, without batting an eye. Worried, Helle glanced at him from the side in disbelief.

• • •

Two things puzzled the Lemnian agents: Hermes, because he had disappeared without a trace; and their boss, the Consul. The last hint of Hermes' whereabouts had come five years earlier, when they intercepted a garbled message about an iron gate on the far side of Europe that had apparently dissolved into thin air, since it was nowhere to be found. They noted that Hephaestus showed little concern. He seemed equally unconcerned by his daughter's disappearance, and the resultant search had been merely pro forma. It's true he was engaged in extensive projects, but wasn't his daughter the only goddess he enjoyed talking with? And hadn't he characterized Hermes as a dangerous adversary?

They were right on one point: Hephaestus was working harder than ever. But he used his work to hide his own point of view. Hermes and Helle meant nothing to him, because everything would come to an end soon anyway. He assumed they were in the Underworld, trying to free Anteros. Hades was probably holding them there. They may even have been soft-headed enough to offer themselves as hostages, so Anteros could return and cause trouble. In any case, he would arrive too late. Hephaestus laughed delightedly; he remembered how slow the god was, too slow to be perceived. It would take him two thousand years to cause any real trouble. He wouldn't get far in a mere century.

Mankind was ripe, the bombs were armed. The gap between rich and poor was greater than ever, vulgarity and selfishness were practically religious dogma, and the death wish had reached epidemic proportions. Doctrines, religions, sects, gangs, politics, arms sales: the engine of Hell was running smoothly. Now technology had provided the detonator: "Immortality for the Few," eternal life for a handful of rich old men utilizing a steady stream of new young bodies from among the poor. He had calculated the consequences. The only possible outcome was the one he wanted.

VII

A FINAL HASSLE

In early 1994 Helga Herdhitze flew back to Vienna from New York. Like many United Nations employees, she had been allowed to visit the New York headquarters for a three-day orientation course. She had flown to Charles, then stopped in a few major cities she wanted to see before returning to work.

She was now twenty-three years old and still hadn't been to Athens, which surprised her, because she was firmly convinced that Athens was her place and her destiny, although she could not as yet say why. Why had she let so much time pass; why hadn't she at least taken a weekend off for a visit? Of course, she would still have to work at least a year as an interpreter in an area where millionaires were swooping down on cities and villages, driving whole peoples into the abyss for generations to come. The office where she worked was on a street that had been named Avenue of Friendship following the war. That friendship had lasted barely two generations. Helga was happy to feel rage for a change, and not just despair. Now and then she had a moment to mourn and reflect. Then hope would grow anew.

She walked alone in the woods, which was said to be dangerous. She sat on a rock at the wayside and studied the interlacing branches of a powerful old tree, beneath which the path led toward a clearing. Would it be better simply to walk on, or to stay seated and write (a catechism perhaps, for herself and others)? Sketch out an alternative vision of the world, the very opposite of this one? She saw quickly that that was nonsense. Opposites were two sides of a coin.

It would be better to go on until things brightened again. Hermes himself was the message, not anything that might be said to be his teachings. For the first time in a long while, she started to spin her story out further. No one could take it from her, no one knew it. He was a god of seized opportunity, of action. "If you don't like what you see," he said, "stop talking and do something about it." She stood up and walked on. She couldn't be a tree, and she no longer wished to be.

She'd learned Greek in the meantime. Would they let her study in Greece? If she could figure out things anywhere, it would be in Athens. Could she take a break and fly there for two days? Perhaps toward the end of April, during Greek Easter.

• • •

Since Hermes had given his hat and sandals to Hades as a gift, he couldn't travel as far or as quickly as before. Helle, Anteros, and he found it difficult to make it even as far as Lithuania. The city of Kaunas was a good hiding place, since it contained almost no new metal. The only difficulty was finding eyedrops for Anteros. He was still suffering from the effects of Tartarus' darkness. So far he could stand daylight for only a few seconds at a time, and only with the help of the eyedrops. As long as he was blind, it was impossible for him to slip into a person's brain. To move about freely, he needed to disguise himself. Hermes had a host in readiness with an ear for the

gods, a docile young Lithuanian by the name of Romualdas, innocent of all erotic knowledge, which was important. Hermes didn't
want to place too great an initial demand on Anteros.

They had reached the end of November 1999, by human reckoning. Though they'd spent only three days in the Underworld, five
and a half years had passed aboveground. Hades had warned them
about this; it was one of the reasons he didn't pay much attention to
worldly events, which tended to be so far in the past he couldn't
catch up with them. Hades reminded them that Anteros was to be
used only in personal matters, otherwise he would bring him back.

It was Hephaestus' anger at the lack of response by Aphrodite
and Athena that had led to Anteros' disappearance centuries before.
"If he won't help me, he won't help anyone!" Hephaestus cried, and
wove an intrigue that led Zeus to exile Anteros.

Anteros was happy to be on the face of the earth again,
breathing in the pleasant fragrances. He asked if there were still
temples devoted to him, particularly those erected by the Metoeci, a
race of foreigners living (unloved) in Athens. He was disappointed
to hear that mortals no longer knew his name, and to learn that
Athens was closed to the gods, except for Pallas Athena, who was
there and could not leave.

He was already at work on Hermes and Helle. His method was
somewhat complex. He covered Hermes' eyes from behind. At the
same time, he needed to hear Helle's voice, or at least have her scent
in his nostrils. A trace of perfume or a scarf was sufficient. Before
long Hermes would begin to love her, a love beyond lust, Helle
thought. Unfortunately things might move somewhat slowly, said
Anteros, but since they moved surely, that posed no problem for a
god. He could only set mutual love in motion, however, once Eros
or at least the goddesses of friendship and charity had done their
part: "I don't have the arrows of Eros, the pale-blue letters of Philia,
the libations of Agape! I can't manufacture emotions, only their
echoes."

They were living in an attic above the Devil's Museum, the

only museum in the world devoted to depictions of the devil. Hermes and Helle took turns caring for Anteros. They took him on walks now and then, describing what they saw. Kaunas was a beautiful city, with churches and buildings of long-standing integrity. The surface devastation of Lemnian multiplication had passed them by.

Hermes went through the Devil's Museum with Anteros at night. What he couldn't see he could feel with his staff, and light only hurt Anteros' eyes anyway. As he was describing the sculptures and paintings, Hermes noted that the devil wasn't simply hated but was sometimes secretly loved as well. Since the devil was an imaginary being combining traits of both Hermes and Hephaestus, it made no sense to ban Hephaestus completely from the world. It would be enough to introduce a love virus into his system of hate and indifference, while liberating him and winning him over to a higher cause.

"If there are problems with my father, it's because he's lonely," said Helle. "I'll go and talk things over with him. After all, I love him."

"If you love him," Hermes responded, "we could use Anteros on him right away! But will he still talk to you?"

Helle wrote her father a letter saying she'd never really turned against him and asking to see him again. But evidently Hephaestus wanted nothing to do with her, for there was no reply. They started thinking about what they could do. They saw in a newspaper that the connoisseur Ignaz Knidlberger—that is, Aphrodite—was to deliver a lecture in Vilnius, just a few miles away. Helle went to the lecture and pushed her way forward toward the heavyset man hosting the goddess of beauty, who promised to put in a good word for them with Hephaestus.

"When will you see him?" Helle asked.

"In two weeks. He's coming to Moscow to see the newest volcanic eruption at the grand opening of the Trismegiston, a multiplex cinema."

That gave Helle an idea. "Anteros and I will come too! If you can win him over, we'll show ourselves."

They began preparing day and night in Kaunas, since everything had to be ready within two weeks. Still no letter from Hephaestus.

"Do you love him a little yourself?" Helle asked.

"He's your father," answered Hermes, "and since I love you . . ."

"You call that love? You're in for a surprise," she said with a laugh. "But we should try something else."

"What?"

"To get him to love you too. Of course, if you don't feel any love for him, nothing will happen."

"I'll do my best. Keep reminding me of his lovable traits; I tend to forget them."

The days passed rapidly. Anteros was sometimes able to see for a few seconds at a time, but whenever he tried to slip into the ear of the young Lithuanian, he always wound up falling on the pillows Hermes had piled up below.

"What's the point, anyway?" asked Anteros. "I have to place my own hands on Hephaestus to have an effect. Romualdas's hands won't work."

Hermes was insistent: "You've got to be able to see, enter ears, and speak English and German too, in case you have to drop out of sight. Anyway, your lessons are over for the moment: I need to get inside his head and learn Russian and Lithuanian. Take a break and study the Moscow cinema seating chart. We can't afford any mistakes."

Hermes got to know Kaunas and its languages, and although his host didn't like talking with Russians, Hermes refused to spare him. "Find a few educated people who speak excellent Russian, please. When my voice comes over the loudspeaker in Moscow, I don't want to sound like a sausage vendor."

"Our local sausage vendor is highly educated. He's a

former cultural attaché who knows literature forward and backward: postmodern, classical postmodern, retrograde postmodern, everything—"

The Lithuanian broke off. He could see further discussion was pointless. He was having a hard time, but strangely enough he knew what a god was and that it would all be worth it, even if it didn't seem that way.

While Romualdas was sleeping—and he slept a lot—Hermes practiced his synchronized text for the Trismegiston in Moscow. Hephaestus had to hear his voice just as Anteros covered his eyes, or the spell wouldn't work. When Helle felt that his Russian was good enough, she tape-recorded him.

In his spare time, Hermes learned to play poker, which was part of the plan. He spent his nights moving through heads in two ongoing poker games in Kaunas, one "nationalist" and the other "internationalist," and read several thick books on the game by touching their spines with his staff. He wasn't sure things were going to work out. He needed courage and was on a steady diet of thyme, yet he confessed one evening: "I don't know if we have any real chance. He can multiply and all we can do is add. He represents progress and I just drag my feet."

Helle only nodded. Even though gods needed hardly any sleep at all, they were thoroughly exhausted. After all, they weren't accustomed to work, and what they were doing now resembled it rather closely.

"Do you really think it's such a good idea to play poker with Hephaestus? You've already shown you're not much of a strategist."

"If I can't fool him, who can?"

"All right, then. All we need is the text for the classified ad," she murmured.

"Mimi." He yawned, rubbing his eyes.

"A classified ad that just says 'Mimi'?"

" 'Mimi' and 'Mama.' Make up something with those words. I

have to lie motionless like a crocodile for a while and think things through."

The next morning Helle swore that Hermes had been snoring.

. . .

Three days before the cinema premiere, Anteros managed to slip into the ear of the Lithuanian. After Hermes left, Helle hopped in naked as well, and Romualdas, hosting two gods simultaneously, carried the bags to the station. If everything went smoothly, they would be back in a week.

Hermes again threw himself into preparations. The richer members of the "international" poker game included the head of a car theft ring, drug and weapons czars, and real estate speculators, but he also saw the sausage vendor who had once been a cultural attaché. At first Hermes had to get used to the Russian and Lithuanian terms, since all the poker books he'd read were published in North America. The "international" game was fifty-dollar draw poker; the other game was a strange high-low stud poker called "Rothschild," where cards were passed but the bets were small and always in Lithuanian currency. Hermes had studied all the variants of poker, from simple stud and draw games, through "Dopey" and "Twin Beds," to "Back-Door Widow" and "High-Low Bimbo." No matter what game Hephaestus suggested, he'd be ready. Of course, he wouldn't be able to identify cards by touching them with his staff, but he could read key cards that flashed by for even a hundredth of a second, having regained his ability to count the spots on a lizard's back at a glance, as he had two thousand years earlier. Catching on to the full catalog of the tricks of the trade was a little more difficult. In spite of the heavy traffic in international scoundrels through Kaunas, it was hard to find enough refinement and dexterity to best Hephaestus. But one day an elderly female American tourist arrived, spent the day visiting churches and photographing the poor, then turned up that evening at the international game, asking naive questions about the rules. Hermes wanted to get into her brain briefly to find out more about her. She turned out to be a retired blackjack dealer from Las Vegas named Nora, who had all the skill he needed. By the first hand, she realized a few high cards had been marked with a fingernail, so she marked a few low ones the same way just for fun. During the first hour she noted a lively and profitable dialectic developing between the head of the car theft ring and a former professor of Marxism-Leninism, into which she quietly entered. She made use of her own special talents, which no one noticed, such as bending a card slightly so it could be felt in the pack, but benefited primarily from her skill as a dealer, shuffling the cards with dexterity and apparent thoroughness, using the "Las Vegas shuffle" and the "undercut stack," which Hermes quickly learned. She also knew how to hold cards in the pack and then introduce them into the game at the right time. She could memorize up to sixteen cards in a series, which was impressive for a mortal. All the while she gave the impression of an average player, making sure that the weakest player at the table, the progressive sausage vendor, won heavily while the better players were left cursing their luck. The cardsharp who had marked the deck, and the two who were in cahoots, all lost steadily throughout the night but weren't broke yet. She watched their little tricks with amusement and even found them slightly touching. After a few hours she slouched in her chair, feigning fatigue, seeing and concealing things even more effectively. In the gray early hours of morning, she suddenly had a run of "luck," leaving the sausage vendor, who by that time was in a state of euphoric faith in his own good fortune, the future, and even God, with nothing but his hot dog stand. She then disappeared, with her a large portion of the fruits of that week's East European traffic in arms, drugs, cars, and real estate. She left Kaunas and headed for Vienna with two bodyguards, a few blurred photos of churches, and a large stack of money. Hermes planted the idea of her staying there for at least a few months, so he could have her at the poker table in the Hermesvilla. If he could involve her in the game with Hephaestus, the resulting confusion would be even more elegant. He hoped that Hades would join in, too, and that he would quickly grasp what was at stake.

• • •

The hardest part was getting the film director to go for a walk in snow-covered Gorky Park, where they couldn't be heard. The easiest was bribing him with a hundred dollars. Since Hermes' text corresponded precisely to the model on which it was based, and fit the film as well, it was necessary only to record it over the other text. It was done in half an hour.

Aphrodite, known as Knidlberger, had received nothing but a politely negative reaction from Hephaestus, but Helle wanted to try it anyway. Romualdas was carrying the papers of the arms dealer from the poker game in Kaunas and bought four tickets in the orchestra. According to the seating chart, which Helle had secretly studied in the internal ministry, Hephaestus would be sitting in the middle of the row in the balcony, behind him two Georgian diplomats with their wives. Helle slipped into the Georgians' hotel and exchanged the balcony tickets for seats in the orchestra. She had learned everything from Hermes, including how to steal.

It was assumed that the diplomats would be too diplomatic to notice and would be willingly guided to the orchestra seats.

Performance time neared. Romualdas, who was carrying two silk tunics, for Helle and Anteros, over his arm, entered without difficulty and made his way to the men's room, where they both descended from his ear and dressed. Then he exited and took his seat. Helle followed a little later, tripping along lightly, chatting with Anteros in a Greek magpie language that only Attic women understood, the surest way to make people think they were diplomats. They took their seats next to Romualdas, who pretended not to know them. Hephaestus had reserved two seats, one for himself and one for his crutches. Helle was seated directly behind him.

When the lights fell, Anteros knelt in front of Helle, behind Hephaestus, and pretended he was searching for something. During a commercial with a lot of bare skin, Helle guided his hands around her father's mighty skull, covered his eyes, and whispered, "Guess who, Your Excellency! But don't peek!"

Hephaestus had no intention of guessing anything. Anteros crouched quickly as her father whirled and hissed at Helle. "A very poor idea! When I want to see you I'll let you know. Watch the film if you want, then beat it!"

Helle's heart sank. How could she get Anteros back into the ruse? She tried anyway. As Hermes' voice rang out with a few introductory words about volcanoes, she repeated the maneuver. Perhaps a split second would be enough. But Hephaestus was ready for her. He motioned to a high-level Cyclops security guard, who rushed to his side. "Throw her out!"

Fortunately the volcano began to erupt at just that moment, and the smoke on the screen darkened the entire room. Helle and Anteros managed to strip off their tunics and slip into the ear that Romualdas held toward them. He calmly climbed over three rows of seats and a good dozen diplomats' wives and headed for the exit, where a low-level Cyclops confronted him: "Your ticket and papers, please!"

Romualdas measured him with a gentle smile and held them out. "Do you know who I am?" he asked under his breath, and nodded toward the chief guard, who was rushing toward them. "You're going to be in big trouble, and here it comes."

"That's all right, then," said the Cyclops, letting them pass. The guests in Romualdas' head were impressed.

"Unbelievable! For someone so young, who's never been with a woman . . . ," said Helle.

"That's why his nerves are still steady," said Anteros.

• • •

"I'm afraid that wasn't such a success," said Helle, when they were in their attic rooms in Kaunas again. Hermes was lost in thought.

"It was a crazy idea," said Anteros, who was seldom so direct. "You can't cover someone's eyes twice in a row if he doesn't want you to. That would be too easy. I could produce love the way Hephaestus turns out railway ties. But it's not that simple, and for good reason."

A message soon arrived from Hephaestus to his daughter, forbidding any further "harassment." So Anteros' spell hadn't taken effect.

Now Hermes wrote his own letter. He announced that he had learned to play poker and challenged Hephaestus to a game for the highest stakes possible. "If you win, you can seize me and send me into exile. I'll go willingly to Tartarus. If I win, I'm free to go to Athens, and you'll leave my people alone. If you don't accept my challenge, then I'll note with respect that you've recognized the limits of your own abilities and are smart enough to avoid playing with me!"

He pictured Hephaestus roaring and throwing his crutches at this deliberate provocation. He'd answer by return mail! Now it was just a matter of waiting and preparing. It would take some time for the mail to arrive, since it would have to go by way of the god of dead souls, whose realm was beyond Hephaestus' control.

Few other messages arrived from the rest of the world, and when they did, they usually contained bad news, especially from the West. Without the guidance of the gods everything was going wrong—every deed, every desire, every thought. It had started decades before. Everyone had a bad conscience, but no one had the slightest idea how to go about creating a good one. The high-water mark of hate had risen. Duels had returned, but they lacked any sense of fairness and ritual, men armed with knives trying to restore their inner balance by fighting to the death over a parking place. In most countries the government allowed people to own guns, in an attempt to secure the vote of the more aggressive elements in the electorate. There was also a suicide sect now, calling itself the Cadaver Corps. Although its members weren't in despair, they were no longer interested in life. They had given up on mankind—first on others and then, after a time, on themselves. The only thing they could offer the world was to cleanse it of their presence. The declining sense of curiosity, which Hephaestus had done his best to undermine, calling it a meddlesome and presumptuous trait, weakened other aspects of life as well. There was no longer any spirit, just a kind of conceptual insurance company. The language of love or passion was memorized like a computerized program for phone sex. Things weren't much better in the East and South. A huge and powerful state had arisen with a true culture of hate, led by the "Inconceivable Infallible," who had forbidden the use of the letter I except in the leader's own name. But since it was hard to avoid using "I"— children in particular sinned repeatedly—the number of executions grew.

"Makes no difference to me," said Hermes, gazing into the distance with Olympic calm.

"It does to me," replied Helle. "I can't forget Helga, my former mortal echo. She wouldn't find it so funny."

"I don't find it funny either. It's boring!" For Hermes that was the ultimate sign of contempt, so it did make a difference to him.

Anteros' sight had returned, even though he needed thick glasses, including a tinted pair. He wasn't a pretty sight, since he still had huge feet. The next-larger shoe size would be a violin case. By day, hidden in the Lithuanian's head, Hermes strolled through the city with Anteros, looking for mismatched lovers. They found half a dozen such couples, including a politician who couldn't find anyone to love him. That was so rare they willingly helped him.

Romualdas, who had remained true to his gods, wanted to be a teacher. "Are you crazy?" asked Hermes. "I can make you one of the richest men in the world."

"As long as the world's the way it is, being rich doesn't bring happiness. I've learned a lot from you, and I'd like to share it with others."

"I can't think what. We have to win. That's the most important lesson," Hermes said.

"Life is more than poker and theft!"

"Where did you get that idea?"

"From you."

"When have I ever philosophized about life?"

"I've figured things out traveling with you."

"Just because you've caught on to a few things doesn't mean you have to be a teacher. A good bluff, a leap across the abyss, is worth more than a year in school."

Hermes was grumpy at times. The poker game cast its shadow forward, the Moscow affair didn't seem to have had any effect, and worst of all, he had to stay in the same city week after week. Helle, the goddess of travel and soft landings, found it equally hard to take.

When Romualdas brought them breakfast in bed the next morning, a sheet of paper lay on the tray, with the words: "Thus spake the Cyllenian." The Lithuanian must have written it in the night. Hermes laughed.

"May we have breakfast before class begins?"

"These aren't lessons! They're statements or questions. I want to interview you and get your response. To help the Lithuanians, among others."

Hermes was too lazy to read in human fashion. He grabbed his staff from the night table to get through this kettle of fish as quickly as possible.

Arm nations only briefly, not for years at a time. But how?

People come up with countless ideas, including some good ones. They're almost all forgotten. They keep reinventing the soup plate. What can be done?

He who defines himself forgets a part of himself. But how can we not define ourselves?

Learn to find, not to seek. How can we turn a simple seeker into someone who simply finds?

Can mortals enter into other mortals?

Is it possible to act without thinking, quickly and correctly, like one of the gods?

Success, you say, is not a matter of duty and careful planning but arises naturally from curiosity and pleasure. What does that mean in practice? Licentious learning? Adventurous education?

"Hassle everyone!" In what sense? And won't you just anger others? Won't you simply create enemies?

Distance yourself from mankind and yet "never give up on anyone." Isn't that a contradiction? Is it possible for mortals, or only for the gods?

What should our attitude be toward mortals who want to die, especially when they want to die "for something"? When is that right and when is it wrong? When should I try to stop them?

What am I to make of the statement: "The best aid is anonymous and merely sensed"? That's true for you, but to be of any help, a mortal has to show himself.

"The gods have lost their faith," you say. Will they ever find it again?

"You have to figure these out for yourself," said Hermes. He'd read for only the space of three heartbeats; he wasn't at his best in the morning. "And putting things into practice? Do the right thing, that's the right practice. If you can do it, it's not because you've practiced it but because you've dared to do it. What's important is my presence in the world. I am the message. Your questions are good ones. They leave one at a loss and thus closer to the truth. Shouldn't you be a journalist rather than a teacher?"

"They're almost the same. A teacher has more free time."

"That's what you think . . . ," Hermes murmured.

"Shouldn't we take a few notes while we're waiting for love to be requited?"

"Too many people have wound up as professors doing that and never did find love, simply because it was so long in coming. Isn't that so?" Hermes asked Anteros, who was just slipping on a size "special" shoe and blinking in bewilderment through his thick glasses. "Do things have to move so dreadfully slowly? I hung on the basalt for two thousand years—no one can accuse me of lacking patience—but you've pushed slowness to the limit!"

The answer itself came too slowly. Hermes rose abruptly and left for a walk through the city, having fled into Romualdas's ear and guided him from the room. Anteros followed, although he felt unloved. But nothing would change without the help of his helping hand.

Deep winter outside.

• • •

In the middle of the night, a whirring was heard above the Devil's Museum, and two restless points of light could be seen through the window. Hades had come to Kaunas to see them. They opened the door quickly, and the god of the dead stepped in, wearing the winged hat and sandals.

"The mail was delayed because I was away. So now I've brought it myself. Here's the letter."

He sat down and launched into his adventures on the road, although they would have preferred to read Hephaestus' reply at once. Since he could fly only at low altitudes in the Underworld with Hermes' hat and sandals, Hades been flying on earth for some time now. He knew how to cloud-hop, and for invisibility he'd brought along his own magic cap, which he wore under Hermes' hat whenever necessary. Since he had visited earth so rarely in earlier days, and then only in a black carriage, with horses that trampled everything underfoot, he hadn't met many living mortals.

"Well? How do you like them?" Hermes asked politely.

"It's strange. I can laugh now," replied the god of the dead, who was known for never laughing. "It's compulsive; I just can't seem to stop."

"What's so funny?"

"It's so . . . touching. They talk and act as if they were immortal, and the next thing you know, their time is up and they've returned to dust. They fall off a cliff, and they're still happily reassuring one another, 'Things have been fine so far,' when they hit the ground."

"Hephaestus wants to make some changes. A few people will be given a chance to live forever. If they want to."

Hades laughed again. "They couldn't stand it. They're not gods. Why would he want to do that?"

"He's a technician. . . ."

They read the letter. Hephaestus agreed to meet Hermes at the villa in Vienna for a game of poker with him, Hades, and one other person, of their choice. He would bring along two of his own people. The date he named was almost upon them.

"Quick," Hermes told Helle. "Call *Le Monde.* We have to put the ad in so the gods will have time to get here!"

"What's the ad for?" asked Hades.

"It's a signal. When the text appears, they'll know it's all set. Helle has arranged everything."

Hades was restless, eager to be off again. He planned to visit China and the Himalayas before the poker game. But when he rose, he closed his eyes in a momentary thought.

"Immortal men," he said. "Immortals against mortals. Didn't you say he wanted to commit suicide?"

Hermes knew what he meant. "Yes; I think he's going to try to do it this way. What do you think—could it work?"

"It's possible. It depends on how much antagonism he can generate. It's not my cup of tea at the moment. I don't find the upper world particularly entertaining. I'd rather be flying: the world may not last for long."

And he was off with a whir.

Two days later the following ad appeared in *Le Monde,* a paper read by many of the gods:

> *Escaped: one crocodile, two meters long, goes by the name "Mimi." Can say "Mama" and "Papa." Report to Hermesvilla, Vienna, by January 15, 2000.*

"And this is the text for the gods?" Hermes asked, shaking his head.

"Only 'Mimi' and 'Mama.' I was so tired that evening."

He took her in his arms and looked into her eyes. Neither one of them spoke. They stood silent, then he kissed her, said nothing, kissed her again, and again was silent.

"Well, has it happened?" Helle whispered.

"I think I've underestimated the fellow."

"Now, of all times, when you have to play," she complained, although she was far from sad. "People who have just fallen in love play so poorly."

"So does a god with a death wish."

• • •

Hephaestus sat smoking in the dark, his card catalog of enemies before him, in the computerized center beneath the old forge in Vienna. Since he was having the plumbing repaired, he'd given the Cyclopes the day off. He didn't want the workers to hear any noise, not even the hum of the generators. He switched on a flashlight and scanned the cards, but he didn't feel like trying to sort them in this feeble light, or making any new notes. He thought of keeping a file someday on the people he liked. What a harebrained idea! He shook his head at his own foolishness. If there were more than three cards in the file, he might as well give up the whole grand plan he'd been working on so long. What was he thinking of? With the operation shut down, his brain didn't seem to be functioning normally. A file in the subjunctive case: If my daughter had remained loyal, I would love her. If he weren't such a typically arrogant Olympian, and typically stupid as well, I would even love Hermes. Now the Cyllenian was wasting the little time he had left playing a game of poker he was bound to lose, and then he would be cast into eternal darkness. Not all that eternal, of course; it would disappear along with everything else in universal death. Hades hadn't grasped that yet. His existence, too, depended on the human imagination. He'd been flying around the world on pleasure trips, entering village inns invisibly to have a drink like the most simpleminded of local spirits. Hephaestus had respected Hades for centuries, but no longer. It was time to put an end to things, and the sequence and timing of events was now in place. It would be his greatest work.

The poor nations, exploited by local oppressors as well, were now sufficiently impoverished. The rich nations were im-mensely rich, producing and consuming huge amounts of energy. Their lead was insurmountable, above all because several elderly scientists and financiers were able to extend their experience through new bodies and fresh brains. Aggressivity had increased at a satisfactory rate. Rich nations not only allowed the poor nations to remain poor but used them as a source of raw material for the bodies and heads best suited to serve as vessels for the immortality of others.

Continue another thirty or forty years in this manner, then organize the atomic terrorists, stage the collapse of international finance by means of supercomputers, and arrange the inexplicable "coincidences" that render atomic blackmail serious, making sure nuclear power plants actually explode. And it would work, if the ancient ones, grown tired at last of life in younger bodies, secretly arranged it. Just for fun, he would throw in a few not quite extinct volcanoes, so that the sun would no longer penetrate the smog, and the frost would destroy what life remained on earth and with it all the gods. It was crucial that the members of the new immortal elite, all of them over one hundred and thirty years old, become as fed up with their extended lives as were most of the gods. Hades and Hermes offered the only real problem. They seemed content to live "forever" for some time yet. But the poker game would take care of Hermes. He wouldn't be in the way much longer.

He thought again of the card file. "Of course I love you—I love all of you," he muttered, with a grin. "I'm granting you death, something immortals have longed for in vain. If you feel like thanking me, better do it quick."

• • •

A week after Greek Easter in May 1994, a young woman in an Athens hospital was visited by an American who had flown all the way from Atlanta. He brought her a portable CD player and his newest hits. He played the drums.

"How's it going, baby?" he asked.

"A little mishap, a holiday hassle, but they'll pull me through. How about you?"

He realized she wouldn't want to hear about his hit shows, his wife, or his kids. He asked her how it had happened.

"I'd been walking around Athens for several days. I'd already seen so much, but I wanted more. I was walking down Hermes Avenue for the second time, and it's a long street. At the Temple of Hephaestus—the only one in Athens that's still well preserved, by the way—I started to cough. What came up was blood, pure blood. My eyes saw so much blood—it seemed for a moment like it was too much for my mouth. That was it. Tuberculosis; a little late to find out. I had been losing weight for months and didn't know why. But I had so much to do, I thought it was the work."

The hospital was in the northern part of the city, an old building with pine trees outside the windows. Helga studied their branches as she listened to Charles's music.

He told her he would drop by the next day, after a brief outing. "Is there anything I can do? Can I get you something?" he asked before he left.

"Not really." She smiled. "It's not important."

"Go on—what is it?"

"I'd like a deck of cards. Sometimes I invent a sort of comic book story, and at the moment it's a grand poker game, with the fate of the world at stake. It passes the time; I'm too tired to read. . . . But please, only if you don't have to go out of your way."

"If I do, the god of detours will help me."

When he was gone, Helga thought more about her story. Perhaps it should end happily, but then again, perhaps not. If things went well, the mischief-maker wouldn't be cast into Hell. He was still needed.

Measured against truth, every story was just a form of comforting nonsense, ironic at best. Truth was tragic. Love died, mortals died. The world was cruel. It didn't pass away, only those things in it that mortals found important passed away. But even so, she might as well bring her story to a close.

After a week Helga's strength diminished markedly. She had three illnesses at once now, to the doctors' astonishment. She lay in intensive care for a week, then showed some slight improvement. But she was no longer certain she would ever leave the hospital.

At night she tossed and turned, tangling the sheets as she always had, and the nurses shook their heads. By day she lay still, no longer going through the deck of cards, hoping to give her body one last chance by something very much like prayer. She watched the almost imperceptible movement of the tiny bubbles in the slender intravenous tube.

One day there was a knock at the door and an unexpected visit from Jean-Claude, the French mathematician from the ship. "How's it going?" he asked.

She shrugged and whispered: "It looks like I went wrong somewhere. But we'll see."

Jean-Claude was still with his Greek playmate. He'd completely fallen for her, Helga could tell. He was running an accounting department in Paris now, thanks to a little nepotism. He confessed to writing novels in his spare time and said that since he was the great-grandson of Connétable, he shouldn't have any trouble getting them published.

She would have preferred to hear about his girlfriend, but Jean-Claude steered clear of the topic. Presumably he had all too conventional ideas about proper topics for discussion with the seriously ill, or perhaps he thought those who were ill were no longer curious about such things. Nevertheless, he was visiting her and meant well. She was thankful for any company at all, thankful for each minute. But Jean-Claude spoke in flowery phrases and spent far too long worrying the nurses with his damn bouquet instead of telling her what was going on in the world. Not every insurance accountant is a born storyteller. Suddenly feeling faint, she closed her eyes, and he noticed. "I really should go and let you rest," he said, then added with a smile: "Hit the road with Hermes—but I'll be back."

Toward evening Helga grew angry. To have to give up life at barely twenty-four was too much. There was still so much she wanted to know, so much that could happen, unexpected, crazy things. Now that she understood a little about the world, it would surely be good for it if she could live awhile longer. She'd always rejected suicide as a waste of something that wasn't hers. Never give up on anyone, especially yourself! Her anger, seeking an outlet, turned at last toward her father. I'm dying in pain and suffering, and he just threw his life away. She would have liked to tell him off. A builder, an inventor, who couldn't find a way to go on living! It was nothing less than betrayal.

Her anger subsided as darkness fell, and the pine branches moved eerily in the glow of the streetlamps. A waste? An odd argument, really, vanity mixed with the fear of death. She might as well claim she had earned the right to live because she could speak eight languages. No doubt it was better to forgive. Life was a gift, a windfall, a thief's booty. It couldn't be held for long; no one had that right. Sometimes a brief life might be a greater gift than a long one—

who could say? That was something no individual could decide, and it was best not to ask. The verdict would be handed down elsewhere. End of debate.

She heard her name. It was Hermes. She couldn't see him, but she knew. In her story, he was still in the Underworld. . . .

"How's it going?" he asked.

"Well, you know," she said. "I'm dying, more or less."

"Can you sleep with the pain?"

"Yes. But apparently I dream too much. They're worried I'll fall out of bed. So they want to tie me down at night. I always toss and turn in bed; it's not a problem."

"They won't tie you down. The laugh will be on them," the god said cheerfully, laying his staff gently on her forehead. She fell asleep at once, and they set out together.

VIII

ATHΣNS FOOL!

Hermes remained in the city without Helle, as she had wished. She was already in Santorin, where the other gods were due to arrive later. She wanted to have a quiet look at the place she had first seen ten years earlier through Helga's eyes. Perhaps she simply wanted to get away from Hermes for a few days, a hint that his love was becoming somewhat smothering. And there were preparations to be made for the grand festival.

Hermes was living on the top story of a building at 136 Hermes Avenue, in a poorer area of the city. On the ground floor of the once imposing corner building was a gas station, and on the second story, directly beneath him, the conference room of the Association of Greek Archaeologists. Because there was so much to excavate in this country, they didn't confer often. Hermes could stroll back and forth on the conference table and look down into his street. He had a good view of the Temple of Hephaestus, the only well-preserved temple in Athens, and the Agora and Acropolis.

He couldn't get his mind off Helga, whose young soul he had guided into death, although according to her story he was supposedly stuck in the Underworld at the time. Like other mortals, she never really understood that a god is truly omnipresent. But since some of the finest tales arise from this misconception, it would be wrong to change it.

He knew that Helga would have enjoyed the poker game, even though the god she cared about lost so dramatically. Hades, who visited Helga now and then on the Blessed Isle, reported that she knew something about poker. They played for pearls, and sometimes for love, both of which were abundant. Hades had only one fault to find with Helga: she was too curious. She kept checking the balance sheet to see how much she was winning, and that sometimes cost her. But on the Blessed Isle that was no problem.

Hephaestus was the best poker player in the world, and he'd taught Hermes a powerful lesson. The entire game had been closely followed by a dozen gods and ten videocameras, and each slip or effective bluff could be reconstructed, as could errors of over- or underconfidence, and all the clever tricks Hermes tried: the arrangement with Hades and Nora from Las Vegas, the fake shuffle when Hermes was dealing. The crowd may not have seen it all, nor even Hephaestus, but the cameras did. The review would take place only after the game was over, however, and could not change the outcome. On the following day the videos revealed that Hermes was one of the wiliest con men ever, and at the same time showed that was precisely why Hephaestus won. The slide-rule-wielding blacksmith hadn't resorted to tricks, but stuck instead to mathematical probabilities.

Hermes left the building, crossed the street, jumped over the tracks of the number 31 tram line to Piraeus, and strolled to the temple to pay his respects to Hephaestus. Of course, he can't beat me quite so easily now, he thought, but I'm still a second-class god when it comes to poker. I'll have to live with that for a long time.

Even Hera was in the audience, wrapped in a robe the color of unbaked dinner rolls, perhaps the very dress that drove Zeus to America. And of course there was Ares, who had practically lived with a deck of cards in the trenches over the past few centuries. He was still dangerously old, and everyone urged him to switch into the head of a young and powerful man. "Or woman," added Aphrodite, who had picked a man again after Knidlberger's demise. But Ares loved taking risks. He was still the god of war, and it showed in poker too, which was why he lost his chips so quickly and was reduced to the role of kibitzer.

Hermes had no desire to pick up a deck of cards anymore, let alone chips, and the proud claim of the blacksmith god still rang in his ears: "I am a system, and no one beats me!"

After passing through the remains of the old Agora (where he had once felt at home, at least more so than in that pious Manhattan of the Acropolis above), he wandered along Hephaestus Street, a short lane filled with secondhand shops and lengthy sales pitches. He turned off into Astingos Street and made his way back to Hermes Avenue, where paradoxically he found more ironmongers than in Hephaestus Street. In front of one of the shops he saw a white Styrofoam lamb turning on a spit. Such sights had long since ceased to strike the creatures of Hephaestus as strange. The antispirit of multiplication and division deconstructed everything and then focused only on a specific part of the whole. A Styrofoam roast! A divine eye could only turn away.

The Athenians had one thing right, however. They named the most appropriate street after him, a street of cosmopolitan exchange. It began on Constitution Square, directly beneath the buildings of parliament—the former royal palace—continued for some distance in high fashion thanks to fancy hotels, furriers, and perfume shops, and then became increasingly middle class. An old cloister, surrounded by bars, was followed by an increasing number of closed shops with rusty roll shutters pulled down, and right in the middle of them a "Theater on Hermes Avenue." Workshops became more numerous, situated mostly below street level and reached by a narrow set of stone steps. More and more Hermetics could be seen—trapped adventurers, repressed visionaries, headstrong men with a gift of gab lying fallow. Beyond the intersection of Philippou and Karaskaki the commercial image became even more run-down, ending in construction companies, construction sites, and then the bus depot, where Hermes Avenue came to an end with two squat rectangular smokestacks. That had been his path yesterday, the first time, when he discovered the old building with the gas station.

Now Hermes was walking somewhat aimlessly down the street in the other direction, in spite of his appointment with Athena. He would spend the next hundred years here, so he had plenty of time. At the corner of Astingos he sat down at a table in front of a motorcycle shop that offered tea in addition to power bikes and parts.

Three weeks had passed since the poker game, and he still couldn't shake the image of Hephaestus' final straight flush, fanning out with irritating slowness, goose-stepping its way smartly from three to seven, and always in diamonds. Was there ever a more annoying color than diamond red? On the table before him lay the final poignant tableau of the four queens, arm in arm, revealed in vain, embarrassingly exposed, four female flops, who could no longer help their god. He would have been better off learning to play in Las Vegas and forgetting Lithuania. And a bit of friendly advice from Hephaestus: "No one is easier to beat than a self-confident con man. I find it rather sad that the only games these days are on computers, where you don't do anything but tap keys. Your classic cardsharp was always good prey. Too bad. You may be the last of the breed!"

A defeat captured on film for all to see. He was the old Hermes, behind the times, who hadn't caught on. Even for him, the god of clever self-reduction, it was hard to take. His fate in the poker game was a reflection of the fate of his Hermetic followers throughout the world. Being fearless, and believing in their luck, they boldly conned their way through life and were immediately recognized by a superior controlling logic, which spotted their irrational moves and gently outmaneuvered them, or drove them toward neck-breaking adventures. In Hephaestus' system, swindlers were simply fools, and fools were simply swindlers. Perhaps he'd accepted the invitation to play poker only in order to prove, once and for all, that Hermetics were no longer needed in this world, nor Hermes himself.

Athena was already sitting in a fashionable roof garden restaurant—and she was smoking. Her host of many years had died, and she now appeared in her own form, as Hermes did. If a new world was to emerge, encouraged by the guidance of the gods, she would no longer have to mask her divinity with such care. That was a pleasant prospect, for friendly conversations tended to lose a good deal when they were filtered through other minds.

Athena's dress was expensive, informal, and elegant. Hermes understood why she hadn't wanted to meet him among the bikers. Her divine visage alone would have caused their jaws to drop, and it had a similar effect even here. After she had complimented him on his now permanent and attractive dark skin, she asked him about Vienna.

"Fine. I spent a lot of time ice-skating."

The ban Hephaestus had placed on Athens had been lifted for only two days, and Athena still didn't know the outcome of the poker game. She had heard a rumor that Hermes' freedom and the fate of the entire world had been at stake. If so, he had obviously won.

"I lost! Hephaestus won," Hermes replied. "He made a turkey of me. But the only thing he won was what *he* was playing for. I played my game during the breaks and while we were eating. In high-stakes poker the style is quite elegant, with a good deal of formality and conversation. I was on a winning streak, I had my best cards ready, my bluff had taken the legs and crutches from under him. Of course, I would have been happy to have beaten him at cards as well. I'm not wise enough to lose intentionally. Even if some now say I did."

"How did you manage to bluff him?"

"First of all, he thought I was there to play poker, which was crucial. He didn't doubt that for a moment, until it was too late."

"Did Anteros affect him?"

"He didn't show up during the game, having left in a huff when that arrogant rascal Eros referred to him as 'Ossi.' No one could figure out what the problem was, since both names had 'os' in them. But his influence was already taking effect on Hephaestus, so there's no doubt it helped."

"What were your trumps?"

"The other gods. Ares, for example, who has some experience in the matter, explained that mortals who live forever don't gain in wisdom and tire of life but after about one hundred and twenty years simply grow more isolated and wretched. They spend their time hunched over, talking to themselves, hitting themselves in the head because their lives seem unbearable. 'They'll fill the psychiatrists' couches,' he said, 'but they won't rule the world.' That made an impression on Hephaestus, who had pictured things quite differently. Then Apollo arrived with a report on current research. . . ."

"Is it true you're monogamous now and that Helle, who was missing for so long, is your sole wife?"

Hermes was taken aback. Apparently she had no burning interest in his manly duel.

At that moment Apollo entered the roof garden, also in his own form, although he wasn't nude, as one might expect of the god of light and translucence. He was wearing his national military outfit, with long white socks and the famous short skirt, and caused more of a stir than Athena.

"Please excuse my appearance. I'm still not up to selecting contemporary clothes. I found these things in the National Museum." They obliged and asked him to sit down.

"At last we dare to sit together," Hermes said with a wink.

"When you mentioned the true oracle, he caved right in. How did you know he'd substituted a false one with an opposite wording?" Apollo asked.

"I didn't. I just tried the idea, and he collapsed and admitted it. Like a murderer caught in the act."

"Too bad you couldn't have been there, Athena!" said Apollo. "Comrade Herdhitze fell off his chair, his crutches slipped from his hands, his lips started to tremble, and he sobbed like a child. He'd done it all wrong, he couldn't go on, he'd lost all desire, he was all alone, and on and on. We had to comfort him and tell him he was a great guy and should continue on with Zeus and the rest of us. He said he loved us all but there was nothing left for him but Tartarus. Then Hermes hit on the right tack. He told him that figuring out how to harden steel with goose droppings had been a stroke of genius, a really first-class discovery, and that those forged iron doors on Notre Dame were something you really had to take your hat off to. Then Hephaestus stopped crying, wiped his damp cheeks with a smile, and said, "Well, I guess you're right there.""

"The best part came long before that," Hermes said, "during the break. An unexpected report from the astronomers in Sydney. It was science itself that defeated Brother Vulcan at the last moment."

Since Athena picked up her ears at the word "science," Hermes explained. "The news isn't good, Athena. On August 14, 2116, a meteor five kilometers in diameter will strike the earth, destroying all life on the planet. Apollo found out about it just before the poker game. The heavenly body will accomplish what Hephaestus desired. So he can retire and await the end in dignity with the rest of us. We still have over a hundred years."

"It's time to go," interrupted Apollo, the god of punctuality.

"Father arrives in Palea Kaimeni this evening, and I would hate not to be there."

Athena was interested in other things. "Isn't Helle jealous that you're here alone and meeting me?"

"No."

"And can you stand being here without her?"

• • •

Helle scanned the sky. Clouds stretched across the islands of Santorin, with the sun breaking through here and there. At least the cloud cover would allow Hades to arrive in time to greet Zeus. She was standing on a high plateau on Palea Kaimeni. Until yesterday, it had lain silent and lonely as the grave over the centuries, which made it an excellent meeting place. Mount Olympus was always overrun with tourists, camping out on the holiest sites.

She watched as a small flotilla of sailboats approached the island along the seaway to the southeast, carrying bartenders, musicians, and supplies of nectar and ambrosia, as well as human aliment for those who had become accustomed to it, not to mention several kegs of wine and beer. A motorboat was arriving with Hephaestus at the emergency harbor, which meant she would have to hurry down to help him up the mountain. He originally wanted to come in a helicopter, but the other gods had forbidden it.

Several had already arrived. Artemis strolled along Schmidt Cliff, casting her critical eye on the eternally smoking garbage dump on Thira. Hestia, who was preparing a much more welcome fire here in the middle of the high plateau, was finding it difficult to locate flammable material. With the exception of a sparse scattering of macchia, no wood grew on the island. They would have to wait for the barge to bring firewood. Anteros was just raising his finger to explain "balance in the positive sense" very slowly to Eros, who was no doubt listening only because he found it stylish to stage a reconciliation scene with Anteros. Ares knelt at the edge of a cliff, observing with motionless patience a busily burrowing black beetle, then noting on a small card: "*Raiboscelis azureus*: active by day in spring." Looking up from his notes, he saw that a Cycladic lizard *(Podaris erhardi)* had popped the object of his investigations into its mouth and was disappearing with it beneath some mossy fern *(Selaginellaceae)*.

It was hard to say whether the festival was taking place because the world was improving or because the gods had come to a new understanding. Even prior to the events in Vienna, mortals had begun a sudden and surprising transformation, and in the ensuing three weeks the change had affected the entire world. Those in whom Anteros had awakened mutual love were now noticeably calm, wise, and active. The mortals who had served as a host to Hermes had ceased searching and discovered instead the art of finding, a productive indolence. They ceased to be victimized by work and instead found joy in success. The pitfalls of a project were no longer listed in advance. People relaxed, dozed off, imagined a scenario in which everything worked out, then acted on their vision. Jean-Claude wrote under the pseudonym "Le Connétable" and was so successful he hired his own accountant. The young man who had given Hermes headaches was now filling the concert halls with his guitar; Nathalie Rittberger was president of the Federal Republic; Rosangela was a good architect; the blacksmith from Freystadt Oberpfalz was champion of the senior division in Latin American dance; the priest from the confessional in Venice directed a top variety show in Paris. Romualdas was studying engineering and pantomime in Athens and was already alarmingly better than his teachers.

Hermes' presence had taken effect at a surprisingly late date, however, a fact that Anteros couldn't help noting.

Even without divine intervention the barometer of discord had noticeably fallen, while the tendency toward selfless, anonymous charity grew, and greater goodwill toward foreigners, misfits, and outsiders. A respectful tolerance developed between Hermetics and Apollonians. Although it was clear no one knew about the oracle, it was equally clear that they could live together once again.

Hermes, the fearless pirate, had triumphed. But he had no thought of assuming command or becoming some kind of general secretary. He would wander about as before, on the lookout for the unusual, playing practical jokes, avoiding work, and yet still a god among gods, for thanks to him, good was no longer simply the avoidance of evil. Those who had no fear of the abyss and the unknown, who were drawn to strange worlds, who loved taking risks, reassumed their rightful place in the cosmos through Hermes.

Having admitted the superiority of addition over multiplication, Hephaestus now preferred to spend his time discussing tubers, guelder roses, and ferns. His computers had concluded that the golden age of multiplication was over. He now taught that its future role would be limited to a few of its more primitive functions.

So there was good cause for a festival. The gods would no longer be bored. It was now clear why they had been so fed up. It wasn't the world of mortals that was boring; it was the merciless piling up of products, which overwhelmed everything else, instigated by an increasingly isolated and decrepit Hephaestus, hiding behind a mountain of work. The future looked better. If only it could last a bit longer! The one hundred and sixteen years remaining before the meteor would strike seemed terribly brief to the gods.

• • •

Athena looked around for Anteros and recognized him by his huge feet, although it had been a long time since they'd met. She'd always told him to keep his hands off her, although various gods fell in love with her and tried to get him to awaken a response, one of them being Hephaestus. Anteros stood his ground and didn't force himself on her. She appreciated that.

"Anteros, what in the world did you do to Hermes? He loved me for centuries, and I didn't mind at all. Now he only wants to talk about Helle and how great monogamy is. Don't you think you may have overdone it a little?"

"I'm confused. I thought you were the proud young virgin who wanted to stay single."

"In principle, yes. But I don't really like seeing it so strictly respected these days. And what I like about Hermes is that he loves all women—and can imagine loving me too, even if he doesn't talk about it."

"You're a difficult case, Athena. I can't undo anything. But I could, if I ever get the chance, incline him a bit in your direction . . . just a bit perhaps. I'll have to think it over. I'm not used to confusing matters."

"You'll have to start practicing," Athena said with a smile.

• • •

Hermes and Helle returned from the cliffs and rejoined the others. It wasn't the right season for an outdoor festival, but Hephaestus had figured out a way to heat the sea and the cliffs by means of subterranean canals—just moderately, otherwise the odor of sulfur would have been unbearable. And Aeolus provided a cheerful warm wind, which was welcomed without reservation.

Zeus arrived by late afternoon, accompanied by a small storm, of course, but clearly ready for a celebration, shoving aside the clouds upon his arrival and providing a sunny evening. He was presented with a conference plan of sorts and frowned when he saw that it was printed. He opened it at random to page 28 and read the following:

XII 7 c: We must discipline the local spirits. The level in mortal wine and liquor bottles is lower than we can permit.

He threw the conference plan into Hephaestus' fire. He had no interest in taking actions or making proclamations, and least of all in following a daily schedule. The festival began with music, and good old Charles, now the most famous drummer in the world, had been imported from the U.S.A. Many gods renewed old acquaintances—referring from time to time to human handbooks as a sort of *Who's Who.*

Hermes stopped Anteros, who seemed to be trying to avoid him. "Hold on, I need to talk to you." He lowered his voice. "You know I always loved Athena, even if it was only Platonic. I respected her wish to be alone and free. But since our reunion she seems overly distant. She hardly listens. If you get the chance, could you awaken a little longing in her? Just for me, of course."

"I'll see what I can do," Anteros replied, and thought: Here are two people in love who want me to arrange things so they love each other. What a perfect deal, if I were a businessman. And another thought occurred to him. There were some things he'd never tried. Why not do something on his own? He'd been in love with Helle ever since Kaunas and Moscow. Perhaps he could influence her visual perception so that his shoes would appear a few sizes smaller, and lend his thick glasses a little sex appeal. He clambered his way in the dark to the highest point on the island, directly above the cliff on which Hermes had been chained for so long, and observed the flickering lights of Thera and Therasia. No, he thought, I probably won't get anywhere with Helle, even if I work more slowly than normal.

• • •

Hephaestus went to his father, Zeus, to say what everyone wanted him to say.

"I did a lot, Father. I took on more than I should have. I

haven't come to apologize, however, but to implore you to rule again, and to cease delegating power to others. The world is improving, offering the gods more entertainment than in the past. I'm sorry to have called you out of your peace and quiet, but I finally realized that it was necessary. No one can take your place."

Zeus nodded in agreement, with a slight hint of impatience. Everyone knew that the only long speeches he liked were his own. And he also realized his absence was partially responsible for the way things had gone.

He cut Hephaestus short. "Of course, my son, I'll gladly return. Every god is another's call for salvation, no more and no less. And from what I hear, we wouldn't have made it this far without Helga Herdhitze and Johann Joachim Winckelmann from Stendal. So from now on, both birthdays will be celebrated on the ninth of December with a poker game. Hades agrees that Helga may return to the earthly world on that day to take part."

The phrase "Hades agrees" had been heard often that evening, with the undertone of solemn assurance, for the prince of the Underworld remained an unreliable fellow. But now he nodded clearly to Zeus. The Helga matter was settled.

Zeus had spoken with carefully calculated modesty, yet with a strength in his voice that made it obvious to all that he had not forgotten how to take center stage, to be decisive, to command respect. Hermes sensed, however, that Zeus was already longing to be back with his freckled Nelly in Sparta and at the Bow and Arrow Club in New Athens. Moreover, there was some question whether the present world was in need of a boss.

Hephaestus was released with a blessing. Relieved, he returned to the others, danced his father-daughter bear dance with Helle, and drank a good deal of beer. In the end he even tried to sing. But since he had been relying for centuries on writing, then technology, and finally his data bank, he could recall only snatches of melody, and a few individual lines, most of them in German; he got no further than

"Heigh-ho, Heigh-ho, how blue the sea," "I've got just you in mind," "Here are the roses of Tyrol," and then had to continue with "La la la la," until he lost the melody as well. What was touching was that he even tried.

"I know I can't sing," he called over to Hermes, "and to tell the truth I never could do math either. And you, my dear friends, as I long since noted, can't read the cracks in stone or tell the future."

Everyone laughed. "We can't even go without sleep," Hermes replied. "That's the way it is. You've finally learned what 'Hermetic' means. From now on, you won't have to wince every time you hear the word. Yes, Hephaestus can't do math, but he's there, and that's what counts. Hermes can't do anything either, but the fact that he exists has an effect. Apollo is no mere pedant's dream; a waiter's good only if he's not really a waiter; a writer—"

"Enough, you sower of confusion!" the other gods cried. "We know everything we need to about you, as long as you don't talk about yourself."

"You see through me, you're my betters," Hermes said respectfully. "Now that you are back in action, I'll be your messenger again, and not one whit more reliable, I promise you that. Hades has agreed and is returning my winged hat and sandals. . . . Where is Apollo? I had something to ask him."

"Here I am," came the reply, as Apollo stood up beside the fire. "What do you want to know?"

"You have almost no contact these days with the latest science and research labs. How did you manage to come up with that news about the coming catastrophe when you were in Vienna?"

Apollo, the god of perfection and pure truth, drew a breath.

"I made it up."

Unbridled laughter rose for the second time in three thousand years. When gods laugh aloud, things get very noisy. Fifteen sheep fled in panic over the cliffs. The tourists on the neighboring island thought the postcard volcano was about to erupt. The brave ones pulled out their cameras, the timorous raced for the boat. Even in Thira, on the stone benches by the war memorial at the Taverna Mythos, a few people lifted their heads, looked out across the bay, and wondered what, in that lonely place, could be the cause of so much laughter.

Author's Note

The stories of the gods and heroes that arose among the people were never set down precisely, since they originated in an age less dominated by writing than ours. No storyteller felt slavishly bound to a narrative tradition. Only in this way was it possible for changing conceptions of individual gods to lead to equally new stories. The transition from a largely matriarchal society to a predominantly patriarchal one resulted in a substantial change in the world of the gods and led in turn over the centuries to a refinement of the life elements incorporated by the various gods. Thus Hermes, the god of fertility, of shepherds and their herds, originally no doubt simply a phallic symbol, developed into the god of thieves and orators, of sure-handedness, messenger of the gods, protector of nightly journeys, crossroads, and intuitive solutions, even a guide of souls into the Underworld.

Because I've taken the liberty of spinning out the stories of Greek mythology beyond tradition, I would like to mention a few details here that are entirely my own invention. I can guarantee that the following figures and events do not appear in traditional mythology:

That Hephaestus invented the wheel in the course of inventing a "wheel man." That Hephaestus took over command from Zeus or usurped control from him. That Hermes, for whatever reason, was ever chained up anywhere (which happened only, if at all, to Prometheus). That Helle was the daughter of Hephaestus and not Athamas (but Nephele, the goddess of fog, is indeed said to have been her mother). That Helle survived her fall into the Hellespont. That gods slipped into the right ear of mortals (but they could, in the classical imagination, take on "any human form"). That gods had no knowledge of multiplication and division. That Hades had luminous eyes. That Anteros made a practice of awakening requited love (there may have been an actual shrine to him in Athens, however, erected by the Metoeci, the so-called foreign citizens of that time). And even a superficial knowledge of Greek mythology tells us that Athena could not have smoked. In closing, I should note that Stendhal's night of love with a certain Minette in the former building at Schadewachten 19 in the village of Stendal in Altmark has been mentioned only by Jürgen Eggebrecht ("Huldigung der nördlichen Stämme," published under the title *Vaters Haus* by Kurt Desch in 1971). One hopes that scholars will soon pursue this burning literary question.

MUNICH, MAY 1994